"Filled with humor and heart. This is how you do fake dating."
—Rebekah Weatherspoon, award-winning author of *Xeni*

"Sexy, humorous, and filled with witty banter, Etta Easton's charming debut dazzles! Fans of the fake-dating trope will absolutely love this book."
—Farrah Rochon, *New York Times* bestselling author of *The Hookup Plan*

"Etta Easton's *The Kiss Countdown* is a funny, fresh, and voicey debut that will keep you smiling—and swooning—until the very last page. I adored it!"
—Mia Sosa, *USA Today* bestselling author of *The Wedding Crasher*

"Easton delivers a sparkling fake-dating rom-com that is both delectably tropey and utterly believable.... *The Kiss Countdown* is a tribute to unexpected romantic connections, crackling chemistry, and the value of family." —*Entertainment Weekly*

"In Etta Easton's lovely debut, the struggling Houston event planner has three months before her new fake boyfriend, Vincent, leaves the country . . . for outer space. . . . This charming NASA-adjacent romance is certain to win Easton loyal fans." —*Elle*

"This book is perfect for lovers of positive representations of Black love. And what's cuter than an astronaut coupled with an event planner? Yes, opposites do attract in this fun read, indeed!" —*Essence*

"A sweet, sparkling love story unfolds in this debut novel written by Etta Easton!" —*Woman's World*

"Easton takes her time building comfort and trust between the leads, making their love affair feel cozy and grounded, even as the plot around them moves at a fast clip. Easton is a writer to watch." —*Publishers Weekly*

ALSO BY ETTA EASTON

The Kiss Countdown

THE LOVE SIMULATION

ETTA EASTON

BERKLEY ROMANCE
NEW YORK

BERKLEY ROMANCE

Published by Berkley

An imprint of Penguin Random House LLC

1745 Broadway, New York, NY 10019

penguinrandomhouse.com

Library of Congress Cataloging-in-Publication Data

Names: Easton, Etta, author.

Title: The love simulation / Etta Easton.

Description: First edition. | New York: Berkley Romance, 2025.

Identifiers: LCCN 2024029847 (print) | LCCN 2024029848 (ebook) |
ISBN 9780593640241 (trade paperback) | ISBN 9780593640258 (ebook)

Subjects: LCGFT: Romance fiction. | Novels.

Classification: LCC PS3605.A863 L68 2025 (print) |
LCC PS3605.A863 (ebook) | DDC 813/.6—dc23/eng/20240715

LC record available at https://lccn.loc.gov/2024029847

LC ebook record available at https://lccn.loc.gov/2024029848

First Edition: March 2025

Printed in the United States of America

1st Printing

The authorized representative in the EU for product safety and compliance is Penguin Random House Ireland, Morrison Chambers, 32 Nassau Street, Dublin D02 YH68, Ireland, https://eu-contact.penguin.ie.

THE LOVE SIMULATION

CHAPTER ONE

What is it called when you know someone is playing in your face but you still manage to sit there and maintain your composure?

Etiquette? The height of professionalism? I've got it—a superpower.

When I took on the role of vice principal at Juanita Craft Middle School nine months ago, I knew I'd have my hands full with rowdy students and entitled parents. The years I spent as a guidance counselor prepared me for *that* part of the job. It's taken a while, however, to get used to the teachers trying to butter me up whenever they want something they know I can't give, and Angie's been the main one out to test my patience.

Angie, Angie, Angie. Out here trying to get me to break school policy. Again.

I push my braids behind my back and suppress a sigh. "It's true. In the grand scheme of things, one chair won't make or break our budget. But if we get a new one for you, we'll have to get a new one for every other teacher. I'd gladly place the order for a truckload to be brought in, but the budget has already been set, and unfortunately it doesn't include room for chairs."

"You know what, Miss Brianna? I might believe you *if* I

didn't know for a fact that you just ordered one for Mr. Torres in December. Now he's got good armrests, wheels that don't squeak, and can lean back without worrying about flipping over. You know whose chair doesn't have all that?" Angie crosses her arms over her chest and glares at me. Her actions are made even more dramatic with the way the armholes of her robe billow just past her elbows, where soft tulle meets down feathers.

Yes, our computer sciences teacher is serious about staring me down here in the teachers' lounge, under the bright, buzzing fluorescent lights and eggshell-colored walls, while she's wrapped in an article of clothing that looks like it belongs on the set of some old Hollywood movie about rich widows.

To be fair, today is Pajama Day, and I myself am in a footed one-piece. So while Angie's outfit is a little over-the-top and will likely do more to distract her students all day than squeaky chair wheels ever could, it is school-appropriate with a silk pants set underneath, and to put it plainly, she looks fabulous.

Fabulous or not, she's still not convincing me to break policy for her. I do wish I could buy all the teachers new chairs, but I already had to fight the principal tooth and nail until he agreed to include in the budget what the school desperately needed—a library upgrade. I'm not certain he won't go back on his word at the slightest provocation. For some reason, it's hard to drive the point home to Angie, even though she's worked with the principal longer than I have.

"You know we didn't replace Mr. Torres's chair for no reason. In case you forgot—which I don't see how you could since you reenacted it for everyone—his chair really did flip him over when he leaned back. Even then, he still had to provide a doctor's prescription stating he needed a reliable chair for his bad back before the purchase was approved."

"Oh yeah, I did forget about that." Angie grimaces, then her demeanor shifts as she leans forward like we're sharing a secret. "But come on. Brianna. Girlie. You know my back is bad too."

Now I'm positive she's playing in my face. I tap into my superpower again and don't react, when all I want to do is bust out laughing. Because, bad back where? Back bad who? It certainly didn't seem like Angie had a bad back at the spring dance. She was poppin', lockin', and droppin' with more spirit than our little pep squad. She even tried to get me on the dance floor with her. When she showed up at school the following Monday, her complaints about the watered-down punch and bad lighting had been loud and clear, but there'd been no mention of any bodily aches and pains.

"If you really have a bad back, then get your doctor to write a prescription," I say, hoping that will get her to drop it, at least for now. It's the end of the school year, and I am done thinking about budgets and requests from teachers and maintaining a professional facade. Done. In my mind, I'm already aboard my fourteen-day cruise in the Caribbean.

Angie huffs, but the fight has left her, so she stands without another word. The robe cascades around her legs, train flowing, and she looks like an African goddess as she moves toward the other side of the room, where there's a vending machine with sandwiches and cold pastries fit to feed royalty. When I'm sure she's lost all interest in me, I finally allow a small smile to slip out.

Before I was a vice principal, I loved cutting up with the staff or complaining about spending too much of my own money on supplies I needed to do my job effectively. Now everything has changed. Even though many of the teachers are around my age, there's a clear line between professional and personal I have to be careful not to cross. Especially if I ever hope to advance my career and catch up to my siblings.

Angie begins hitting the side of the vending machine while yelling about her stuck granola bar, but I turn away to glance at the clock mounted above the TV to see how I'm doing on time. About fifteen minutes before the students begin arriving, which means *he* will show up at any moment.

I readjust myself in my seat, straightening my back without making it so stiff that my body language screams "the kids aren't around, but I'm still judging you for not poring over lesson plans at your desk." My aim is to look respectable yet easy-breezy, so I pull out my phone too. If any staff members glance my way, it should look like I'm taking advantage of the quiet of the teachers' lounge before the students storm in and not like my presence this morning—along with every other morning for the past nine months—is all for show.

As I pull up my email, *he* walks in, and the rhythm of my heart changes, beating to a cadence that chants *Roman, Roman*. I clench my stomach muscles tight to maintain my posture and keep still.

Brown eyes on brown skin in dark brown plaid pajama pants—I swear the monochromatic color scheme has never looked so good.

When I first met him, I thought he was one of the gym teachers. No one can look at him and think he does anything but work on that lean, athletic physique all week. But I was wrong. He teaches eighth-grade science. Assuming

Roman was the gym teacher was my second mistake where he's concerned. The first was landing the vice principal role over him.

"That's a Black king right there," Angie says above me, and I almost jump out of my seat.

I play it cool though, looking up and frowning like I have no clue what she's talking about. "What was that?"

Angie smirks. "Girl, you know what I'm saying. I heard you humming and everything while checking him out. But don't worry, I won't tell anyone our little VP isn't immune to the magnificence that is Major Pain Jr."

Was I really humming while looking at Roman? Because she's read me like a text in all caps. Hell. I hope it wasn't something obvious like *Hamilton*'s "Helpless." And double hell. These are the kinds of moments I miss having with teachers. If I wasn't the vice principal, I'd raise my hands in agreement and shout "*I know that's right!*" But there's no way I can do that here, where half a dozen teachers are within earshot, without looking highly inappropriate.

I elect to remain silent, and Angie shakes her head in disappointment. Then her eyes soften and she bends closer to me. "I want you to know that I'm really going to miss you. I know you won't say it back because you're not supposed to have favorites or anything, but, well, I know I'm your favorite anyway." She winks and sashays out of the teachers' lounge, and I'm left shaking my head again.

Once the last of her robe disappears through the door, I turn my gaze back toward Roman. He's standing by the single-serve coffee maker with the English teacher, Kareem. They always meet here in the morning before the students begin arriving, though, admittedly, it usually takes me a while to notice Kareem. For all I know, today he could have walked in doing the "Cha-Cha Slide" or cartwheels and I completely missed it, only able to see Roman. Even though Kareem is the more talkative and outgoing of the two, that's the only area where he's got Roman beat. Everything else about Roman's presence is just so much *more*. More commanding. More distinctive and arresting. More irresistible. Not that it's a competition between the two, and not that I should be noticing anyway.

Roman scans the room and stops when his gaze lands on me. Our eye contact is brief, lasting two, maybe three heartbeats, then I'm the first to look away. It's back to emails, but now I'm not focusing on the actual messages. My attention is divided between the words on my screen and what my peripheral sees at the coffee maker as Raven, another English teacher, walks in. She greets first Kareem, then Roman with a hug. Why she needs to hug them every single morning, I can't say. Not that Roman seems to mind. As the three stand there chatting, I can't help but notice how Roman's eyes are always a tad softer when Raven is talking. The observation makes my stomach twist with jealousy every time. And yet here I am, every weekday morning, watching their interactions.

After a few minutes of them all catching up, Raven and Kareem turn in my direction. I hold my breath and wonder if they're about to say something about me watching them, but they don't. They offer me small, almost sad waves before leaving for the language arts wing. Um, okay. That was so weird, I almost get up to ask them what's going on, but seeing Roman now standing alone keeps me in the teachers' lounge. I'll find out what's up later. Right now it's time for our little dance. I turn my phone screen off, get up, and head to the coffee maker.

"Good morning, Roman," I say.

Roman selects a random K-Cup, never caring about the

flavor as long as it's not decaf, sets it into the coffee maker, and closes the lid with a snap. He presses the start button and turns to me. "Vice Principal Rogers," he greets in turn, his deep voice already pulling at everything in me.

Where Angie is overly familiar, Roman is painstakingly formal with everyone, even when the students aren't around. Instead of first names, it's Mrs. This or Mr. That. For me, it's always *Vice Principal* Rogers. I figured out pretty early on in the year he wasn't doing it to show everyone he's better than them, but to erect a buffer. And in that regard, we're similar. Only, I keep my distance from everyone so the lines between admin and teachers aren't blurred. Roman, the son of a principal who isn't well-liked or trusted by the teachers and staff, does it to protect himself. With the exception of Kareem and Raven, the teachers aren't falling all over themselves to share the latest gossip with him or air their grievances, afraid he'll tell his dad.

I open the cabinet and am not surprised when I see my favorite tea flavor set too high for me to reach without climbing on the counter. I look at Roman in silent question and he springs into action like he was waiting for his cue. He takes a step closer, and I breathe in his scent, which is rich, sweet, and masculine. It overpowers the smell of the coffee brewing right in front of us, but not in an obnoxious way like our struggling eighth graders who drench themselves in Axe body spray, hoping it will cover up a multitude of sins. Then again, if I could bottle up Roman's scent, I'd be tempted to forgo the water-and-soap route and bathe in nothing but it.

I inhale deeply again, then tip my head back and watch as first he reaches for the lemon ginger. When I deliberately clear my throat, he sets it down and grabs the rectangular box of blueberry-flavored tea. When he hands it to me, I take the box's opposite end, as always, leaving no opportunity for our hands to touch. Even though there's no skin contact, the eye contact is all there, leaving me almost breathless.

"Thank you," I say.

Roman doesn't say "You're welcome" or offer me a smile, which is both a blessing and a curse. A blessing because every time we do this little morning dance, I'm sliding a toe over the line between teachers and administrators I'm not supposed to cross. If anyone ever noticed how we meet in the same spot every day and began spreading rumors that something else was going on, it would spell trouble for my career, and I'm sure Roman would gain no goodwill from the teachers who already treat him differently. But it's also a curse because he's got a great smile.

I first saw it when we were chaperoning the fall dance. We stood on opposite sides of the gym when "Back That Thang Up" by Juvenile came on. Millennial teachers, led by Angie, weren't able to resist the call. They stormed the dance floor while students, suffering from secondhand embarrassment, cleared out. I stayed on the sidelines and watched, wishing I had someone to turn to in that moment who could laugh with me and appreciate that the DJ had at least used the nonexplicit version of the song. Then I looked ahead and found Roman's eyes on me. He was standing alone like I was. Rather than the flat look he normally sported, his eyes were lit up with humor. He shook his head like I did, and our silent conversation commenced.

Can you believe them?

They are way too old to be acting like this.

Who chose the DJ anyway?

I'm pretty sure Angie's three seconds away from snatching her wig off and whipping it around her head like a lasso.

By the time the song was over, we were both grinning like fools, and some inappropriate obsession had taken root.

More than anything—how sexy he is, his amazing smile, or how good he smells, which is incredible—it's that memory and the feeling of the connection we shared that's continuously drawn me to him. This morning routine where my day doesn't truly begin until I see Roman has always been a dichotomy of knowing it's highly inappropriate and unprofessional to feed into my crush and yet hoping the fact that he shows up every morning and plays along means it's not one-sided. I haven't begun to scratch the surface of who he really is outside of being a teacher and the principal's son, but there's something about him that fills me with longing.

Roman pauses mid-stir with a wooden stick in his hand and lifts an eyebrow to me in question. I turn my head back to the microwave so fast I almost give myself whiplash from the weight of my braids swinging over my shoulder and landing on my chest. This part of our morning ritual is supposed to be a simple exchange of greetings while I wait for him to make his coffee then take my turn. It should *not* involve me getting caught staring like a creeper.

Glad that my hair is now blocking my face so he can't see my embarrassment, I stifle a sigh while opening the cabinet above me to grab a Styrofoam cup. Roman is rummaging next to me, and I know now he must be putting the lid on his cup and preparing to leave. He'll go to his classroom to get set up for first period, and I'll go on about my duties having given my brain the serotonin boost it needed.

"So what are your big plans to celebrate getting out of here?" I hear Roman say.

I look around to see if he's talking to one of his friends who has come back, but no. He's looking directly at me.

"After everything is wrapped up for the district, I'm going on a cruise." After that perfectly normal response, I grab my K-Cup. "We're stopping in Cozumel, Yucatán, Puerto Costa Maya, and Belize. It's a fourteen-day cruise, which is on the long side, but I know it'll be worth it. Oh, and I say 'we,' but I really mean *me*. It's a solo trip, but I'm sure I'll meet other people there."

Ugh, and there I go. I try to channel that same superpower I use when teachers, students, or the principal says something outlandish and I have to stay cool, but for whatever reason it doesn't work around him.

Roman looks at me, eyes shining in amusement. I know his smile is there, trying to break through, and my heart answers in a gallop.

"Good morning!" a chipper voice says beside us.

"Oh! Good morning, Mrs. Bland," I say, greeting the social studies teacher and taking a step back. I don't want her getting the idea there is something going on between Roman and me.

"Don't mind me. I just need some creamer."

Her arm stretches between us, and she grabs a small cup of half-and-half. She smiles at me, though it falls flat when she glances at Roman. Roman doesn't seem to care or notice her as he stands there and takes a gulp of his drink.

"In case I don't get a chance to tell you later, it's been great working with you this year," she says.

The whole interaction is uneventful and only lasts about ten seconds, but when she's gone, the air coming off Roman is noticeably chilly, despite the fact that we're in the beginning stages of a heat wave and the AC is finnicky. Is he upset Mrs. Bland didn't speak to him? On the same token, he didn't speak to her. Other than Kareem and Raven, he rarely speaks to anyone else. Did *I* somehow hurt his feelings by stepping away? I would have done the same with any other teacher I was speaking to if someone else had come up. Okay, maybe I wouldn't have stepped away from any other teacher like they were on fire and I was afraid of getting burned, but there definitely would have been some foot-shuffling going on.

Roman's gaze is flat when he looks at me, and I know he's about to head to his classroom.

"What are your plans for the summer?" I ask, wanting to drag this interaction out a little longer. Why not? It's almost the end of the school year and I'm feeling a bit reckless.

He looks at the door a second, then back to me before he shrugs. "Nothing special. I signed up to teach summer school."

"Nothing special? The kids absolutely love you. I wouldn't be surprised if some of them sign up just to take your course for the fun of it. You're great at what you do, Roman."

He looks almost bashful when I stop talking, and I tuck a braid behind my ear. My response might have been a little over-the-top and *could* be misconstrued as flirting, but I told him the truth. Even if the teachers don't welcome him with open arms, the students love him. As a teacher, he knows how to be serious but not rigid. Engaging and fun without letting the lessons fly off the rails. It's obvious so many of the boys look up to him, and on more than one occasion I've had to pretend not to hear a few of the girls going on about how much "drip" he has. I'm only too aware that he would have made a great vice principal.

This morning, however, the fact that we've been circling around each other all year—Roman maintaining a respectful and aloof distance, and me admiring how amazing he is at his job while also wishing he'd simultaneously look at me and ignore me to force me to maintain proper distance—doesn't seem to matter.

"Thanks," he says.

"You're welcome."

Roman nods and begins to walk away, but stops, and instead takes a step closer to me. He's a head taller than me, about six feet, and I tilt my head up to look at him.

"Before summer starts, the teachers get together at Big Lou's to celebrate making it through another year. Raven and Kareem finally convinced me to check it out. You should come through too."

I try not to do that thing when I smile—the thing where I end up grinning so hard my normally full upper lip disappears and I'm nothing but gums and shiny teeth. But I can't help it. And I know I've spent all school year actively trying *not* to get too close to the teachers, but no one ever invited me out somewhere with the promise that Roman would be there. I think it would be feasible to hang out with everyone for one special occasion.

"I was going to order pizza from Big Lou's for all of the teachers on the last day," I say. "But meeting up with everyone there sounds a lot better."

There it is—a small tilt of Roman's lips letting me know he's pleased I took him up on the offer. His smile isn't quite as generous as the one he gave me at the school dance, and it's nowhere near as wide as the one I'm still sporting, but it's there, and its very existence puts my reputation at risk as wild, foolish ideas begin racing through my head. Like the idea that he wouldn't mind if I were to stand on my toes and touch his juicy curved lips. With mine.

"Brianna, there you are!"

I'm jerked out of my Roman-induced haze by the librarian, Mrs. Yates. She's rushing over, obviously upset about something, with her face flushed like she wants to cry. Or strangle something.

I clear my throat, and this time the distance I put between Roman and me is more than warranted. "Mrs. Yates, what's going on? What's wrong?" I ask.

"Is it true that you're leaving?" she demands.

I frown. "I'm going on a cruise in a few weeks." That's hardly anything to cry over.

"No. I mean here. Craft Middle School. Is it true that you're resigning so you can take up the vice principal position at that new arts school?"

All I can do is blink at her. The possibility never even crossed my mind. "Mrs. Yates, no. I'm not going anywhere."

"Wait, what do you mean, no?" Roman cuts in.

I snap my head to him. What's up with his outburst? In fact, what's up with both of them? How does my going on a cruise to Mexico translate to leaving the school for good? And leaving for a new position at that?

"I *mean*," I say to Roman, "I'm going on a trip for two weeks, then I'm turning right back around to prepare for the new school year. Why would you think otherwise?"

Roman runs a hand over his head but doesn't say anything, so I turn to Mrs. Yates for answers.

Those same delicate fingers Mrs. Yates uses to caress book spines and turn pages with the gentlest of touches are wielded like a weapon as she points to Roman. "He told me."

I understand why the library has so few books returned late, and it's not because the kids aren't reading as much. They're probably afraid to see this side of Mrs. Yates. For a second, I'm ready to sprint to my office and make sure I don't have any library books on my shelf. Then her words hit me with the force of a sledgehammer, and I realize I'm not under attack. Roman is.

"Roman," I begin, almost at a loss for words, "why did you tell her that I'm leaving?"

He looks uncomfortable, running a palm over his head again, and I swear, under that fine melanin complexion he's blushing. But I can't get distracted by how good he looks even when flustered. I need answers, and his demeanor is quickly veering from flustered to guilty.

"My dad told me you were," he finally says, and lets out a heavy sigh. "But your reaction is telling me that's not the case."

Hell no, it's not the case. And I have no idea why Principal Major would even say that.

I glance from Mrs. Yates, who seems relieved, to Roman, who's once again closed off. Is that why he was open and friendly only moments ago? He thought I was leaving and was obviously ready to waltz right into the vacant vice principal spot? Whatever I thought I read in that half smile was the product of foolish hopeful thinking.

The worst kind of heat spreads from my ears downward, making my stomach cramp, and I can no longer bring myself to meet Roman's eyes.

"That explains so much of this morning," I mutter, trying to breathe through the embarrassment and hurt stinging in the backs of my eyes. Now I see why the teachers were acting weird, and I especially see why Roman was acting out of the norm. Like he was happy to talk to me. I guess he was just happy to think the vice principal spot was about to have a vacancy.

"It's not like that, Bri—" Roman starts, but gets cut off by Mrs. Yates.

"If you aren't leaving after all, does that mean the money for the library isn't really gone?" she asks.

I snap my head up but don't ask Mrs. Yates to repeat herself. I heard every word loud and clear, and now there's a sour churn in my stomach that seems to make an appearance every time Principal Major is up to something.

I stare straight at Mrs. Yates with my best game face on. "I don't know what's going on, but I promise you, I'm going to find out."

CHAPTER TWO

The school's front doors have opened, ushering in the familiar sounds of kids laughing and shoes scuffing against the floor as I approach the administrative suite where the assistants' and Principal Major's office are, feeling like the world's biggest fool.

I still couldn't bring myself to meet Roman's gaze before leaving the teachers' lounge. It kills me that I was so ready to show up at the upcoming party because it was *him* who asked, when I would've had no problem saying no to any of the other teachers. Nine months of formality should have told me there was something more to his change of attitude. I got my hopes up, and it's left me feeling low and sad. Like the girl who just got duped by the cool guy. This could be my villain origin story. But as I come to stand in front of Principal Major's door, I try to block the image of how open and inviting Roman seemed and suppress every last ounce of emotion as I prepare to do battle with his dad.

I knock on the door and hear a faint "Come in." Steeling myself, back straight and chin up, I turn the knob and walk in.

"Good morning," says the cheerful voice at the other end of the room, and I narrow my eyes. Even if I weren't already on edge, Principal Major's greeting would have been more than enough to let me know something isn't right. "Just the young girl I wanted to see."

And now my left eye is twitching. This man just cannot help himself, but I learned long ago that it's a reaction he's looking for. He's like a poorly trained dog who's learned that bad behavior is rewarded with attention. With each interaction with him, I have to remind myself of that so I don't slip and say something about not being able to teach an old dog new tricks.

I cross my arms over my chest. "I'm glad you're happy to see me, because we need to have a serious conversation."

"We most certainly do." He looks too eager as he leans forward, with his elbows on his massive oak desk. "There has been some moving and a few shake-ups with the new middle school set to open in our district for the next school year. I heard from the principal at Angelou School of Arts. She's still looking for a vice principal. I'm sure you've heard how they'll be doing all that New Age learning. No homework. Classrooms with chairs on the floor instead of real desks." He barely suppresses rolling his eyes. "It seems right up your alley. Well, I already put in a good word for you, and they're eager to talk more. You're welcome."

I wonder, where did he get his audacity? They don't have it at Amazon or Walmart. I've checked. And yet, he's got it in spades. So assured of what he's saying, like it's a foregone conclusion.

"Why would I take their vice principal position when I'm perfectly content here? This is my job, and these are my kids, however much you may wish otherwise."

"Are you perfectly content here, Miss Rogers? Really?"

"Of course," I bite out automatically.

Everyone seems to be on a roll with the ridiculous questions today. *Am I leaving? Am I really content here?* The real question is, why wouldn't I be? This has been the exact change of pace I wanted after I realized that being a guidance counselor wasn't the fulfilling career I hoped it would be. As vice principal I get to help everyone. Teachers and students. It's only on the rare occasion that an unshakable sense of wrongness hits whenever I pull into the school parking lot, and that I attribute to the stress of dealing with Principal Major.

It's impossible to drum up any excitement in working with the man who told me during our first meeting, "You weren't my choice for vice principal, but don't worry. I don't expect you to be here for long anyway."

The nine months younger, bright-eyed Brianna had no idea why he didn't like me on sight. Was it that he wanted someone older than thirty? Someone taller? Was it my braids? Come to find out, it was all of the above, plus the fact that I'm not his son. Principal Major wants me gone so Roman can take my place and has been doing all he can to make my year here miserable. Too bad for him my career plans don't involve getting bulldozed over by a bully. If he wants to be my biggest hater because I'm ruining his plans to rule the school with his precious boy, he can stay mad while I work my way to the top.

"Yes, I am content here," I repeat. "In fact, I love it."

Principal Major stares, clear skepticism crinkling the corners of his eyes, and I know he doesn't believe me. I meet his gaze straight on to prove how serious I am, fighting that uncomfortable tinge I get whenever I have to look at him for too long. He's not an exact older version of Roman, but the broad nose and honey-brown skin tone they share make the resemblance unmistakable. Seeing Roman makes my heart rate soar, but having anything to do with

Principal Major makes me think I need to schedule a doctor's appointment for high blood pressure.

"Anyway," I say, and clear my throat. We could face off all day, but I need answers. "What is going on with the library remodel? Mrs. Yates told me it's been scrapped, but there's got to be some kind of misunderstanding."

"Oh, no. There's been no misunderstanding."

I stare at him for a full minute before finally gritting out, "Come again?" That sour pit in my stomach is back and stronger than ever. I know I'm going to hate whatever comes out of his mouth next.

"Mrs. Yates is correct. We've made the decision to scrap the library remodel and go in a different direction. We're going to upgrade the football field."

For a few seconds there's only silence between us as his words register, then all I can do is laugh. Full-on belly-cramping, tear-inducing, breath-shortening, cheek muscle–quivering laughter. I laugh so much that I have to grip the edge of the desk so I won't fall over. A football field upgrade for middle schoolers in place of a library is the most absurd thing I've ever heard. When I finally get ahold of myself, I straighten up, ready to congratulate Principal Major on finding his sense of humor. Then I get a good look at his face, and the hilarity of this situation is gone. His face hasn't cracked so much as a smile line.

I wipe away the moisture from the corners of my eyes, hoping by the time I'm done here they don't turn into real tears. "You *can't* be serious," I say.

"Of course I'm serious," he says with a frown, like *I'm* the one being irrational by thinking this is some huge joke. "When enrollment opens for the new middle school and students who straddle the line between our zone and theirs get a choice of which school they'll go to, how do you think that will go down?" He holds up a finger to keep me from responding. "That's a rhetorical question, by the way. They're going to pick the new and updated school every time. There's got to be some reason kids want to come here, or we'll lose our funding. Do you think bonds just come along every year? That's another rhetorical question. No, they don't. So I've decided to keep this school relevant and the money coming in. We'll be known for our state-of-the-art football field."

I shake my head. "There is so much wrong with everything you said. I can't even . . . State-of-the-art football field? These are middle schoolers! No one is looking to draft them. They don't even have a choice in what high school they go to. This would be the most ridiculous use of money I've ever seen."

He looks me up and down and scoffs. "Says the young girl in a onesie."

My face heats, and while I have to admit to myself that having jeans on hand for this conversation would have been immensely better, I don't back down. "It's called school spirit, get in on it! Better yet, get a clue. These kids don't need a new football field. They need a functioning library. They need new books and computers. You said the library remodel was a sure thing. You—" I abruptly stop talking as my voice begins to shake.

Two summers ago, a Category 4 hurricane caused significant damage to the school. Most notably, part of the library flooded and a good percentage of the books were destroyed. I don't know why the insurance money wasn't used to fix and recoup what was lost. What I do know is that when I took my position here, they were using part of the library for detention and in-school suspension. They were using the library as a place for punishment. *Punishment*. I knew right then and there that if I didn't do anything, I'd never see the library functioning fully and whole. I thought it was a miracle when Principal Major agreed that changes would be done with the bond money. Obviously, I thought wrong.

"I did agree," he concedes. "But I saw the plans for the new school and had to make the tough decision to pivot. Without kids filling our classrooms, without them *wanting* to fill our classrooms, we lose funding. If we lose funding, do you know what else we lose? Don't answer, that's a rhetorical question." I glare at him, and his stupid rhetorical question bull. Everything he's saying is a load of bull. "We lose the ability to pay what teachers we have left; we lose the ability to buy the books and computers that you want to fill a new library with. This is how I'm securing my school's future." He offers what I assume must be his attempt at an empathetic smile, but it misses the mark by the length of a football field. "Look, I know the library and the books and all the other artsy stuff is important to you. That's why I think it's best you put in for the other vice principal position," he says with a raise of his barely there eyebrow. Just like his barely there soul. "I believe you'll find it much more to your liking. But I know you're stubborn and think you can still get what you want. That's not going to happen, Miss Rogers. Just so you're aware, I had a meeting with Superintendent Watts. The football upgrade is a done deal. The contractors have been chosen and paid, and they'll start working on the field as soon as the kids break for summer. Your energy would be better spent elsewhere, like on, say, interview prep."

Not only did he go back on his word, but he kept plans for the new football field hidden long enough to finalize everything. And it's all been so calculated. From the way he dangled the library upgrade in front of my nose like the most delicious piece of cake, only to snatch it away, to his whole shtick about me being a better fit at Angelou School of Arts.

As much as I want to rage and yell and threaten to grab a folding chair from outside, I know I won't be able to get one word out without my voice shaking from the pressure to cry. And no matter how much my eyes burn and my body locks up, I'd rather walk across hot coals than shed a single tear in front of this man. He is the exact type who would see it as a weakness rather than the most natural bodily response to extreme emotions. And right now, I am extremely full of rage.

Instead, I stalk back to the door and slam it on my way out.

"HEYYY, MISS ROGERS," A STUDENT YELLS WHEN I STEP OUT THROUGH the glass doors of the administrative offices. "I like your pajamas!"

I let my head fall as I smooth down my outfit with still-shaking hands and do my best to hide any traces of anger and disappointment. The hall is full of students, and right now I need to be present in welcoming them.

"Thank you, I got it from . . ." I trail off when I realize the student speaking to me is wearing the same one-piece pajama set as I am.

I blame social media for this. I'd planned on coming in some simple plaid pants and a white shirt. But after searching for "Pajama Days Ideas for Teachers," I kept getting bombarded by ads of the footed pajamas. In the ads, the lady wearing them always looked comfortable and stylish.

I couldn't help but be influenced. To keep it VP-appropriate, I ordered a size up and paid extra for overnight delivery. Unfortunately, I don't think it gives "grown, comfy, and stylish" so much as it gives "kid whose mom ordered a larger size so they can grow into it." I would have stuck with my original outfit, but I was running late after dealing with my dog, Sheba's, morning shenanigans.

"Oop! Not you twinnin' with the vice principal, Jaz," a student in red-and-white-polka-dot pants with a white top and a black bonnet says to my "twin" with a snicker. She looks at me then ducks her head to hide a smile as she hurries away.

Considering how brutal these kids can get with their jokes, I'm counting it a win she went light on us.

"Good morning, Trenton," I say to one of our quieter sixth graders passing by. His Miles Morales pajamas match his black-and-red Jordans. "Nice shoes."

He smiles shyly, though his shoulders straighten. At the little boost to his ego, my spirits lift as well.

I continue greeting the students coming in. Smiling to let them know that even though the year is almost over, I haven't checked out and we're glad they're here. That they're more than simply bodies we need to show up and fill quotas for funding.

I notice Monique, a seventh grader who loves spending time in the library (the part not used for detention), standing in front of her open locker. She seems lost, with a confused scowl reflecting from her small locker mirror, so after a few seconds I walk over to her. "What's going on, sweetie? Do you need help?"

She shakes her head as if coming out of a daze before turning her bright brown eyes to me. "Miss Rogers! I'm glad you're here, because I have quite the quandary."

I love everything about this girl. From her juicy twists to her vocabulary.

"I was the only one who did the extra credit in English," she says. "So I get to take home a book from Ms. Pierce's library. I already know I'm going with Angie Thomas, but which one should I get? My brother said *The Hate U Give* is too grown for me, but I'm not a kid," she says indignantly, stomping her sparkly unicorn slippers. "Then again, *Nic Blake and the Remarkables* has dragons . . . Ugh, what should I do? This will be my first read of the summer. It's a very important decision."

I bite the inside of my cheek to keep from laughing. Not that I would be laughing at *her* but at how seriously she's taking the matter. Then again, what am I talking about? Books *are* a serious matter, and Monique reminds me of how excited I was when it came time to decide what books to read as a young girl. Back before I had full control of my own funds and my TBR pile wasn't high enough to reach the moon. But back then, I went to a school with a sizable library, so whatever books I couldn't get my parents or older siblings to buy, I could check out.

"Well?" Monique prompts, as clearly I'm taking too long.

"That's a hard one. *The Hate U Give* is a classic, but on the other hand . . . dragons." I move my hands like two sides of a scale. "You really can't go wrong with either of the two."

She lets out the biggest huff she can while attached to a backpack that's at least 20 percent of her weight. "Thanks, but that doesn't help me." I snap my head back as she slams her locker shut and sets off, her twists bouncing with each step. These young teens. I swear.

At the same time as Monique turns right to go around the corner, Roman comes from the opposite direction and turns down the same hall I'm standing in. He wears pajamas like everyone else, but his unmistakable male form is clearly distinguishable in the sea of still-growing boys.

"Hey! Save the moves for the court," he yells to a student so busy bouncing an invisible ball and crossing over anyone in his path that he almost runs into Roman. But Roman's got that deep stern tone that seems to reach kids on a primal level, so at his words, the student immediately falls in line.

Once the student is out of sight, Roman's head swivels to me. We lock eyes, but the rush of butterflies I usually get when seeing him is missing in action. It will be a long time before I get over the hurt and humiliation from thinking our morning meetings were something special, and imagining that if we were in different roles, there would be a chance to explore just how deep our connection could grow.

Roman's eyes stay fastened to me as he moves down the hall with purpose. All I know is I don't want to face him right now.

"I need you to make sure the announcements are on my desk by the time I get back," I hear Principal Major say to one of the secretaries. He's about to head out to where I am.

Stuck between the possibility of another showdown with the principal or facing off with his son, I do something a leader should never do. I hightail it out of there.

Rather than go down the hallway in the direction of my office (because of course Principal Major made a point of sequestering me away from the other administrative personnel), I go right out the front doors. I hear Roman's, "Principal Major, a word," which sounds no less foreboding than when he told the student to quit messing around, as my feet hit the concrete. I don't know what Roman wanted to say to me, or if it had even been his intention to talk to me.

But now he and his dad can talk all about how their scheme to get my hopes up for the library worked.

It takes another twenty minutes to get to my office. After greeting students getting off their buses and encouraging them to get to class on time, I continue my walk around the campus, going past the band hall and gym, finally making it to my door. It smells like blueberry muffins, and my stomach rumbles even though I already had breakfast. The perks of being located right next to the cafeteria.

My office is remarkably smaller than Principal Major's and pretty much every other administrator who gets their own space, so I have to squeeze between the wall and my desk to get to my chair. When I land in my seat, I let out a deep sigh. The fact that the library remodel isn't happening is still sinking in, but I don't have time to sit with it fully yet. There are still teacher evaluations that need to be completed, I have a scheduled meeting with Principal Major that I may accidentally forget to show up for, and I need to call back two parents who are concerned about the need for their kids to take summer courses. And that's all before lunches start.

First things first. I pull up my email and see I've received thirty-five new messages since checking it while in the teachers' lounge. One would think that the emails would lessen as the end of the year rolls around, but nope. My inbox stays consistently flooded. While I do a quick scan of the subject lines to see what I can get rid of without opening, a new message from Principal Major with a blank subject line pops up. I have no choice but to open it in case it's something important, then grind my teeth when I see it's full of attachments of all the contractor receipts for the football field upgrade.

My mom used to get on my siblings and me whenever

we'd use the word *hate*, but I swear (something else she'd get on us for) there are days I absolutely hate dealing with Principal Major. When he follows up with a link to Angelou School of Arts, at least I get the satisfaction of steering that one right into the trash.

And that's enough of that.

I exit out of my email. There has to be something I can do to stop this madness about a football field and make Principal Major stick to what we originally agreed on. This calls for a conversation with my mentor. I pick up the phone on my desk and hit the number programmed for Superintendent Watts's office.

I'm sure most vice principals don't typically call up the superintendent so freely, but Jeanine Watts has been my mentor for years and went to the same alma mater as my parents. She's always shown her unshaken faith in my ability not only to succeed in this role but to keep moving up. Principal Major said she already signed off on the football field, but my hope is that once I explain the original plans for the library remodel, she'll see it's a better use of the school's money and make him go back to the original agreement. While I'm at it, I may even ask her to find a new school for him. If anyone needs to transfer, it's him, and preferably far, far away from here. But the conversation doesn't happen. The answering secretary lets me know the superintendent isn't available. I'll try calling her again, a hundred times if I have to, but as I set the handset back on the receiver, my chest tightens and I know I'm on the verge of giving in to my emotions.

God. If I lose the library, what was even the point of this whole year? I didn't abandon my old school and position with the intention of battling with my principal every day or floundering my way through disciplinary action meetings or holding off parents from attacking teachers (and some-times vice versa). I came here to make my mark and make a difference. And now it all seems to have gone up in smoke.

I scrub my hand over my face, then reach for my cell phone to send a message to my sister.

ME: Code Yellow. Can I come by after work?

Code Yellow means one of us is about to have an emotional breakdown. Seeing as out of the two of us, I'm the emotionally volatile one, it's always me using the code. But my sister never lets me down. Within a minute of sending the message, my phone vibrates with a response.

CAMILLE: I'll have the wine ready.

Already I feel the weight on my chest lighten. All I need is a good cry and sister time, then I'll know how to proceed.

CHAPTER THREE

Have you ever thought of investing in a handkerchief? Or maybe several?" Camille asks.

I use my fingers to wipe away the remnants of tears, having long given up on the tissues. They kept falling apart in my hands, making me wonder if Camille switched from the brand she normally keeps around for these sessions. I must look a mess, but God, how I needed this.

After this morning's revelation, my day didn't get any better. I still had to suffer through meetings with Principal Major. Now that the cat's out of the bag and I know his real plans for the budget, he was only too happy to delegate to me the task of taking over communications with the contractors. I also had to break the news to Mrs. Yates that the library remodel isn't happening. The conversation was hard for both of us, and I hope this isn't the nudge that pushes her into retirement. She's been great at making do with a less-than-functional library, but if I'm disappointed, I can't imagine how she's feeling.

"I don't need any handkerchiefs," I grumble at Camille. "You just need to stop skimping and get the good stuff. Look at this." I grab a handful of tattered wet tissue from my lap and give her the stink eye, but the effect is lessened by the involuntary double-hitched breath I take.

Camille watches, unimpressed but not impatient. Maybe it's the effect of being the baby in a family of six, but outside of a professional setting, I've never felt the need to hide my feelings. Hurt, happy, sad—I grew up knowing it was safe to let my emotions out. After sitting here on Camille's rattan lounge, crying for the last half hour and blubbering my way through the day's events, I must admit I feel ten times lighter.

"Can you try going above the principal?" Camille asks. "Contact Jeanine or try writing a letter to the school board."

I take in a shuddering breath. "I already tried that. I spoke with Jeanine this afternoon. First, it took hours just to get her on the phone, and when I finally did, she told me the library remodel would be reconsidered next year. Her contract is almost up, and if she wants the school board to renew it, she can't afford to look wishy-washy. The school board has already closed their offices for the year, so even if I reach out, nothing will be decided until it's too late. And you should have seen how the principal was gloating down the halls today. He really thinks this last stunt is going to run me off for good." I start pulling the tissues apart even more.

"First of all, eww. Watching you play with those is giving me the ick." My sister wrinkles her nose and eyes my lap, appearing every bit the bougie, stuck-up princess her peers in school used to accuse her of being. When I hold one tissue up and make a point of looking her dead in the eye as I pick tiny pieces apart, starting at the edge and not caring if the little confetti-like pieces fall back into my lap or land on the porch, she gives me a look that says *bougie or not, you'll catch these hands if you keep trying me.* Then we hear a soft cry from the baby monitor placed on the closed firepit, and she gets up, pushing my head to the side on her way to get Zara.

"Hey!" I protest, but she's gone before I can do anything.

Three minutes later, Camille comes back with my three-month-old niece held to her chest with one hand and a small wastebasket in the other. She lets the wastebasket fall to the ground beside me with a hollow clang before settling back into her spot to nurse.

It's only the momentary wash of guilt that settles over me as I look at Zara's chubby little form that urges me to pick up my trash rather than anything Camille's attitude could do to move me. Envy is part of the human experience, but I can't help but feel like crap because I've been so envious of my sister for years. She's got everything—the house, the wonderful job where she's her own boss (though she does work with our mom), the loyal and protective husband, and now the perfect angel of a baby. We're only two years apart, but Camille has always been so sure of herself and what she wants out of life, it feels like she's decades ahead. Her, and our older brother, Vincent. I'm behind, stuck in this rut, trying to find a life and a career that's half as fulfilling as theirs seem to be.

My eyes start to water again, and I grab two tissues. Maybe layering will help with their durability.

"Well, if the library isn't happening, what are you going to do?" Camille asks.

I let out a bitter laugh. "There's nothing I can do. I guess I'll go back to school on Monday, suck it up, and do my job."

"You could always apply for the school of arts."

I gasp and cross my arms over my chest, waiting for Camille to take her traitorous words back. "Don't get mad," she says. "Just hear me out. And don't do that thing with your chin."

The thing with my chin—opposite to the thing with my

lip—where the bottom of my chin scrunches and makes my lower lip disappear into a line. There's usually chin trembling involved, and Camille knows I can't control it. Not that I'm trying to right now. If she's going to agree with Principal Major, best believe she's getting the full impact of my disappointment.

"Bri, I cannot with you today. You know I'm only trying to help you out."

"Help me out by agreeing with my archnemesis?"

"Stop being dramatic, I'm not agreeing with him," she says, her voice ratcheting up an octave.

"That's literally what you just did!" My tone matches hers, and if we were teens living at home, this is the exact moment Mom would yell at us from wherever she was in the house to not start something *she'd* have to finish. If we ignored Mom's warning, she'd make us do chores until our anger at her brought us back into each other's good graces.

With Camille being a mom now she must have unlocked the power to stop sibling squabbles before they go off the rails, because she takes in a deep breath while switching Zara to the other side. "Look. I'm just saying, you've been complaining about your principal all year. And when you're not complaining about him, you're mooning over his son. It's not healthy, Bri."

"I do not moon over Roman!" Even though she's my sister and would never judge me—or if she did judge, she'd still be obligated to love me—I never told Camille I have feelings toward Roman. I'm trying to get like her. Admitting to a childish crush doesn't exactly scream "career woman making big strides to a fulfilling career."

"Riiiight. And Lance wants to solve the overpopulation of wild hogs by taking up hunting." She smirks after mentioning her husband's fear of the animal. "You're always telling me how Roman consistently has the best teacher evals or how a hundred percent of his class showed up for lab day or how you want to get your hands all over his ass."

"You know I've never mentioned his nice ass to you!"

Wait, have I? Shoot, I've thought about it often enough, I might have slipped up around Camille.

"Uh-huh. See, I only said 'ass.' You're the one adding unnecessary adjectives. I bet at school you talk to everyone nice and normal, but when Roman comes around, your voice gets all soft and you start rambling."

"Camille, I swear if you don't knock it off . . ." I try staring her down, but the effect is ruined by another involuntary double breath.

She laughs as she begins to burp Zara. "Fine. I'm done. In all seriousness though, what is even keeping you there?"

"How about the kids? I can't just leave them to fend for themselves with an administration that doesn't care if they have access to books and reliable technology."

"Yes, books are important, but what about the thousands of other kids around the state losing access to libraries and banned books within their own schools? You can't help everyone. You may as well find a job where you'll be appreciated and able to make a difference. So again, that school of arts doesn't sound so bad. The only reason I can think of you *not* wanting to at least interview for it is—"

"Do not say it's because of Roman," I warn. She's got precious cargo in her hands, but I've got good enough aim to ball up some tissues and hit her in the forehead.

"Calm down, I wasn't going to say Roman. I was going to say because you don't like the principal telling you what to do. Or anyone, for that matter."

"Don't try to make it sound like I'm difficult. Of course I don't like anyone trying to tell me what to do. I'm not a kid," I say, sounding suspiciously like the student Monique. But unlike her, I am indeed a grown woman and have cause to be indignant when people try bossing me around. "Besides, *no one* likes being told what to do."

"Sure, but you were the only one of us who, when we were kids and Momma said put on stockings to wear to church if it was too cold for bare legs, would pick the brightest-colored ones you could find. They never matched your dresses, and everyone knew you only picked them because you were mad Momma told you to do something."

I try not to cringe, thinking of pictures my parents still have up that serve as prime evidence. Pink-and-purple-striped stockings paired with a white dress with sunflowers. "Wow, I was a brat, huh?"

Camille snorts. "Was?"

Zara finally lets out a burp that seems physically impossible given the size of her body, but it must be all good since Camille switches from patting Zara's back to rubbing it and cooing, "Good job, sweetie. Get it all out." After a while, Camille gets up and stands in front of me. "Here, take her. Or is that too bossy?"

I roll my eyes. "Give me my favorite person in the world."

Camille places Zara in my outstretched arms, and I tuck her in close to my body, breathing in deeply. Vanilla, sun rays on my skin, the first sip of warm tea. That hit of baby serotonin is everything that is right in this world. I don't know if I'll ever have kids of my own, but holding Zara makes a good argument for why I should.

"I'm not trying to pick on you or anything," Camille says. She sits on her cushion with her feet up and legs crossed, eyes closed and head resting on the back. I don't know how she does it. My superwoman sister went back to work as an obstetrician six weeks after having Zara. She works full-time, plus some, since babies don't arrive on a schedule, then comes home to take care of Zara, is in the process of opening up another practice to care for the underserved women in our community, and still makes time for her little sis. "I just want you to be happy," she continues. "We can do this for another year." She sweeps her hand to the wastebasket, obviously meaning I can keep coming here to complain about Principal Major. "Or you can find something that suits you better."

"Don't you think that at a certain point I need to find something and stick with it? Teaching wasn't enough for me. Neither was being a guidance counselor. I can't keep hopping from position to position. You and Vincent have grown up and gotten your lives together while I'm out here like the token wild child, unable to settle down. I need to get it together."

"Hey, you'll find your way. Life isn't a race to see who can get it together first. And believe me, I don't have it figured out nearly as much as it may seem."

She rubs her face. For a moment I see exhaustion pull at her eyes, weariness turn the corners of her mouth down. Then she looks at Zara in my arms, and love wipes out all other expressions. Camille has never been as emotional as me. When we were kids, she was always the strong one, keeping what she felt close to her chest. But when she looks at her daughter, it's like she remembers who her strength is for, and that cape of hers just keeps rippling in the wind.

"Why don't you take the summer to think about what it is you really want to do," Camille says. "If it's staying as vice principal with your current school, fine. If it's moving on, I promise you that will be fine too."

If Camille says it, it must be true. And frankly, I'm too tired to argue anymore. I'm still not ready to concede defeat and walk away like Principal Major wants me to, but for now, he's taken the fight out of me.

CHAPTER FOUR

A week later, I'm on my way to monitor first lunch. The scent of baked cheese enchiladas smothered in canned chili has been seeping through the vents and cracks of my office door for the last hour, and I am almost salivating in the hope that the kids won't try wildin' out today so I can enjoy a plate.

"Excuse me, where is your hall pass, little miss thing?" one of the gym teachers, Paul, says while coming in the opposite direction holding a tennis racket.

I don't waste time looking around; I know he's talking to me. As the distance between us shortens, I wait for it to hit him. When it does, his eyes bug out and his face goes red.

"Oh, Miss Rogers, sorry! I didn't realize it was you," he says in his country drawl.

I nod and offer him a tight smile. "It's okay, Paul. I get it." Today's spirit day theme is Dress like Your Principal, and while most of the kids who participated are in slacks and a button-up to imitate Principal Major, the eighth-grade girls took it to the extreme in dressing like me. I've come across countless mini-Briannas walking around with their cute goddess braids in varying colors from jet black to honey blond, and maxi skirts paired with cowboy boots. Add in the fact that today I'm wearing a yellow maxi skirt with brown cowboy boots *and* I forgot my lanyard at home, and it's been a hilarious morning of confusion watching the teachers try to figure out who the real me is. So Paul thinking I was a student walking around is understandable.

"*Little Miss Thing* though?" I raise an eyebrow at him.

"Oh, ah." He flushes even redder. "Yeah. It won't happen again."

I nod and Paul goes on his way.

When I walk into the cafeteria, it's already at full volume, with kids shouting at each other across tables and claiming their spots while still in line.

Angie is on lunch-monitoring duty as well. She passes me with her upper lip raised to her scrunched-up nose, signaling that she's smelled something bad. Before moving on, she complains, "Why is it so chaotic *and* musty in here?"

I cover my mouth before I can bust out laughing. She really should be used to the smell of teenagers still learning about self-care by now. I've become pretty much noseblind to it, which is why I can only smell the food.

"Miss Rogers!"

I scan the crowd and see Monique waving me over from her seat at one of the long brown tables. I walk to her and bend down. "Hey, Miss Monique. How can I help you?"

"I don't need help today. I just wanted to show you the book I picked out!" She reaches into her backpack and holds out her book like a trophy. "*Nic Blake and the Remarkables.* And look, she looks just like me!" Monique holds up one fist like the girl on the front cover with a high puff, then goes on to tell me how she put her own hair up this morning and even managed to get the edges just right. "I asked Mrs. Yates if she can get a copy of *The Hate U Give* so I can check it out next year. She didn't seem too sure, but I hope she can. I read all the good books already, there's nothing left. I'll probably end up donating this one to the school when I'm done so y'all can have *something*." She shrugs and I fight to quash the lump in my throat.

It's a shame that donations from a child is the best our library can hope for. I don't want to think about the canceled upgrades anymore, but how many great books are these students missing out on by not having a fully functional library here? How many of these students would benefit from seeing characters on book covers that look just like them? Camille made the point that there are thousands of kids all over the state losing access to libraries. Instead of helping me accept that I can't help everyone, the desire to do something about it is even stronger. Without the budget approval, I just don't know what that "something" would be.

I stand up straight and take in a slow breath. "Let me see that pose again," I insist, and Monique crosses her left arm over her chest. "Yass, that's what I'm talking about!"

Monique grins and I give her a high five, the only acceptable form of contact with students, before continuing to move through the tables. Eventually I stop walking and lean against a wall where I still have a good view of the whole cafeteria. Jordan, a math teacher, stops a few feet away from me. He's talking to Roman's friend Kareem. I would move along to give them privacy if it weren't for two points: One, I'm nosy. It wouldn't be professional for me to gossip with the teachers, so I have to listen in when I can to keep a finger on the pulse of what's going on with everyone. Two, a small part of me hopes they mention Roman. But I try not to dwell on that.

"But it won't be a waste of your summer," Jordan is saying,

and I don't need any other context clues to know what they're talking about. Jordan is trying to recruit Kareem for a Mars simulation program.

After Christmas break, Jordan asked permission to represent the school in a six-week challenge where teachers try surviving in a Mars-like environment. It was easy enough to get the okay from Principal Major and the superintendent, but the real challenge for him has been assembling a team. Jordan, who loves all things space but for whatever reason decided to become a math teacher instead of pursuing a career with NASA, thinks I, as the sister of a real-life astronaut, walk on the moon. I was one of the first people he tried to get on board, but even if I wasn't adamant about boundaries with the staff, I'm not willing to give up my summer break for anybody, especially after the year Principal Major put me through. Unfortunately for Jordan, most of the teachers he's asked feel the same way.

I continue scanning the cafeteria and only halfway listen in as Jordan tries pleading his case.

"Come on," Jordan says. "Teachers who participate in the simulation and make it through the full term get twenty thousand dollars. Easy money, bro. And if the team successfully completes all of our tasks before time is up, the school gets five hundred thousand."

Wait a minute. I come to attention immediately at his words. Jordan didn't tell me anything about getting money for participating, and he sure as hell didn't say a word about earning money for the school.

If our school had an extra five hundred grand, Principal Major wouldn't be able to justify *not* using it for the library.

Kareem apologizes to Jordan after making it clear, Dr. Seuss–style, that even if the grand prize were a million dollars, he would not, could not be caught dead in an enclosed space with five other scholars. Just thinking about it makes him shake his head and want to holler.

As Jordan sighs as Kareem walks away, I slide right into his personal space.

"If you're about to ask me if you can leave because you finished lunch early, the answer is no. You know the rules . . . Oh." Jordan blinks when he gets a good look at my face. "Sorry, Brianna. I thought you were a student. What's up?"

"I couldn't help but notice that when you told me about the Mars simulation, you didn't mention anything about the money."

He frowns and scratches at his short locs. "I didn't? Dang, I guess it must have slipped my mind. What can I say, you know? I'm doing it for the journey and not the money. Some experiences are priceless, am I right?"

"Oh yeah, no doubt. I love experiences. Anyway, so what you said about the money is true then? There's a prize for teachers *and* the school?"

"Yeah, there is. Wait—did I forget to tell everyone else about the money and that's why they turned me down?" He gives a self-deprecating shake of his head.

As I open my mouth to ask more questions, Jordan's eyes widen as he looks somewhere over my head. "Marcus, why would you throw cornbread at the back of her head?" He sighs and stalks toward the cornbread-throwing fiend.

I consider stepping in to help so Jordan and I can get back to our conversation but think better of it. Jordan may be easygoing and at times forgetful, but he's been teaching for eight years and knows how to get the kids in line. And while variables have changed regarding the Mars simulation—in the amount of $500,000, to be precise—that still doesn't mean I'm willing to throw my whole summer away and join him. I might have flitted around trying to find the right career for a while, but I've never had aspirations to explore, or pretend to explore, space. Besides, Jordan probably won't be able to pull a full team together anyway. And if he does get the team, we probably wouldn't win the grand prize. I remember him explaining how only 30 percent of teams complete each objective. The whole thing would be a waste of time.

Throughout the other two lunch periods, in between grabbing a plate of enchiladas and stopping any more potential fights, I replay each reason why joining the simulation is a bad idea. But as soon as I'm in my office, I send Camille a message.

> **ME: On a scale of 1 to stealing peaches from Old Man Willie's yard reckless, how unhinged would it be to join a Mars simulation for the summer?**

EMAILS ARE ANSWERED, PARENTS ARE CALLED BACK, I'VE CHECKED IN on three classes, and still Camille doesn't respond. I'm sure she's busy with things that are infinitely more important than what I've got going on—like bringing life into the world—but can't she sense my emotional turmoil? With only a few days of school left, I need to make a decision about the simulation. I can't go to my mom. She almost went into a midlife crisis when my brother went on a mission into space last year. My dad would say he supports me no matter what without giving me his actual opinion, and Vincent wouldn't see any negatives since he thinks space is the bomb. The only person I can count on to look at this objectively is Camille.

I give it a few more minutes before I can't take it anymore. I get up from my desk, squeeze against the wall to get to the door, and march out. When I'm in the math wing and at Jordan's classroom door, I peek through to see if it's a good time to talk. It looks like the students are playing some type of relay game where teams try to solve a math problem on the board as quickly as they can before moving on to the next person. Once it's over, the winning team members high-five one another while the other teams slink back to their desks. As Jordan erases the problems, I knock on the door. He sees me, then quickly writes more problems on the board for the students to work on and excuses himself.

"Did you catch that? Impressive, right?" he says as he steps into the hall. "I promised the kids that whichever team won would get full-size candy bars, but everyone did so great I'm just gonna give them all one."

I smile at him. "Candy, the great motivator."

He smiles back, and I can't help but appreciate how he's always got a great attitude whenever we speak. If only his presence made my heart pound the same way it does when I see Roman.

Ugh. I cut that line of thinking right away. After my talk with Camille, I made the decision that I'm not thinking about Roman anymore. I'm getting over this crush, and I'm not fixating on a different teacher. What I really need is to find a well of men who don't report to me and who I can be attracted to without any complications.

"So," I say, "we never got to finish our conversation earlier." I wait for his eyes to register in recognition. "About the Mars simulation."

"Oh yeah," he shouts, then lowers his voice back to acceptable hall levels. "Did I win you over? Do you want to join as part of Team Jordan?" He squints and shakes his head. "I gotta keep working on the name. How about Team Craft? Yeah, the name of the school works better."

"Before I commit, I have a very important question. Well, I'll have several, but first: When we complete the simulation, who decides what the money for the school gets used for?"

"I'm not sure. I'd guess the school board."

"How about this—we stipulate that when we win, the board will use the money to remodel the library."

Jordan nods. "I like your vision and I like your attitude. I'm all for it."

I didn't want to do this, but Principal Major forced my hand. "Then let's shake on it." I stick my right hand out and Jordan clasps it, shaking vigorously. "Well, okay. I guess the next step is to get the rest of the team together."

He grins wide. "We're already halfway there. After talking to you earlier, I realized that I *hadn't* told anyone about the prize money. I went back to a few people and already got a yes from Simone. She'll be our medical person."

Simone is one of our nurses. I haven't spoken to her much during the year, but she seems nice and has a calming presence.

"We still need two more, but I'm confident we'll have a full team." Jordan looks about ready to burst as he rocks on his heels.

"Great. I'll let you get back to your class, then."

Once Jordan heads back inside and the door closes behind him, I bite down on my lip to fight a smile. I'm going to get that money for the library remodel. Take that, Major Pain.

CHAPTER FIVE

Before I can claim victory in the battle for the library, I have to make sure there's no red tape in the way.

When I get back to my office, the first thing I do is call the superintendent's office. She's available to speak to me right away, and if that isn't a sign this is meant to work out, I don't know what is.

"Hello, Brianna," she answers when the secretary passes me through. She sounds weary, like she's waiting for me to beg her to reverse the decision about the football field again.

"Good afternoon, Superintendent Watts," I sing. "Don't worry, I'm not calling about the library." Her breath of relief is audible, and I correct my statement. "I mean, I *am* calling about the library, but it's not what you think. Do you remember signing the approval for Jordan Wilkerson to represent the school in a challenge run by NASA?" At her affirmative hum, I'm hit with a sudden burst of nerves, but I inhale a deep breath and spit it out. "Well, I've decided to join his team."

I can practically feel her hard stare through the phone as everything on her end goes silent. Her voice is carefully controlled as she asks, "Are you sure that's a wise choice?"

With Principal Major forcing my hand, it doesn't matter

if it's a wise choice. It's the only choice. Though clearly Superintendent Watts thinks it's a terrible idea. I get where she's coming from. On a personal level, she's got the warmest of personalities. She loves her husband and kids and will talk off anyone's ear about her grandbabies. But when it comes to her duties as superintendent, there's no playing around. She's all business, making sure everyone stays in line and in keeping with policies.

You come from a family of greatness, she once said to me. *So, it's given that* you *will be great too. I want to help you because it's not only a vice principal I see when I look at you.* Her eyes shone the same way my mom's had after Camille performed her first C-section. *I see principal. I see superintendent. I'm not just mentoring you for this role, Brianna. I'm mentoring you for what comes after. You've got everything you need to succeed. But what you don't need is a scandal. Keep out of trouble, and you'll go places.*

When I asked her how she's managed to climb the ranks and stay out of any controversies, it was simple: draw a harsh line between your personal and professional life.

The point's been driven home over and over again. *Guess why the admin from Corpus was fired. She knew her favorite students were stealing computer parts but didn't report it. She got too close, too personal, and now she's out of a job.*

Did you hear about the teacher suing her district? She claims some teachers are part of an exclusive clique and terrorize teachers they deem uncool, led by the vice principal, and is suing for emotional distress.

Everyone's talking about the principal from California who was asked to step down. Her husband showed up during an assembly and started accusing her of cheating in front of everyone.

Actually, that particular principal had been carrying on

affairs with the married band director (whose wife taught art at the same school) *and* the government teacher. It was only a matter of time before the whole situation imploded, which, I guess, goes to prove Superintendent Watts's point. There need to be certain lines that aren't crossed. Boundaries that must be maintained.

And I have maintained excellent boundaries all year.

Mostly.

Okay, excellent where Roman isn't concerned. I mean, it's not like anything has ever happened between us. A few smiles and appreciative glances do not a scandal make. And since Roman won't be part of the simulation, there's really nothing to worry about.

"I'm sure it's the best choice," I finally answer her. "You know it's been my goal all year to do something about our library. Think of how good the school will look if we do well in the simulation, all in the name of our kids and community. Think of how good *you* would look if your protégé is part of the team."

I may be laying it on a little thick with that protégé business, but Jeanine's curious "hmm" tells me she likes the sound of it.

"Tell me more," she says, and so I do.

Twenty minutes later, I'm practically skipping down the halls. That's what feeling like you're ten times lighter will do for a woman.

I make a right turn on my way to Principal Major's office when I almost collide with someone. I come to a halt, already prepared to tell whatever teacher or admin to relax and that I'm not a student, until I get a good look and my stomach does a flip. It's Roman. He didn't dress up for spirit day. He's in dark-wash jeans and a gray long-sleeve Henley shirt. He looks good.

"Oh, it's you," I say. My voice comes out involuntarily high, and I clear my throat. "I mean, hi, Mr. Major. Er, Science Teacher Major . . . *Mr.* Science Teacher Major."

Roman's brows crease as I test out saying his name formally. It sounds and feels wrong, but last week proved how allowing myself to become too familiar with him only served to hurt and embarrass me. The first step in getting over him is distancing myself. No more mornings spent waiting for him to make an appearance in the teachers' lounge and no more using his first name when speaking to him.

But . . .

"Vice Principal Rogers." He nods in acknowledgment, though if I'm not mistaken, not only does he look taken aback by me calling him mister, he also looks a little disappointed. "I wasn't sure you were you at first," he says, not moving on. "I could have sworn I saw you like five times today. I was convinced I'd fallen into the Brianna-Verse."

I haven't heard Roman make a joke all year. Now, with him not only saying my name but bringing the Spider-Verse into it, I gnaw on my cheeks to keep from grinning like a fool. This is exactly why I need distance from him. My reaction to him is too quick.

I take another step to the side so I can get past him.

"I, uh," he continues before I can get too far. "I haven't seen you in the teachers' lounge in a while. Or the science wing."

Oh no, not my heart doing cartwheels while in my mind I'm doing a little jig from TikTok, full of body rolls and poppin' hips.

Nope. Nooo. Bad Brianna. If Roman is the type of playboy who only likes when a girl chases after him, then offers up just enough crumbs to keep her interested when she pulls back . . . well, my name ain't Gretel, and I'm not about to feed into his ego to let him know it means something that he's noticed my absence.

"I've been busy trying to close everything out for the end of the year," I say.

He nods. "Yeah, of course."

"Is there anything else you need?" I ask when he continues to stand there.

"Yes," he answers right away. "I wanted to apologize about the other week. Vice Principal Rogers. Brianna, I'm sorry."

On second thought, maybe I am as foolish as Hansel and Gretel taking off into the woods, because my name on Roman's lips could lure me into the deepest of forests with the desire to do the wickedest of things.

"I should have gotten any news from you firsthand before believing my dad and talking to anyone else about it. I . . ."

He stops midsentence as my back goes straight and I hold a hand out, palm facing him. That's right, Roman's dad. Roman's presence is so alluring, so distracting, that I forgot why I was down here.

"It's okay." I relent just a little. It feels unnatural to be so rigid with Roman. "It means a lot to me that you would apologize after realizing your mistake. And I believe you when you say it won't happen again." Roman dips his head in agreement. "Perfect. Well, I'll let you go, then. If I don't talk to you before break starts"—which I won't; it's going to take some time before this crush is out of my system if one conversation with him has the ability to turn my insides to goo—"have a great summer."

This time I don't give him room to hold me up any longer. I step around and continue on, past the attendance window, through the administrators' half-empty desks, and right to Principal Major's door. I knock two times and open it without waiting for an answer.

Principal Major snaps his head up from his computer. "Miss Rogers? What are you—"

I hold up a hand, just like I did with Roman. Principal Major looks both shocked and outraged, and it's like I've unlocked a new superpower. Hell yeah. I'll need to put my palm to good use more often.

"I have something to say," I announce. "All year you've done nothing but try to make my job miserable, even going against what you must know will benefit students. All because I took the VP spot you want your precious boy to have."

"If you wanted to resign, an email would have sufficed. No need to burn bridges while you're at it. But if this is how you want to go out, by all means, then, continue." He leans back in his seat and regards me with cool eyes.

I smile sweetly, ensuring my dimples are on full display. "Oh, I'm not resigning. I wanted to let you know I'm not going anywhere. And you were right when you called me stubborn, because I haven't given up on the library either. I found another way to get the money, and I estimate by this time next year, Juanita Craft Middle School will be known for its new state-of-the-art library."

I turn around and stride out of his office with my head held high, leaving the door open on his confused and annoyed face. He doesn't know my plans yet, but by the time he's got it all figured out, it will be too late for him to stop me.

I'm still operating off the high of Principal Major's outrage when I get back to my office. I collapse into my chair and smile up at the ceiling, not remotely bothered that the panels above are in obvious need of replacement. I open the drawer with my cell so I can send Camille a play-by-play of what just happened. But when I turn the screen on, I see there are four missed calls and five text messages from her, each reading more and more concerned.

> CAMILLE: **Old Man Willie? Girl, what are you thinking of doing?**

> CAMILLE: **Call me so we can talk about whatever it is you're considering.**

> CAMILLE: **Hello? Where are you??**

> CAMILLE: **Did you really send me that message then disappear?**

The phone buzzes in my hand, and one last message pops up.

> CAMILLE: **What have you gotten yourself into this time?**

I STARE INTO THE YOUNGER SPITTING IMAGE OF MY DAD'S FACE THROUGH the screen. Dark brown skin with contrasting light brown eyes. These days, there's a little gray at his temples, which I'm sure he'd say makes him look all the wiser. Rather than get back to Camille (at least right away—I will eventually call her before she decides to show up at my school), I reached out to my older brother, Vincent.

His eyes glitter with excitement and his mouth twitches. "I have to say, my little sister joining a Mars simulation was not on my bingo card for this year."

I roll my eyes. "You don't even play bingo."

"You don't know my life. I do lots of things." I continue staring at Vincent and he smiles. "Fine. I don't play bingo. Yet. So, did you tell Mom about the simulation?"

"No. I'll just text her later."

"No, you should call her. And let me be on the phone when you do. Better yet, let's do one big family conference call."

I narrow my eyes. "Why? It's not that big of a deal."

"After all the fuss she made about me going to the moon, you better believe she'll think it's a big deal. I, for one, can't wait to see you take the heat instead."

I shake my head. At least Mom had good reason to worry about Vincent. The daredevil among us did what some only dream of by becoming an astronaut and then making history by going to the moon for six months. There was actual cause for her to be legitimately worried about him. But worried about me? I'm still going to be in Texas. As large as the state is, I can't imagine she'd think it's as big of a deal.

"It's really not that serious," I say, and there's no way he can convince me otherwise. But before he can try, I go on. "So, about this simulation. What should I expect? Nothing but jars of mushy baby food? Alien invasions?"

Vincent looks up to the ceiling and squints as he thinks. "Before my mission, we gave them a list of our favorite foods and they were able to get it manufactured into the flavors we like. It may not look appetizing, but once you get over the mush texture, it's not bad. I tore down on the hamburger flavor after a while."

I push away my burger from the cafeteria, which wasn't even that great to begin with. "What? I was just playing.

Vince, please tell me they aren't about to send us out there with jars of baby food."

"Jars?" He shakes his head and I'm almost relieved. "That would be too heavy for transport. It's all about being authentic and mimicking exactly what life would be like on Mars. It's in pouches, and you slurp the food. Mimi?" He looks to his fiancée off-camera. "How long did it take me to get used to chewing food again so I could digest it properly? About two weeks?"

"Yeah, that sounds about right," comes her distant voice.

I slide a hand over my face and sigh. "This is honestly going to be way more challenging than I thought."

I thought they'd be sending us with the kind of dehydrated foods I use for camping or taking long hikes. God, this better work out, and we'd better win that money for the library, or I swear I'll . . .

I hear what sounds like Vincent sneezing, and when I look up, I see he's trying to hold in a laugh. I sigh and shake my head. One would think after having thirty years of experience with him trying to play around, I'd be able to pick up on when he's being unserious. Maybe I would have if Amerie hadn't cosigned on his joke.

"You two just can't help it, can you?"

Amerie comes into the frame, popping her head on Vincent's shoulder. "Sorry, Brianna! I couldn't resist."

I give her a mock glare. It's hard to be fully annoyed when they're so cute together. Vincent managed to find the one person to go along with his absurd sense of humor.

"The simulation, Vince. What can you tell me?"

"Okay, okay." He kisses Amerie's hand before she pulls away, then focuses on me. "I have some friends who have either facilitated or participated in the simulations. It's not that hard physically, but it is mentally. You need to go into the experience prepared to be away from home in every sense of the word. You'll be isolated. You'll have days when you're so bored that you wouldn't mind watching water boil or paint dry. Speaking of, you should take some art supplies or some good books. As far as the team goes, there will be days when everyone gets along and days when everyone will be at each other's throats, insulting the way they cough or breathe. But when you look back, you'll see them as family. That's just how it goes."

I can't help but frown, hearing Superintendent Watts's warnings in my head about scandals and career trajectories.

"What's that look for?" Vincent asks.

I shrug. "It's just the part you said about teammates becoming family. I mean, I'm only going to be there for six weeks. I like the teachers I work with and everything, but I'm not going there with the intention of becoming besties with anyone."

Now he's the one giving me a look, and I don't like it. Like he's thinking, *Poor little Brianna. Afraid to go up and make new friends.*

"What?" I say. "All the people you went on your *very real* mission with were astronauts, so y'all had no choice but to become family. I'm a vice principal doing this *fake* simulation with my teachers. Our stakes are not the same. I'll still need to maintain proper boundaries so when we return to school it's not weird."

"I see where you're coming from," he says. "I really do. But I've learned, pretty recently, that there needs to be balance. It can't be all work all the time. We're humans and we need those connections. If you ask me, it's actually the best part of being human. Camille has told me that since starting your new position, you've been pretty isolated. None of us want that for you, Bri."

Wow, now I have to worry about Camille and Vincent talking about me behind my back. Like I'm some sad hermit who does nothing but work and then comes home to my dog. Which, granted, I do. But I'm not the only adult who's unfulfilled and still trying to find their way to happiness.

I study Vincent through the screen. He looks happy. Like, truly happy. I can't help but marvel at the fact that not long ago, it would have been so hard to get him to find enough time to sit down and have a drawn-out conversation with me. He would have been putting way more hours into his work and training than was needed. If ever there were a poster child for work-life imbalance, Vincent was it. But that was before he met Amerie, his then–fake girlfriend turned real fiancée.

If I could be like Vincent, I would. But he's always known what he wants and has never had to deal with the likes of someone like Principal Major trying to hinder him. If I go into the simulation with the idea of cozying up with the teachers, I'm worried it will affect how the staff at school and Superintendent Watts see me and in turn derail my career.

Vincent looks past the screen again and smiles softly at Amerie.

Then again, letting people close does seem to have paid off for Vincent. Maybe I'll think about taking his advice.

Not that I'm going to tell *him* that.

CHAPTER SIX

I love it when I get what I want. And I'm not just stating that from the point of view of the youngest child who is therefore doted on. I'm saying that from the point of view of someone who just really loves the thrill of winning.

While standing in front of the library's old, worn doors that are so crooked we have to use a chain after school hours to keep them closed, I smile at Principal Major, and he smiles back. My smile is real, and I'm sure it radiates nothing but the elation I feel. Principal Major's, on the other hand, reminds me of how Sheba snaps her teeth together each month when I try to get her to take a heart-worm prevention pill, no matter what kind of treat I wrap it in. But oh, the taste of watching Principal Major trying to stomach putting up a celebratory facade today has been delicious.

"Just a few more shots," the district photographer says. "Look here and smile. On one, two, three." A series of flashes has me seeing bright dots in my vision, but my smile remains still in place.

"Is that it?" Principal Major asks. His tone isn't exactly gruff, with him being on his best behavior in front of Superintendent Watts, but the strain is there.

"Wait, did we get enough 'before' pictures in the library?" I ask, just to get on his nerves. I'm going to milk this victory as long as I can.

Superintendent Watts laughs and winks at me. She obviously knows what I'm doing, and I'm not ashamed. If I can put up with Principal Major's attitude for nine months, he can get through a dozen or so pictures.

"How about we head outside and join the rest of the celebration?" Superintendent Watts suggests.

"Finally," Principal Major mutters. "Miss Rogers, I'm sure you can close up in here." He gestures for everyone to follow him through the doors and leaves so quickly I'm beginning to wonder if he's got something against libraries as a whole.

"Do you need help?" Superintendent Watts asks me.

"Don't worry, I've got it. I'll see y'all outside in a few minutes."

Superintendent Watts and the rest of the crew going to the Mars simulation—Jordan, Simone, and our newest recruits who joined in the nick of time, Angie and Renee— follow after Principal Major, and I'm left by myself.

I find the heavy chain on top of one of the desks. Instead of grabbing it and closing the doors right away, I take a moment to stand still and soak in the quiet of the library. I let the scent of books (and what I suspect might be a trace of mildew) wash over me. Accomplishment washes over me too. If everything goes according to plan, this will be the last time I see the library like this. Old, dreary, sad, and in desperate need of more love than Mrs. Yates can give it.

I start walking along the shelves, looking at the colorful spines, then can't help myself and act like I'm a little kid in the library again. I close my eyes and run my finger along the book spines before stopping on a random one. The book I pull out dates itself with an illustration of a boy with messy brunette hair and crooked glasses, and despite the clear protective plastic, the hardcover is falling apart and about ten years past ready to be retired. When I open the book to the copyright page and see it was published in 1992, I shake my head. It doesn't get any better when I randomly select six more.

There is no reason for me to have to pick up nearly ten books before finding one that has someone with a brown face on the cover. We've got too many books out in the world for that to be a reality for kids at this school.

"If books are supposed to bring joy, why do you look like you're in physical pain?"

I start at the sound of Roman's voice, but don't turn to him. I slip the book I'm holding back in, ensuring it's in the exact same spot I got it from.

"I don't know what you mean," I say.

All I needed was to be able to get through the remaining school days, and then I would no longer need to worry about running into him for the whole summer. But now I look to my left and there's no way for me to escape. The shelves are pushed together to make space for detention, and this particular row intersects into a T. Not only is it a fire hazard, it means the only way out of this aisle is through Roman.

My pulse quickens at the realization that he must have sought me out. There'd be no other reason for him to be in here. I don't know why he would, though. I thought we said everything that needed to be said outside his dad's office.

Realizing that he's obviously content to stand there and not say anything, I finally turn and face him. It's a mistake. His unwavering gaze is on me, saying a dozen little things at once. Like, he's sorry and please forgive him and don't write him off like all the other teachers have. But, God, do

I want to write him off. Just barrel past him and escape like I did before.

But I also don't want to be that vice principal who becomes unapproachable once someone makes one mistake.

"What can I help you with, Mr. Major?" I ask, once again not using his name so that the part of my brain controlling my attraction to him gets the hint that this man is off-limits and someone I need to keep at arm's length. Though being alone with him in the library doesn't help either of those goals.

Roman doesn't answer right away. He stretches his arm in front of me, though not close enough to touch, and pulls out the book I was inspecting before. It feels like it's been forever since I last got a whiff of him, and my senses feel the effect double time.

"*The Body Book for Boys*," he reads, lifting his eyebrows.

My cheeks heat in physically painful embarrassment. I wasn't paying attention to the titles of any of the books I picked up, only the condition they were in.

"Maybe I'll make this a requirement in my class for next year," Roman says, his joke easing some of my discomfort. "Having to suffer through three class periods after gym classes ain't for the weak."

"Only three? Lucky you. According to Angie, it's bad all day."

My lips begin pulling into a smile until I remember I'm not supposed to be on any kind of overly friendly terms with Roman. I let the smile fade before it can fully bloom. As my smile vanishes, so does the light in Roman's eyes. He sighs and slides the book back on the shelf. Only he isn't as meticulous as I was, and it ends up in the wrong spot. I try to leave it as is but eventually cave and right his wrong.

"Someone needs to learn to respect libraries," I mumble

under my breath while grabbing *The Body Book for Boys* and placing it where it belongs, two slots to the left.

"Sorry," Roman says.

"It's fine. At least you kept it here in the reference section and not somewhere like, say, crafts."

"Naw, I wasn't talking about straying from the Dewey decimal system."

I snap my head to him, eyebrows raised. We love a king who throws library terminology around as easily as discussing the temperature outside.

"I mean," he continues, "I'm sorry for telling people you were moving."

We're back to that again. I just want to forget about that morning. "I know. You already apologized and I accepted, remember?"

"I remember. I just know that it bothered you, and I didn't want us to end the year with this animosity between us."

"There's no animosity between us," I lie. He quirks a dubious brow and I shrug. "Okay, fine. Maybe a little. I guess I've just been hurt since finding out your dad canceled all the plans for the library. It seems like something you could have told me anytime I saw you in the morning."

"I didn't know about the library," he says, and this time *I* raise a dubious eyebrow. "I'm serious. I know everyone thinks me and my dad have this super-tight relationship, but it's not like that. He doesn't tell me his plans. He just does what he wants and expects everyone to roll with him." He shakes his head like it's something he's experienced a lot of from his dad. Honestly, it sounds exactly like something Principal Major would do. "If I had known, I would have told you. I respect what you're trying to do here, Bri—Vice Principal Rogers. Everything you've done this year for the students and teachers, and the way you've put up with my dad. And now that you're about to give up your summer to make sure the library still comes through, it's just . . ." He pauses, his eyes searching my own, and I get the feeling he's seeing *me*. Not Vice Principal Brianna who battles with his dad every day, but the woman trying so hard to just make a mark in the world so she'll feel a little less insignificant. "Amazing. I want you to know that I think you're amazing."

He stops talking, and I hold my breath, wanting—*needing*—him to say more. I need him to elaborate on all the ways he thinks I'm amazing so I can luxuriate in the way my insides are going all warm and tingly.

Maybe he reads it in my body, because he takes a step forward and goes on. "I don't agree with how my dad has handled things this year. Especially where you're concerned. You deserve so much more, Brianna. You deserve—"

"Miss Rogers!" comes a high-pitched voice.

Simultaneously, Roman and I jump apart. We turn to find Monique standing at the opening of the aisle where Roman was before.

Monique looks between us, and at first I'm worried she'll say something about us being alone. I can imagine her little voice singing, *Miss R and Mr. Major sittin' in a tree, K-I-S-S-I-N-G.* Honestly, I don't hate the image that evokes, but it would spell bad news if she went around yelling about anything she thinks she saw.

Blessedly, the sweet child blinks up at us innocently and cements her place as my favorite student. "Miss Rogers, there you are. I was looking all over. The food trucks are here, and the superintendent asked me to escort you out there."

"Thank you, Monique," I say, and look over at Roman. "I guess I better close up in here and head out."

Leaving the seclusion of the shelves, I grab the chain and head for the doors. Roman stands just outside the library. He looks at Monique, who's apparently taken her job to heart and isn't returning to the celebration without me, then he looks at me. It feels like we're leaving a million things unsaid, but it's probably better this way. I turn away to close the door and he makes his way down the hall.

"Is Mr. Major your boyfriend?" my ex–favorite student asks as we pass empty lockers.

Roman is ahead of us but luckily not in hearing range. I tear my eyes away from his sexy-as-sin walk and try to look composed as I answer. "Of course he's not. Why would you ask? Because we were back there? We were just talking about books and the new library." It's probably way too much of an explanation and a simple no would have sufficed, but Monique doesn't seem to mind.

She shrugs. "Oh, okay."

When we reach the front of the school, where the drop-off circle has been converted into a mini festival, Monique goes off on her own and I let out a breath. I inhale again, and the scents of turkey legs, smoked chicken, and street corn cause me to salivate.

Once our crew was complete and everyone agreed the grand prize money would be put toward the library remodel, Superintendent Watts insisted on a celebration both in honor of school officially being over and to send us off on the simulation. Much to Principal Major's dismay. Students, parents, and teachers walk around with food and balloon animals. There's a booth from one of our local independent bookshops with colorful books displayed on tables and a tent with NASA employees in blue-and-white shirts surrounded by curious students. My heart is so full as I take it all in, and I don't know whether to explore or eat first.

Before I can decide on any direction, I see Superintendent Watts walking my way. She smiles and waves to students running by with cotton candy, then stops beside me. "Look at how excited everyone is. You keep making moves like this, you bring home that money for the library, then I don't see how anything will be able to stop you. Not an unyielding principal"—she pauses and clears her throat—"or his ambitious son."

I'm almost positive I make no outward movements or sounds, but when she brings up Roman, my muscles lock. Did she somehow see us in the library together? Did Monique report back with the news? I knew I was too gracious in calling her my favorite student. I hope she's not running around telling anyone she can about what she thinks she saw. *Scandal! Scandal!* flashes before my eyes, but I blink it away and try to remain composed.

"Honey, I get it," Superintendent Watts goes on. "He's young and he's got it going on with his smooth walk and bedroom eyes." I want her to stop. "But there are plenty of men with the same attributes. You're a rising star, Brianna." She levels her eyes at me, making sure each word she says has maximum impact. "Don't let the wrong decision set you off course."

I swallow, feeling like a Goody Two-shoes in trouble for the first time. "I won't," I say. And I mean it. I have no plans of doing anything with Roman that would jeopardize my career.

Superintendent Watts must believe me, because her eyebrows relax and she gives my hand a brief squeeze before walking away.

I let out a slow breath. In hindsight, I should have left

the library once Roman apologized. Bulldozed right through him if I had to.

But then I would have missed how he held his breath while waiting for me to accept his apology and how his eyes softened when he called me amazing.

God, I am a mess. At least this is the last day I'll see him for a couple of months. With my mind focused on completing the simulation and winning the money, I will be way too occupied to worry about him.

On that hopeful thought, I start walking around again. I wave at students and accept wishes of success from the grown-ups. They're as excited as we are at the prospect of a better library. I slow down as I come upon the bookshop's booth. They've got a wonderful, diverse selection of Middle Grade and YA books, as well as a table loaded with essential bookish items: bookmarks, tote bags, reading lights. I pick up a cute book-themed kaleidoscope and aim it at the sky, twisting the end to see changing prisms with red, green, and yellow. When I set it back down, I see a kid with shoulder-length locs shove a graphic novel in front of his mom's face.

"Can I get it, Mom? Please?" he asks, nailing her with puppy dog eyes.

She makes him sweat for a moment but eventually caves and says yes. I clench my fist in victory. If she hadn't bought the book for him, *I* would have been tempted to, and then I would've gotten stuck buying books for every other kid out here to make it fair.

I keep walking and spot Principal Major talking to Renee. Renee looks uncomfortable, and while I sincerely hope she isn't getting chewed out for some arbitrary reason, I don't have the energy to go run interference. I do, however, have the energy to give Principal Major a mocking wave when he glances my way and scowls. Jerk.

Next I come across a group of people dancing around a speaker. Scratch that, it's Angie dancing while a handful of people stand around recording her. I don't remember her ever mentioning being a professional dancer, but she is on point with those moves. Her arms alternate between fast and slow movements without missing a beat. She's doing the Beychella "Everybody Mad" dance. It's not the same song, but I'd recognize those iconic movements anywhere, and she's nailing them better than any majorette could. Watching her almost makes me wish I could jump right in, but I am not trying to be the vice principal who goes viral that way. I'll have to live vicariously through Angie and be glad she can dance so well without her back bothering her. Ha.

I smile to myself and look around, unsurprised when my eyes land right on Roman as he stands on the other side of the circle, holding a huge turkey leg in one hand and a white cup in the other. It's the fall dance all over again as we both stand on the outside with no one to cut up with but each other. I'm not upset at him anymore, and despite Superintendent Watts's warning, I wiggle my eyebrows as if to say, *Where does a computer sciences teacher learn moves like that anyway?* However, something gets lost in translation. Instead of answering, Roman walks around everyone and comes to stand with me.

He holds the cup out. "Corn?"

I swallow back my shock as I look from the cup of corn, with its layer of cotija cheese and chili powder, to the turkey leg to Roman's lips, then force my eyes back to his and shake my head no. "No, thank you."

He shrugs and bites down on the turkey leg. It's the biggest piece of poultry I've ever seen, but he handles it like a champ.

"Is it good?" I ask.

I take his muffled "Mmm" as confirmation before laughing and turning back to Angie, who's now dancing with some students.

I play it as cool as I can, but my mind is racing. I'm all too aware of Roman's presence beside me and my hammering heart that won't give me peace whenever he's around. And why is he hanging around like we do this all the time? Why did he seek me out again?

Answers float in my head, but they can't be right. He didn't seek me out because he likes me. He doesn't feel the connection I've felt tugging between us all year. Then again, he did call me amazing. I don't think I'll ever forget that. He also seemed sincere about not liking how his dad treats me.

Superintendent Watts passes by with a colleague and catches my eye, glancing between Roman and me with a frown. A silent warning not to get caught up in any trouble. I know she means well, but I can't help bristling slightly. I don't need anyone trying to warn me not to get too close to Roman. We're standing here watching Angie dance. It's not like we're about to do anything crazy out in the open.

When a breeze stirs the air and a fresh wave of Roman's cologne washes over me, as I inhale as much of the scent as I can, I consider the possibility that the superintendent is right about her warning. I fake a cough and take the tiniest step away to put some distance between us.

"You sure you don't want any?" he asks.

One of these days I'll learn not to meet his eyes, because they get me every time. I look at his outstretched hand that's once again offering up the corn and want to erase the distance I just put between us. Maybe I'm too easy when it comes to Roman, but I can't think of a reason I should hold a grudge against him. I need to get rid of the crush I have on him, and I will, but not today. Today I'll savor one-upping Principal Major, as well as the support of our community and their belief that we'll do well in the simulation. And I'll share some corn with Roman.

"Actually, I think I'll try it after all," I say, and take the cup from him.

CHAPTER SEVEN

The next two weeks are a whirlwind. I'm so busy filling out end-of-year forms and other business to officially close the school year, there's little time to second-guess my decision to join the simulation. I was initially set to take my cruise before returning for summer school; however, now that I won't be coming back until August, Principal Major will have to handle hiring new teachers and onboarding them, overseeing summer school, and dealing with any issues that arise as construction for the new football field begins all by himself. Or, more likely, he'll have Roman step in for a few weeks and take over the vice principal role. Whatever they decide to do for those six weeks has nothing to do with me, and I'm honestly glad for the break, even if there's going to be less wind in my hair than I anticipated.

I take a deep breath as I pull into a parking lot located at the Johnson Space Center to meet with the team. Today, we'll get fitted for our space suits and sit through orientation. Tomorrow we'll get shuttled to our new home, or habitat, for the summer. Just me and four of Juanita Craft's finest getting cozy for six weeks.

I pull the visor down and check my reflection in the small mirror. Even though I'm no longer going on the cruise, I kept the hair appointment I'd scheduled and got my braids redone early this morning. It's left my head a little tender, so I gingerly sweep the honey-brown braids behind my back and get out of my car.

"Good afternoon," I say to a man sitting at a front desk when I walk into the unmarked brick building. "I'm here for the Mars simulation orientation."

After I show my ID, the man points me down the hall to where a set of double doors are open.

I walk into a large conference room. There are five treadmills, two rows of desks facing a large screen on the wall, and two portable changing rooms, where my team is gathered. I set my purse and keys down on the nearest table and walk toward everyone.

Jordan is the first to see me. "Hey, you made it!" he greets. He looks as ecstatic as a kid at Christmas who just got the video game system their momma swore up and down they wouldn't be receiving as he does some movements in his suit. According to the preliminary paperwork I read through, they'll supply the outfits we'll be wearing. Basic long-sleeve coveralls for inside the habitat, as well as a space suit, with helmet and oxygen tank included, for any work we do outside. Jordan has on the blue coveralls.

"I made it," I say.

Simone is next to Jordan, doing some high-knee marches to test the fit of her coveralls. Like me, she's in her early thirties. She has light tan skin with a pink undertone and the most gorgeous spiral curls. "Hey, Miss Rogers," she says, slightly breathless when she sees me. "Glad you could make it."

"Thanks," I say. "And just Brianna. If we're all going to be cooped up together for close to two months, I think we can use first names."

"Hey, Brianna," Angie says as she steps out from one of the changing rooms. "Ooh. Or should I say Miss Body-ody-ody?"

"Brianna," I plead as my body flushes. We were instructed to show up in formfitting exercise clothes the coveralls and space suit would go over, so I came in navy leggings and an athletic shirt. It's another outfit I was influenced to buy off social media. Unlike my pajamas for spirit day, this outfit does everything it's meant to. It snatches, lifts, and yes, gives me *body*. I didn't think it'd be a big deal since no students are around, but leave it to Angie to point out that my goodies are out for all to see. "Just . . . call me Brianna."

She shrugs as if to say *suit yourself*, then turns to Jordan. "When should we expect the football players to show up?"

Football players? That's random. Considering the whole reason we're here is because of an unneeded football field, if any players show up, I'm going to riot. I turn to Jordan as well. He cringes, looking decidedly guilty as he moves by the other changing stall, and says, "How's everything fitting?" He's deflecting. I try catching his eye to get some idea of what is going on, but he dodges me.

"It's pretty good. A little tight in the biceps though," a deep voice from behind the other changing screen says. A voice completely lacking the high pitch of what I know Renee should sound like.

I stop caring about whatever it is that Jordan's obviously hiding as my stomach begins to knot up. I have to be hearing things. This room looks like the ordinary, run-of-the-mill conference room turned training space, but there's something wacky about the acoustics in here. Or maybe my braider did my hair too tight, and instead of giving me a headache, it's affecting my stereocilia. Or . . . or . . . I'm trying to think of any other explanation, but at this point I'm only denying what I know to be true.

Roman steps out of the other changing room.

Hell to the mother-loving no.

Scratch that—hell *yes*. It's like my heart flatlines then surges again when I get a good look at Roman. He has on the same long-sleeve coveralls as the others, but *my God*. The fit is indeed tight on his biceps. And abs and thighs. Even though Roman's physique is more on the slim side, like a runner's as opposed to a bodybuilder's, the coveralls highlight how toned he is. How utterly and completely divine.

Maybe one day I'll look back over my life and realize that when it comes to Roman, I'm no better than the men who openly leer at women just trying to walk around and live their lives. But today is not that day.

"Yeah, I think I need the next size up," Roman says, moving his arms across his chest in such a way that it's obvious how wrong I was. NASA isn't providing us with simple, everyday coveralls. No siree. These things must be made from superior fabric. The kind that by all accounts should have ripped into shreds the moment Roman closed the zipper, let alone flexed. The kind of fabric you'd see on some infomercial claiming how indestructible it is, followed by a tank rolling over it or a cat using it as a scratching post, only for someone to then hold it up and find it perfect and perfectly clean. The kind of fabric that . . . Okay, I'm done. Even I know I'm doing too much.

Roman does the same high-knee march Simone did.

Seriously, who sourced the fabric? Can I get it on Amazon?

"Maybe two sizes up," Roman says. "It feels like I'm about to bust a seam or . . ." Whatever else he was going to say is cut off when he turns and spots me.

He stares, looking so surprised to see me that for a second, I wonder if I'm even supposed to be here. Because one of us is surely out of place.

Then he blinks, and his eyes move away from my face to travel the length of my body. Awareness zings my skin like little prickles of electricity, mirroring the path his gaze takes, and I'm suddenly very cognizant of the fact that he's never seen me in anything tighter than slacks. And with the coveralls so snug on him, I can see the moment he inhales, then swallows. Then licks his lips. It's the exact same moment my insides turn to literal goo.

If we were on school grounds, the look he's giving me would be highly inappropriate. But here, in this room and in different clothes, it's like we're seeing each other in a new light. I don't know about him, but it sure as hell doesn't feel like I'm looking at a science teacher right now. I'm looking at a man whose attention sets my body aflame and who I want to give many babies to.

"Brianna," Roman says. He schools his features and makes a point of not straying from my eyes. "You made it."

For all the gawking and big talk going on in my head before, no response comes out. Evidently, I don't recover as smoothly as him. All my thoughts have up and poofed. Simply peaced out to leave me standing here speechless and wanting.

Roman clears his throat and begins to look increasingly uncomfortable with my silence. "We just started trying on the clothes, so you haven't missed anything important."

I shake my head to get rid of the tunnel vision that's only allowed me to focus on him. With my eyes open to the other people in this room and the fact that seeing Roman today is the last thing I expected or wanted, I ask him,

"What are you doing here?" My heart is racing full speed at the impact of what his presence means.

"I heard y'all were down a man," he says, like it's the simplest of explanations.

"Yeah," Jordan confirms. "Something came up and Renee couldn't commit after all. I tried calling every teacher I knew. I even went to the school to see if I could talk one of the teachers getting ready for summer school into changing their plans. Then I ran into Principal Major, and he suggested Roman."

While Jordan explains, the gears in my head begin turning, clicking right into place when he says "Principal Major," and I can't believe he doesn't see it.

Oh Jordan, you sweet, sweet summer child.

I'm not going to lie, Roman had me good with his little performance at school. With his talk of me being "amazing" and not liking how his dad treated me, I thought he was being genuine, but it was all a ploy to get me to let my guard down. Well, I've learned my lesson—playing with Roman is playing with fire. I won't be burned again.

I look at him, allowing myself one more moment of appreciation. One moment is all it can be. He can claim he's here to be our last man, but I know once the simulation starts, we'll be working on different teams.

———

"YOU CAN'T GO," CAMILLE SAYS. SO EASILY TOO. LIKE IT'S THE FINAL word on the matter just because she wills it.

I sigh. "You've already said that. Repeatedly. And I already told you that *yes*, I can. I have to."

Camille leans against her quartz kitchen countertop. She's wearing a pair of crisp white scrubs while getting some morning snuggles in with Zara before work. Camille isn't even wearing a burp cloth in case she gets drool or spit-up on her, like she knows her perfect baby wouldn't dare mess up her momma's outfit.

"Brianna Odette," Camille says in that grating tone she uses when she's about to tell me how to live my life. She's been using it all morning, now bringing my middle name into it, and I have just about had it. "I'm serious. Going through with this simulation after finding out the teacher you've been crushing on all year is joining is just asking for trouble. Do you honestly think this is a good idea?"

Honestly? No, I don't think it's a good idea, if for no other reason than that I'm not sure what I'll do to Roman if I have to be near him for weeks on end. The more I think about him joining the simulation, the angrier I get. Angry, hurt, and humiliated. One thing is certain: that crush I had on him is gone. Gone. Even if thinking about the hungry way he looked at me with my exercise clothes on makes me shiver, his unexpected and unwelcome appearance ensured all other soft feelings I had toward him dried up.

How could he seek me out in the library and act like he was on my side, only to throw it all in my face? Like I didn't see his dad talking to Renee at school, where he most likely said something to get her to drop out. This is all clearly a calculated move on Principal Major's part, and Roman, for whatever reason, is playing right along. "Having or not having a crush on Roman is irrelevant. I have to go and make sure he doesn't sabotage everything." What better way to derail my plans than for Principal Major to get a man on the inside to do his dirty work, hoping once again to try to break my spirit? "Without that money, the library really will be a lost cause. Don't you see that I just can't walk away from that?"

"No, I really don't. Why put yourself through all this nonsense?" Camille asks.

Brown eyes, the same shade and shape as mine, study me. Tenacious, dependable superwoman Camille doesn't understand that I need to see at least one thing through, and getting the library built is it. Roman notwithstanding, if I can help get our team through six weeks of tasks and isolation to win the money for the library, then I can do anything. Then I won't be the young, flighty Rogers child still trying to get her life together while her siblings conquer the world. I'll be that rising star Superintendent Watts spoke of.

But I don't say any of that because, again, Camille won't understand.

We both turn at the sound of footsteps as my brother-in-law, Lance, strides into the kitchen.

"Hey, sis," he says to me.

Lance is about five feet nine, with dark brown skin and wire-rim glasses. He's been part of our family ever since I can remember. Growing up in the same small town as us, he and my brothers were best friends. When my oldest brother, Tay, passed away and then Vincent distanced himself from the family, Lance was still there for us. Most especially there for Camille when she decided keeping everyone from falling apart even further rested solely on her shoulders. They made it through the hardest of times and are now living their happily ever after.

Lance walks up to Camille, kisses her forehead, and massages her shoulders, then takes Zara out of her arms. As he holds her at arm's length, making funny faces, Zara's eyes widen. No baby giggles yet, but the recognition is certainly there as she scans her dad's face and smiles.

"Ready for your meetings today?" Camille asks Lance.

She steps close and embraces him, wrapping her arms around his waist. As he smiles down at her, she slides her hands under the hem of his blue button-down and grabs the waistband of his Golden State Warriors pajama pants.

"Woman!" he yelps with a grimace when she lets the band hit his back with a pop.

Lance uses one arm to secure Zara to his chest and the other to tickle Camille, and I slide off my stool to give the happy family their privacy.

I try to tell myself not to be jealous and that one day the time will come when I'm expressing my love language to a partner through fun and games. But I can't help but wonder, *when*? When will it be my turn? I force back the image of standing beside Roman and looking up as he went to town on his turkey leg. It wasn't adorable, and he's not the man for me.

I look out the back door window and see Sheba standing there patiently, her brown eyes barely visible through her golden fur. Camille agreed to watch her while I'm gone. When I open the door, she politely walks in and comes to me for some cuddles.

"Who needs a partner when they have the best girl in the world anyway?" I whisper as I bend down and scratch behind her ears.

Sheba and I have come a long way since she was a curious puppy I had no idea what to do about. If anyone saw her, they'd never guess the same well-behaved dog once attacked someone. Well, *attack* is a strong word. More like *mauled with love*. I'll never forget the day a year ago when we went hiking with my family and my brother's now-fiancée, Amerie, jogged away from the group to catch up with Vincent, who'd taken off like the Lone Ranger. Sheba managed to slip free from me and ran after Amerie, causing her to fall and sprain her ankle. Amerie held no grudges, realizing Sheba only wanted to give her kisses, but I felt horrible.

After the trip I spent two thousand—yes, *thousand*, as in the cardinal number that is the product of ten and one hundred—for a personal behavior specialist and trainer. As it turns out, I was the one who needed training in how to deliver consistent and confident commands. The difference is night and day.

I didn't think I'd ever be one of those people harping on about their dogs being their babies, their dog being the one to rescue *them*, or how petting their dog helped them relax after a long day, but . . . yeah. Sheba has been all that and more. Especially this year as I've adjusted to a life more isolated from coworkers and friends. I can't always show up on Camille's doorstep since she's got her family to take care of, but I can always count on coming home to someone happy to see me.

"Don't forget about me while I'm gone," I tell Sheba before standing up.

It seems Lance has taken Zara upstairs and is probably getting ready to conduct some meetings from his home office. Camille is alone in the kitchen, back to making me uncomfortable as she studies me with her arms folded over her chest.

She pushes off the counter and walks over to me, then reaches out to smooth my braids and sighs. "If you're determined to see this through, just be careful. You're smart and capable of anything you set your mind to. Including kicking ass in the simulation. But you're also sweet and gentle and led by your heart. I'm worried that with Roman around, it's going to lead you right into heartbreak. Then *I'll* have to get involved because he hurt my little sister."

"I'm not a little girl who needs her big sister watching out all the time." I shrug my shoulders high up to my ears, and Camille gets the hint to stop messing with my hair. Before she can take a step back and call me a brat, I grab one of her hands and squeeze. "But I appreciate your concern. Even if I don't show it, I always have and always will. I am going into this with every single one of my guards up, focused on nothing but making it through the next six weeks. And don't worry about my heart, because I haven't, nor will I ever, give it to Roman to break."

CHAPTER EIGHT

A
s I wait to load my bag into our "shuttle," I will my heart to stop beating so hard.

Really, it's a mixture of nerves and excitement. We're about to set out, and our little adventure to save the library will officially begin. There is so much riding on this being a success. So many kids whose lives will be impacted—in good or bad ways—depending upon our ability to complete each objective before the six weeks are up. We can't mess this up. I won't let us.

The increase in my heart rate may also have something to do with the fact Roman is standing right behind me.

While Angie works on fitting her bag, which is clearly double the size we were instructed to bring, into the back of the fleet van we're being transported in, I strike down the urge to glance over my shoulder at Roman. It's not even that he's standing close to me, because he's not. Each time I've taken a step forward, he's remained rooted to his spot on the asphalt like some silent sentry. But among Angie's grunts and curses and the excited chatter coming from Jordan and Simone, who are already strapped in and ready to go, I *know* he's looking at me. I feel his eyes on me. On my hair, my back, my ass where the extra helpings of enchiladas migrate to.

It's some special sensory superpower I gained after noticing Roman's reaction to seeing me in workout clothes. I'm painfully aware that with every step I take or each time I shift my weight to the other hip, he's watching the movement. It's making the tiny hairs on the back of my neck stand on end and grating on my nerves.

I don't want to, nor can I afford to, feel any kind of excitement from his attention. We may not be at school, but I'm still his vice principal, and if that isn't reason enough to ignore whatever is going on between us, I also don't trust his reason for joining the simulation. If only turning off your attraction to someone could be as easy as flipping a switch. My brain knows he's the enemy and will most likely try to ruin this whole experience for everyone, but my body's response to his nearness says, *Okay, and?*

I reach up to the top of my head and unwrap the strands of braids I used in lieu of a scrunchie to keep it all in a bun. The braids tumble down my back like some physical barrier between me and his gaze. There, no more hair-raising awareness.

Angie gets her bag situated and clears out. There's not much space left when I step up to the doors of the van. Duffel bags and containment boxes filled with supplies and uniforms have pretty much taken up any extra room. With a little maneuvering, though, I manage to get my bag loaded and head in to grab a seat.

"Do y'all think the whole school will be watching the livestream?" Simone asks when I step into the van.

"I don't know about the school, but my family will," Jordan says, trying to get comfortable as he's somehow landed between Angie and Simone.

I'm not pleased to see the last row will be just Roman

and me, but when Jordan tries stretching his legs, with a "Nuh-uh, no manspreading," I keep it moving.

"I know at least half the teachers will be watching," Angie then says. "They told me."

As if I don't have enough to stress about. Every move we make—every single one of our interactions and reactions—will be recorded for all to see. I want to make my family proud. I want to inspire the students. I want to show Superintendent Watts, who's given me so much of her time and wisdom, that she made the right choice in backing me. But I'm scared. If we lose, my failure will live on forever. I'll only be known as the not-good-enough Rogers child.

In the middle of my downward spiral, Roman steps into the van.

"I hope you don't mind this here," he says to me as he sets his bag between us and sits down on the right side of the row. "There's no more room in the back."

With him so close, I have no choice but to notice how delectable he smells. It's this kind of spicy scent with notes of chocolate, which I freakin' love. He's wearing blue coveralls like the rest of us since he was finally able to find a size that wasn't too tight, though it's still snug on his chest and biceps. But what really gets me is the fact that he had the nerve to show up with a fresh haircut and trimmed beard. He's here looking all fresh and sexy, and I can't in good conscience enjoy it knowing he has ulterior motives.

I look at his hand resting on top of his bag. I wonder just what he'll do to try and stop us. What exactly were Principal Major's directives?

"Hey," Roman says to me. "You good?"

So, building trust. Look at that fake concern trying to throw me off my game before we even get there.

"Just peachy," I say.

Roman's eyes search mine, but I turn to the window before he can find anything to tip him off that I'm onto him. This isn't like school, where we put aside everything in the morning then have our silent competition once the kids arrive. Here, the stakes are much, much higher, and for me the battle starts now.

I spend the ride alternating between being only too mindful of Roman's every shift, sigh, and slight snore and napping myself, as well as trying to mentally prepare for what we have in store.

The goal of the simulation is to understand how people will cope with life on Mars. Similar to how astronauts stay on board the International Space Station then switch out, the habitat, or "Hab," we're arriving at on "Mars" has been occupied by other teams before us. It will be the job of our crew to complete certain objectives that will keep everything running at top performance for those who come after us. And keep our sanity in such close quarters when we only have one another to rely on.

"And we're here," our facilitator announces seven hours later. Considering it would take about nine months to get to the planet Mars, a half day's drive across Texas isn't so bad.

The van slows as we approach a guardhouse, and I know *somebody* is playing with me, 'cause ain't no way the building they're taking us to looks just like a football stadium. I don't know whether to laugh, knock on wood, or pray to kingdom come.

Rather than clear-cut corners and a flat roof, this structure is a long, imposing oval with a closed domed ceiling. There are no windows or anything else on the exterior that would indicate what's inside, which makes the single door that I can see look tiny, and a bit ominous, compared to the building's size.

"Welcome to the red planet," the facilitator continues once the guard raises the rail for us to drive forward. "You all have come a long way, and now you've finally made it! As you know, the air on Mars is toxic. You'd die in less than two minutes without a proper suit and oxygen."

Simone gasps out, "Oh no!" and Angie cuts her an annoyed look that says, *really?*

Angie has been quite hostile the whole drive. Rolling her eyes and huffing, throwing in something about Mexico every now and then. Complaining when poor Jordan crossed their invisible line and allowed his elbow to hang too far over on her side. I don't know what's going on, but if I have to worry about both Roman *and* Angie, this doesn't bode well for our team at all.

After the van parks in front of the building, our facilitator undoes her seat belt and turns her body as much as she can to face us. "As stated before, even though you all aren't trained astronauts, we believe in your abilities to succeed. Think of this experiment like a game of strategy," she says like she's letting us in on a secret. "It's all mental. It's normal to feel like you're overwhelmed or want to go home, so try to focus on what you all came here for. Remember you're a team, working together to reach a common goal."

When she says *common goal*, I can't help but cut my eyes to Roman. He catches me and frowns. I turn away before he can say anything and continue listening, leaning forward as the facilitator gives us more information.

"First and foremost, this simulation is for education, to study how humans will survive when we finally call other planets home—it's not reality TV. The bedrooms are not monitored by cameras or microphones, so consider those safe spaces." Her voice becomes quieter. "Neither is the computer server room. There's no camera, and the microphones only pick up the sound of the fans. In the greenhouse, cameras are on, but no microphones, again due to the fans. The last blind spot is in the left corner, right next to the lab station." Like the MVP she is, she nods at us once, then goes back to her regular voice. "All right, let's get this thing started. First things first—space suits!"

We practiced helping one another get into our space suits at the orientation, but both the facilitator and driver help us today to save time. Then we load the two crates full of supplies onto a metal dolly, and in what seems like no time at all we're standing at the door.

A sudden spike of adrenaline sends my stomach tumbling and my limbs tingling. I'm really doing this. I'm about to spend six weeks locked up with my work colleagues. With Roman.

I haven't felt this nervous since I went away for college. I left behind my family and all that I knew to brave it out in a different world. At least then, home was half a day's drive away and leaving only meant sacrificing a weekend.

With the world I'm about to step into now, leaving or losing focus will mean giving up the library. But I won't let that happen. I straighten my shoulders, remembering how good it felt to walk across the stage and receive my diploma. Walking out of this simulation six weeks from now will feel just as good because not only will we walk out knowing that we've saved the library, but we'll be heroes. Not to mention how good it will feel flaunting my win in front of Principal Major's face.

"Okay, astronauts," the facilitator says. This time her voice comes through little earpieces we put in. She gives us a rundown of going in and opening the hatch for the Hab.

How once we go through the door, the only time we'll come out is when the simulation is over, or if we "expire" early.

"You're on your own from here," she finishes.

"Yeah, let's do this!" Jordan says, pumping a fist in the air. He seems to be the only one of us not having second thoughts.

The facilitator swings the door open and takes a step back, then we walk through.

Jordan goes in first, pulling the dolly behind him. Simone follows, then Angie, Roman, and me.

"Wow," Simone says as we take it all in.

Wow, indeed.

It may look like a stadium on the outside, but on the inside it's like we've literally left Earth and been transported to the red planet. Because indeed, red is all around. There's hard, flat sand under our feet, but throughout the stadium the ground swells with hills of varying heights. This place reminds me of pictures I've seen of the Mojave Desert, except there's no vegetation and the panels above project an afternoon sky in a pink hue tinged with red, making it feel like I'm wearing tinted sunglasses.

As we take it all in, the door shuts behind us with an air of finality, and now there really is no turning back.

"You guys," Jordan says. "This is . . . amazing."

He walks forward as if pulled by a string and we follow after him, heading toward our settlement.

"Does anyone smell that?" Simone asks.

I take in a few sniffs. "I smell *something*," I say. "But I'm not sure what it is."

We keep walking, getting used to the way our big blocky boots drag through the sand, toward our settlement at the north end of the stadium. Soon we approach a tall metal antenna, some freestanding solar panels, and our Hab. At first glance, it looks like four large tents fused together to make an apartment. But as we get closer, I see that while they look like tents, the exterior is more solid. Clearly not as strong as brick, but not thin like polyester either.

When we get close enough, Jordan abandons the dolly and jogs to the Hab, running his gloved hand over the exterior. Once he's done, a white streak is left, and I realize the Hab isn't red, but is covered in the dust surrounding us.

"Look, this was made from a 3D printer!" Jordan exclaims.

"If it caves in on us while we're sleeping, I'm suing everybody," Angie mutters.

While Jordan's busy spinning in a slow circle, Roman is the one to open the hatch and usher everyone inside. We enter a narrow, tube-like hall where we have to wait two minutes while the pressure stabilizes. It's a tight fit with all five of us, our bags, and the dolly, and somehow I end up right next to Roman. His bag and arm hang by my hip and I hardly dare to breathe so I don't push against him more than necessary. When I make the mistake of looking at him and we make eye contact through our helmets, warmth spreads through my chest, quickly followed by the word *scandal!* and now also *traitor!* flashing in my mind. I turn away just as the second door unlocks and we're finally able to see our new temporary home.

As soon as we step in, everyone starts taking their helmets off. I suck in a deep breath of relief to be away from Roman but instantly regret it.

"Oh God," I say, covering up my nose. "What is that?!"

Angie covers half her face with her hand. "It smells like rotten eggs."

"Yo, no way! Can y'all believe how much thought went into each detail?" Jordan says. He tilts his head back and sniffs at the air like something good is in the oven, and I don't understand it. Is his excitement at being here somehow suppressing his olfactory system? "Mars has large compounds of hydrogen sulfide, so yeah, it definitely smells like rotten eggs. Don't worry, we'll get used to it soon enough."

Angie shakes her head, eyes glaring as she focuses on Jordan. "I can't believe you really got me out here breathing in death! I'd rather be trapped in a room with fifty musty kids than deal with this."

Jordan cringes as Angie stalks off behind one of the open doors.

"What was that about?" I ask. Jordan won't meet my gaze, so I look at Simone and Roman. Neither of them has answers.

"Maybe she's tired and cranky from the long drive," Simone offers with a shrug.

"How about we all get unpacked and settle in," Jordan says. "After, we can meet back out here and go over a game plan."

Everyone agrees. Simone and I follow after Angie, who's found her way to one of the bedrooms. The room is round, with no windows, though there are LED light strips along the bottoms of the walls, and the dome has a sunroof that looks like it's able to open and close to let more light in. There are four beds extending from the walls like little pods, each with half of the full-size mattress embedded in the wall and the other half sticking out.

Angie has claimed one of the middle beds, so I walk to the first bed on the right side of the room and set my bag down. Now that I'm closer, I see that LED strips also line the wall right above the bed. The headboard and footboard are wide enough to place books or other knickknacks on, and there is a screen that can be pulled down for more privacy. There is also a journal on the pillow. In orientation they mentioned how we would be expected to answer daily questions about our activities and the food we eat and record our overall feelings and mood while here. All designed to understand how humans will operate on Mars and to help us keep our sanity.

"Did anyone else find it hard to decide what to bring?" Simone asks from her bed. "It was so hard packing up my life in just eight pounds." Among a few other items, she pulls out framed pictures, books, undergarments, and a purple candle. She catches me eyeing the candle and smiles sheepishly. "I know we're not supposed to have anything flammable. I don't plan on lighting it or anything though. It was a Mother's Day gift, and my kids insisted I bring it. Nothing beats a little aromatherapy when you're stressed." She closes her eyes and takes in a lungful of the candle's scent before placing it on the headboard right next to a framed photo of her family.

"I should have thought of that," I say. She doesn't have to explain herself to me. I'm here to win, not act as anyone's boss or enforce all rules.

I look at Angie, who's spilled the entire contents of her bag onto the bed. I can see why it was so big. She's got a load of protein bars, an adult coloring book and markers, cards, dominoes, hair products, and . . .

I gasp. "Angie, why did you bring an industrial-size box of condoms?" And who is she planning to use them with?

Angie huffs and tosses the box behind her. It lands in the middle of the floor. "Do not even get me started," she says. "I specifically asked Jordan if this simulation was like those reality shows I watch where they have different celebrities and athletes trying to survive different challenges, and he said yes. I *assumed* there would be some football players joining us. I freakin' gave up going to Mexico to be here."

I bite down on my lip to keep from laughing as she slams a fuchsia bra down on her bed. That finally explains the animosity she's had toward Jordan. He was determined to make it here. It makes me wonder if he does actually realize that Roman is most likely a plant sent by Principal Major but chose to overlook it.

I turn back to my bed and begin unpacking my things. Undergarments, a picture of Sheba, and books. "Wait a minute," I say under my breath. One of these books does not belong.

"Ooh, that's a pretty cover. What book is that?" Simone asks.

"Uh . . ." I consider stuffing the book back in my bag, but it's already too late.

Simone crosses the small distance to my bed to see what I'm holding. "*That Time I Got Drunk and Yeeted a Love Potion at a Werewolf*." She snatches it from my hand with the biggest smile stretching across her face. "I never took you for a werewolf lover."

I put my hands against my burning cheeks. "I'm really not."

As in, not *just* a werewolf lover. I love *all* the creatures. All the shifters, dragons, and aliens. My bookshelf at home is completely different than the one in my office at school.

"My sister must have put that in there," I say. "She loves to play practical jokes on everyone." No wonder she looked so pleased when we said our goodbyes this morning. I'd told her when I read the first book in the series, so normally it would have been a treat for her to surprise me with the second one. But not in front of my colleagues. There are some things they don't need to know about the vice principal.

"Aww. My siblings and I all have a decade gap, so we don't have tight relationships," Simone says. "If you don't want to read the book, I'll happily take it off your hands."

I stare at the book a few more seconds. I do really want to read it. "Sure."

Simone must read the longing in my gaze, because she giggles. "I promise I'll give it back before we leave."

"I love that book," Angie says, coming to join us. "Not only is that Felix a werewolf, but he has tentacles." She fans herself.

I am going to kill Camille for this.

I turn back to my bed and work on putting up my clothes and trying to make my pod feel homey. When it's time to meet the guys in the common area, I watch Angie step right over the box of condoms she left on the floor like they're not even there. Like they don't draw as much attention as one of those yellow signs they put on a wet floor. And I wonder who, if anyone, will end up using them.

CHAPTER NINE

I scan the common area as Angie, Simone, and I walk in. It's four spaces—the kitchen, living room, communication station, and lab station—efficiently made compact and squished into one large room, and will be where we'll spend the majority of our days.

Jordan is at the comms station, which has at least a dozen screens, analyzing each switch. I easily spot Roman reading a pamphlet on one of the couches. I let my eyes linger on him a little to make sure he's not making any moves to try to sabotage us already.

A jarring ping interrupts the quiet, sounding from the speakers and echoing throughout the room. We all look at Jordan, the only person actually messing with stuff, while he holds both hands up.

"I swear I didn't mess up anything," he says. "I only touched one button."

We can't have things breaking when we just got here. I take a step to see what is going on, but Roman puts his pamphlet down and beats me to the comms station.

"They're messages from Mission Control," Roman says after a moment.

"Thank God." Jordan wipes his forehead then sits up straight. "I mean, see? I told y'all I didn't mess up anything."

He uses a touch pad to navigate around the screen. "It looks like there are separate messages addressed to each one of us. They must have been transmitted on our way here."

Jordan eagerly selects his message first. It's a video from his mom and dad. They congratulate him on making it this far and sign off with a "*We know you'll make us proud!*"

"Oh, me next!" Simone volunteers. She gets closer to the monitors, and Roman moves off to the side to give her room.

Simone's video comes from her kids. They're spitting images of her, with the same curly hair and light brown complexions. They hold signs that read "I love you, Mom" and "Go, Mom!" Simone swallows thickly and looks like she's on the verge of tears when her video ends.

"Angie's is next," Jordan says.

Angie leans forward, but once the video starts playing, her face falls. Her message is from someone I assume to be her sister, though it looks like she may have been counting on someone else. Her sister encourages her to kick ass and bring home the bacon.

With everyone else receiving messages with two or three family members on video, I'm a little bashful when Jordan clicks on mine and my whole family pops into frame. Mom, Dad, Camille holding Zara, Lance, Vincent, and Vincent's fiancée, Amerie.

"*We'll be watching you!*" Camille says before they sign off, like I need the reminder.

I have to admit, being in this new setting with this group of people I hardly know is weird. Seeing my family's faces is a familiarity I'm grateful for.

"Hmm." Jordan moves around on the screen then looks back at us. "That's all the videos we have," he says apologetically.

An awkward stretch of silence falls over us like a blanket. Roman didn't get a message from his family. Nothing from Principal Major or his mom. Nothing from his siblings, if he has any.

For a second I consider his insistence that he's not as close to his dad as everyone assumes. Did they get into some kind of fight before Roman came, and now Principal Major isn't showing his support? But if that's the case, why is he here?

When I look at Roman, he appears almost unbothered that he's the only one who didn't have a message. I say *almost* because he doesn't meet anyone's eyes and his jaw is clenched, telling me he's at least feeling some type of way. He's got to be, right? Unless this is a play at garnering sympathy from us so we'll let our guard down.

I turn from him, my conscience and sympathy at war with what my brain says is part of his long game.

"It's messed up your family didn't send you anything," Angie says.

Why she says it, I don't know. It's one thing for all of us to silently feel bad for Roman or, in my case, be conflicted about feeling bad, but it's another thing to actually make a comment.

Simone, Jordan, and I must all be of the same mind, as we look at her in disbelief. Angie's eyes swing between us, and she shifts her head back. "What?"

I sigh and shake my head.

Another ping comes through the speakers.

"Oh, maybe that's your message," Jordan says to Roman. He takes a moment to read the screen and grimaces. "Never mind. We got another message from Mission Control. It's a list of the daily tasks and experiments we need to perform. It reiterates what we went over in training."

Simone leans forward to read over Jordan's shoulder. "'We believe you'll help foster a way for future humankind to survive on the Martian surface and handle everything thrown your way with grace, integrity, and ingenuity.'"

Thrown your way. I know we'll face a few challenges, but that sounds especially ominous.

And that's when we hear it. A loud bang, what sounds like a mini explosion followed by the unmistakable sound of bending metal, and finally a loud thud I feel from the ground all the way up my legs.

"What was that?" I ask, and my voice comes out shaky with nerves.

We all stare at one another with wide eyes, but no one has any answers.

"Cameras," Roman says. "We need to turn the cameras on."

Jordan fumbles with some of the switches, eventually finding the correct one for the cameras. A few seconds later, four screens show us a feed of the outside. Dust is still settling, but it's glaringly obvious what the whole commotion was. Something struck and knocked down the antenna.

"That can't be good, right?" Simone asks, surveying the screen.

Part of the antenna is bent in half, with scattered pieces of metal and snapped cables lying on the ground.

"I'm certain it's not good," I say.

"It looks like we just lost our way to communicate," Roman says, and my heart sinks.

———

"ALL RIGHT, WHO'S HUNGRY?" JORDAN ASKS. LIKE AN INTEGRAL PART of our mission didn't just fall apart.

"Are you serious?" I ask him. "We need to do something about the antenna."

"I agree with Brianna," Roman says, which is a new tune. He never agreed with me on anything in front of his dad. Instantly suspicious, I turn to glare at him while Roman frowns, confused. During our little exchange, Jordan walks to the kitchen and begins rummaging through the cabinets. He sets to work on a stove that's little more than the width of his body, while Angie and Simone go to the living room to see what movies and shows we'll be able to watch. I stand in the middle of the common area, watching them. It's like no one is taking this simulation seriously. Food? Movies? We need to be worried about what just happened outside. If the antenna is down, what's to come next?

From the corner of my eye, I see Roman moving around at the comms station. I don't know what he's up to, but I'm going to make sure he doesn't add on to our trouble.

There are two laminated papers posted on the wall near the comms. I walk up and act like I'm studying them, turning my body so Roman is easily in my field of vision.

He clicks around on the monitors for a while, then opens a drawer I didn't see there beforehand. He pulls out a pamphlet similar to the one he had earlier and begins leafing through it. He's so focused on the words in front of him, he doesn't even notice me staring.

After a while it's obvious that all he's doing is reading and I'm probably safe to go find something else to do, but I can't look away from his strong profile. As much as I want to turn off my attraction to him, I'm mesmerized the same way I always am when evaluating his class at school.

Without warning, Roman turns in my direction. I jerk my head back to the papers and try to appear like I was looking there the whole time. It's an emergency evacuation plan, which, actually, is something I need to become familiar with.

I can see Roman looking at me from the corner of my eye. He watches me like I did him, like he's daring me to look back. I don't give him what he wants and eventually he gives up and calls me. "Brianna."

I try to act unaffected by the way he says my name as I turn to him and raise my eyebrows.

He waves the paper he's holding. "Got some good news."

I may melt at the smile he sends my way, but I don't dare trust it. "What's going on?" I ask.

"There's a satellite that orbits our site about every two hours. I ran some tests on the antenna, and it looks like it can still pick up data whenever the satellite is overhead. It will take hours to receive a full message, but it's something."

My muscles loosen a fraction. I'm glad to hear we're not starting this whole thing completely without contact. I could kiss Roman for the relief he's brought me. Which would be a horrible, horrible idea. I settle for a tentative smile. "That's great to hear."

"What's going on?" Angie asks.

"Rom—Mr. Major found out we can still get messages from Mission Control, but they'll come through slowly," I say.

"Well, something is better than nothing," Angie says. "Nice going, Roman."

Roman nods in acknowledgment but doesn't smile at Angie like he did at me, which I find interesting. Evidently Angie doesn't. She narrows her eyes at Roman and walks to where Jordan is still cooking.

"Are you done yet?" Angie asks him.

"I'm getting the plates ready right now," he says. "I hope y'all are hungry, because dinner is served."

We all gather around the high table with backless stools.

"Bam!" Jordan says each time he sets a plate in front of us. "Enjoy your early Thanksgiving meal."

I study the food piled on my metal plate. The turkey slices are a little suspect. The color is slightly off, and there is no seasoning, but the veggies and mashed potatoes look like any other meal. And while I wouldn't exactly call it a *Thanksgiving meal* since it's missing the sweet potatoes, macaroni, and cranberry sauce, it looks filling enough. At least it's not baby food.

"Wait!" Jordan says before anyone can take a bite. "We need to commemorate this occasion with a toast or blessing or something." He looks around at all of us with so much joy, I feel like I might burst. Jordan is living his dream out here. "I'm really glad to be with you all. Um. Enjoy this food for the nourishment of our bodies. May it keep us going and going." He finishes with a forkful of mashed potatoes.

"Nope," Angie says after taking one bite of the meat. She pushes her plate away, slides off her stool, and goes back to our room.

I pick up the meat and take a tentative bite. The taste isn't bad. The texture is off though. Like, way off. Chewy, but tough against my teeth and hard to get down. It probably has more to do with Jordan's cooking method than the actual food itself. A little less time in the pan and it should be closer to what fresh meat would taste like.

"Our first meal on Mars," Jordan says, simply awed by everything as he chomps on a large piece of meat.

Simone is eating the vegetables and seems satisfied.

Roman's expression is blank, so I can't tell if he hates the food or if this is his idea of five-star dining.

It occurs to me that I don't know what kind of food he likes to eat. He doesn't get hyped about enchilada day like everyone else. He never takes his lunch in the teachers' lounge, preferring instead to stay in his classroom during his lunch hour. Is he a steak guy or all about burgers? He's clearly not a vegetarian since his turkey is halfway gone, and he hasn't touched the veggies yet.

Roman digs his fork into the mashed potatoes. Before taking a bite, he glances up at me, and this time I don't look away. I can tell myself I'm curious as to what he thinks of the food, but as he swallows without so much as a grimace, I know the real reason. I like looking at him. I like how there's chatter about horrible techniques that lead to over-cooked but under-seasoned meat, but neither of us engage. But I don't like this feeling of guilt spreading in my chest that tells me as much as it feels like I'm glowing under his attention, I can't trust him. So when Roman raises his eyebrows as if to say, "*Mars, huh?*" instead of answering, it kills me a little to drop my gaze back to my plate and ignore him.

Angie walks back in with one of her protein bars right in time for us to discuss our game plan.

Jordan wipes his mouth and clears his throat. "As you all know, we have daily and weekly duties." Those duties are simple enough. Exercise daily, keep our habitat clear of dust, and keep the solar panels clean. "If we do those and last the full six weeks, we get—"

"Twenty thousand dollars!" Angie shouts like she's about to compete on the Fast Money round of *Family Feud*.

Simone claps, and even Roman's face lights up.

"Yes, twenty thousand dollars," Jordan says. "And if we complete the four main objectives, we get the money for the school."

"Whoo, let's go!" I say, pumping a fist in the air. Everyone stares at me blankly, as if I'm the weird one and Angie didn't just have a similar outburst. Roman lets out a small huff, but I don't trust it. He's probably trying to get me to let my guard down again. I put my arm down and slump in my chair.

"Continuing on," Jordan says. "To win the money for the school, we'll have to find the rover that got lost in a previous sandstorm, gather samples at a predetermined site for our experiments, grow dandelions in the greenhouse, and fix the antenna."

We begin discussing which of the big objectives to tackle first. I think it should be the antenna so our communications with Mission Control come through as quickly as possible and say so. Jordan really wants to find the missing rover, however, and since he's our mission commander and I don't want to start our mission off with an argument, I bite my tongue and agree to follow his orders.

Jordan rubs his hands together like a fly about to grub down on some food. "Great. I'm glad we have that settled. Everything seems straightforward, but we need to be prepared for anything to go wrong at any time. These simulations are as much about how people respond to emergencies as they are about completing the objectives. Remember, we're all a team, and everyone's role is important."

"What *is* everyone's role?" Simone asks.

Jordan blinks like he hasn't considered the question. I know he had certain positions in mind when he recruited (begged) us to join. Simone is our medic, I'm supposed to help keep morale high, Angie is our techie, and Jordan, our mission commander, is supposed to be an all-around specialist and decision-maker. Roman? I guess he's simply here to look pretty, which again makes me positive he's here to do Principal Major's dirty work.

"We'll all work together when it comes to keeping the Hab clean, finding the rover, and fixing the antenna," Jordan says after a while. "Most of these can be done in shifts, like taking care of the greenhouse. We will need a team of two to gather the rocks. If I remember the map correctly, the site is over a few hills. Just going off sheer physical capabilities, and no shade to anyone here"—Jordan directs to me and the other ladies—"Roman, I think you're best to head up that task."

Roman nods once in agreement, and I impulsively shout, "I'll be his wingman!" before Jordan can volunteer himself. "I mean, wingwoman. I grew up hiking all the time, so the physicality is no big deal." And this way, I can make sure Roman doesn't mess up collecting the samples on purpose. Jordan seems way too happy to be here, so I'm not sure if he'd keep an eye on Roman or get distracted by the fascinating hills or tracks in the sand. Jordan may be the commander, but I'm going to have to be insistent on this point.

"Are you sure, Brianna?" Jordan asks, and I nod. "Well, okay then."

I sit back in my seat, satisfied, as they move on to discuss cleaning shifts. When I look over at Roman, wondering if it's begun clicking that I'm onto him and not willing to sit aside while he ruins the simulation, I come up short. Roman doesn't seem nervous. He's not sweating bullets or so much as grinding his jaw. He's sitting there with that same half grin he wore when he invited me out to Big Lou's. Like it did then, it sets my pulse soaring and my cheeks flushing.

For some inexplicable, possibly demented reason, he looks satisfied.

CHAPTER TEN

don't sleep well the first night, slipping in and out of dreams only to wake up bothered. It's not due to homesickness or being in a different bed. It's thinking about the possibility of failure. How if we somehow don't win the money, I'll have to walk back into school and face Principal Major and his smugness and go through another year of being put through hell. How I'll be the Rogers kid who just can't get it together and is considering running away from yet another job.

It's the fact that Simone and Angie are somehow snoring in tandem. Angie breathes in with a rattling, rumbling vibration that sounds like a mountain on the verge of collapse. And if Angie is the mountain, Simone is the chainsaw, hacking away in loud spurts.

I considered moving to the sofa in the common room but thought of how that would put me in closer proximity to Roman, aka the final reason I'm not sleeping well.

He's managed to sneak into each dream I've had. And not simple dreams where we pass each other in the school hall or a running favorite where he waits for all the teachers to leave the teachers' lounge in the morning. Instead of going to his class when the bell goes off, he smiles as he walks up to me, wraps me in his arms, then kisses me softly before wishing me a good day. It's a tame dream, but the idea of anyone doing something so sweet, something that would make me feel cherished and seen, has always made me wake up with a smile. But the dreams I had tonight were anything but tame.

In one dream, Roman has locked the door in the teachers' lounge. Instead of an innocent kiss on my forehead, he grabs my braids to tilt my head back, exposing my neck, where he begins trailing hot kisses. In another, he backs me into a corner in my tiny office, ready for a morning romp before class.

I think the only way to save my sanity and sleep is to get rid of him. We don't need a full team to complete the tasks. That was only required to start the simulation. In fact, during orientation they said they fully expect most teams who compete to lose more than half of their members over the course of the six weeks. I'm just not sure how I'd actually accomplish getting rid of him yet.

I close my eyes, trying to fall back asleep. They pop right back open when Simone lets out a rough snort. I open the screen of my pod. The clock on the wall reads 4:30 a.m., which means by now it's too late to get any quality rest. With my pajamas on—black leggings and black crewneck shirt—I quietly leave the room.

Walking through the habitat is eerie. The only sounds are from the fans and computers. Logically, I know I'm not alone. There are cameras with who knows who watching me move around like a lab rat in this big experiment, and my teammates are within shouting distance. Still, I can't help but jump when I hear a creak.

I look around and don't see anything, so I force myself to shake it off and go to the kitchen. I'm craving a little *normal*, and tea is the same whether you're on Earth or Mars.

I fill a small pot with water and place it on the stove. While that heats up, I'm rummaging through the cabinets, where I find packets of our dehydrated food, tuna, and Spam when I hear a deep voice behind me.

"Looking for the tea?"

From the first syllable he utters, I scream and jump, fearing that the simulation has taken a turn for the worse and Mission Control is about to have us face off against aliens. Then I turn around and see Roman and don't know what scares me more—the thought of fighting off aliens with nothing but metal cups and plates and not-quite-hot water or the way he sends my heart leaping in bounds.

"Whoa, it's just me," he says, like that's supposed to be assuring.

"Why are you sneaking around? You almost gave me a heart attack." I place my hand on my chest while taking deep breaths to calm myself.

"How was I supposed to know you were gonna scream loud enough to wake the whole planet up? And I didn't sneak. We've got to work on your situational awareness," he teases. "Could've been a whole alien in here and you wouldn't know."

I pause for a second. I thought it was eerie to be out here by myself, but it's even more eerie that Roman would talk about aliens when they were just on my mind. It's like we're on the same wavelength. Then again, we are on an extra-terrestrial mission. I'm sure the thought of aliens has crossed everyone else's minds too. "My situational awareness is just fine, thank you." I sniff. "What are you doing out here so early? You should still be sleeping."

"I gave up trying to sleep hours ago. It usually takes me a while to adjust to a new bed. It's just not home, you know?"

I've never had problems adjusting to new beds, and

suddenly I'm filled with all these questions I want to ask him. Did he have to adjust to new beds often? Why? Does he travel a lot when not at school and stay in a lot of different hotels?

Before curiosity can get the better of me, I turn away from him and go back to searching the cabinets.

"What are you doing up this early?" A loud snore sounds from my room, answering Roman's question, so he pivots to another topic. "You were looking for the tea, right?"

"Yeah. I've checked all over, but can't find it."

Roman opens one of the cabinets I already went through but reaches higher and pulls out a metal container. "Blueberry?"

"Thanks." I take the tea from him. "I guess it would have been smart to look up. Then again, I wouldn't have been able to reach it anyway, even if I saw it. Not without a ladder at least. I guess I need to find those next." I bite down on my lips. I'm doing that thing again where I overshare.

Roman hands me the tea then finds the drawer with the strainer and passes it to me as well. The Mars simulation program is all about sustainable living, since we wouldn't have the same resources on the red planet as we would on Earth. For tea and coffee, we have to steep them in (rationed) hot water, strain it, then put the leaves or ground coffee into the compost. Roman just stands there and watches as I unseal the canister and shake some leaves into the pot. His presence is so unnerving I end up putting in way more than I planned and huff out an annoyed breath. I look at him, but all he does is offer a too-sexy smile that throws me off. When has he ever been this open and inviting?

When he invited you to Big Lou's because he thought he was about to steal yo' job! a voice in my head says.

At the abrupt reminder, I turn away.

"I can put it up for you," Roman says when I'm done with everything, pointing at the tea.

"How about we find a place on the counter so I don't have to keep bothering you about it?"

Roman momentarily pauses, but says "Fine" and places it next to the microwave.

I sit down with my cup while Roman heats up water to make coffee for himself. I try to ignore the clanging of cabinets opening and closing and the rustling of fabric as he moves around the kitchen finding exactly what he needs. He sets his cup on the table at the opposite end from where I'm seated, grabs a booklet from another drawer, and sits down.

While drinking my tea, I can't help but notice how loudly he's sipping his coffee. Obnoxiously so, like he's doing it on purpose.

"What are you reading?" I finally give in and ask, only to get him to stop slurping. The sound is almost as bad as the snoring floating in from Simone and Angie.

Roman closes the booklet and gets up from his stool, coming to sit on the one next to me.

I watch with wide eyes as he slides the booklet to me, then look down. "The dishwasher manual? If you're that starved for entertainment, I have some books you can read."

"It's not for entertainment," he says with a smirk. "We're supposed to know how to fix anything here that could break down at a moment's notice. At the orientation they said we should take the time to learn about everything during the first few days here. I read about the rover last night."

I remember them saying we should read the manuals, but I'm surprised Roman is already getting up to speed on things. After all, how much does one really need to know about each machine here in the Hab to sabotage it?

"Right," I say under my breath.

"What's that mean?"

"What's *what* mean? All I said was 'right.'"

"I know what you said, but it's the way you said it. You don't believe me?"

With Roman's seemingly confused gaze on me, I look away and consider what to say. I can act like there was no undertone to my words, or I can just come right out with my suspicions to let him know the jig is up.

In the end, I choose violence.

I set my mug down and swivel in the stool to fully face him.

"Rom—Mr. Major. Come on, let's be real. You and I both know why you're here, and it's not because you want to see the library being remodeled."

"I don't?"

"Nope. You're here because your dad sent you. He wants you to make sure this whole simulation is one colossal failure. That way I'll be too ashamed to show my face back at school, and you can take my job."

I watch closely as Roman's face darkens and he crosses his arms across his broad chest.

Got him.

Maybe now that he realizes I'm onto him, he can save us both the trouble and graciously bow out. Me and the rest of the crew will be able to continue on in peace.

But Roman shows no sign of backing down or of being defeated. He scoots his stool forward, stopping right before his knees knock into mine. I look down. We're not touching, but mere centimeters separate us, and I can feel his body's heat. I have the urge to move my stool closer, ever so slightly, to erase that space. It's like holding two magnets apart, sitting this close and yet so far from Roman, and it feels wrong. Like we're going against physics.

"I'm not here for my dad," Roman says. "I'm not on some secret mission to screw this up for everyone. I'm here for you all. To help the mission succeed."

While Roman speaks, I tear my gaze from our legs and meet his steady brown eyes. The way he said *you all* . . . it was like he put a special emphasis on *you*.

"What do you mean, Rom—Mr. Major?"

He shakes his head. "Brianna, call me Roman. Please. No more Mr. Major or Vice Principal Rogers. Here I'm Roman and you're Brianna."

I cannot—*no*, I *will* not do that thing with my lip. If he wants me to use his first name, fine. It makes sense seeing as we aren't on school grounds. And yes, it feels like the sun has just beamed down on me, bathing me in warmth, a dove landing on my shoulder and all, because of the way he says my name, but clearly he's trying to throw me off my game. Of course someone sent here to ruin everything would deny it. Of course he would put on an air of total sincerity, most likely having picked up on the fact that I want to see the good in everyone. He didn't really mean that he's here for me specifically. Just like he didn't mean it in the library when he said I was amazing. He was trying to get me to trust him then, and he's doing it now.

I can't get my brain working quickly enough to say anything, and when a door opens followed by Jordan coming into view, it's too late.

"Oh wow. You two are up early," Jordan says. He's got a spring in his step like he just woke up from the best sleep of his life. "Are y'all excited for our first spacewalk? I know I am." He moves toward the stove.

Roman has backed up his stool to a respectable distance, and his indifferent mask is back on.

I study him closely, wondering if the conversation we just had actually took place or if it was all some sort of hallucination from lack of sleep. Did I imagine his intense look and the words coming out of his mouth? He always seems to clam up when other people come around.

"What's that?" Jordan asks, pointing to the booklet still in front of me.

"It's the dishwasher manual. We're supposed to get familiar with all the gadgets here." Quietly, I tack on, "Roman reminded me."

"Oh cool. I'll have to make sure to check that out later," Jordan says. "Right now I'm starving. I wonder how good the eggs are."

After saying his name, I look at Roman, who offers a small smile. The butterflies in my stomach are very real and come on quick, and I know that for someone who should be suspicious of every breath Roman takes, I'm walking a mighty fine tightrope right now.

CHAPTER ELEVEN

It's another hour before Simone and Angie emerge. While they were sleeping, Jordan scrambled some rehydrated eggs and bacon. I couldn't bring myself to touch the eggs since I still haven't acclimated to the horrible smell here, so I let the guys have it all to themselves and ate oatmeal while trying not to mentally replay my conversation with Roman. It didn't work.

"Good morning, ladies," Jordan says to Angie and Simone. "Ready to start the day?"

"Sure," Angie says.

"I'm ready," Simone says, only slightly more enthusiastic.

"We have to spend at least thirty minutes a day in the gym," Jordan says. "The gravity on Mars is different, so we've gotta hit the weights to keep the biceps beefy."

"Or *get* the biceps beefy," Simone says with a giggle in response to Jordan flexing.

"It's six in the morning," Angie deadpans.

"Working out first thing in the morning is a great way to wake up," Jordan says.

Angie huffs out a breath and looks to me to back her up. "It's six in the morning," she says again. "I'm not doing a damn thing until I've at least eaten."

"Yeah, Jordan," I say. "I'm with Angie on this one. I never work out on an empty stomach."

"Okay, okay." Jordan holds up his hands. "I know we're still working out the kinks in our new schedule. Though I am a bit surprised teachers would have issues waking up early."

"It's summer break. I should be in Cancún. It's six in the morning!" Angie gets more agitated with each statement, her eyes turning an accusatory glance on Jordan.

"Totally right and absolutely valid points." Jordan steps back slowly, and my opinion of his survival instincts rises. He can obviously sense when danger is near and knows when to back off. "I'm going to go ahead and get my workout in. You all enjoy breakfast and whatever else you need to do, and we'll see you in there in about, what, twenty minutes?" Angie bares her teeth, and Jordan amends his statement. "I mean, forty-five?"

Angie doesn't answer, which gives Jordan leave to take his timeline as acceptable, and he turns to Roman. "Do you want to hit the gym with me now?"

Roman stands from his stool and walks up to Jordan, patting him on the shoulder. "Sure, man. Let's get to it."

I don't miss the way Jordan shakes out his arm as he follows Roman, nor do I miss how Roman's eyes shift to me before the two leave the common room. But I'm still confused and processing my chat with Roman, so I do my best to avoid eye contact.

"Let's see, what should I eat?" Angie says, opening a cabinet. Finding nothing to her liking, she lets out a disgusted snort. "I guess I'm eating another protein bar."

She heads to our room.

Simone goes to the cabinet and pulls out a cup of oatmeal and shrugs. "Oatmeal is oatmeal."

After she gets her food ready, she sits at the table and passes me the book I let her borrow yesterday.

"Wait, you're done already?" I ask.

"Yeah, I read it before falling asleep. I go through these phases where I either read nothing for months or I devour everything I can and finish books in, like, a day." Simone takes a bite of her food, then looks down at it, surprised. "This isn't bad at all." She eats some more, pausing when she's about halfway done. "Do you have any other good ones in your bag? I'm usually not a werewolf girly, but that one was really cute and fun."

Angie walks back in finishing off a protein bar. I hope at some point she'll try some of the food available. I'm pretty sure it's not good for her to rely on so many of those.

"Angie, you were right about Felix and those tentacles," Simone says to her, waving her fingers as if they're her tentacles.

"Of course I was. And I heard you ask Brianna for another. I've got some books you can read. One has an alien that growls," Angie ends with a wide grin.

"I don't know," Simone says, scraping her bowl to get the last of her oatmeal. "Growling doesn't really do it for me. What about you, Brianna?"

I must look like a fish with my mouth hanging wide open, and for that, again, I blame Camille. If she'd never put that book in my bag, I wouldn't have to field questions about growling. How am I supposed to face these women when we're back at school if I talk to them about extraterrestrial romance heroes?

"Come on," Angie says before I'm forced to answer. "You mean to tell me you've never kissed a man who growls? Hot does not even begin to describe it."

"Have a lot of experience, do we?" Simone asks Angie.

Angie's eyes take on a wistful, almost longing look before she shakes her head and smirks. "Yeah."

Simone raises an eyebrow and looks at her skeptically. "I'm supposed to believe that not only have you been with a man who growls but you like it? I'm sorry, I just can't. It's hard to imagine that working well in any scenario outside of a book."

I switch my attention back to Angie, all ears, waiting for her answer while she drinks a portion of her daily water. Inquiring minds want to know.

She wipes her mouth with the back of her hand. "You bet I like it! It's amazing. I'm telling y'all, to be with someone who wants you so bad and knows how to let his more animalistic side come out . . ." She ends the thought, fanning herself. "If you know, you know. Am I right?" She directs the last tidbit to me, and all I can do is blink.

Where the hell would I have found a man who growls like that in my very limited dating life? I've spent the majority of my adulthood trying to land a suitable career, not find some sort of Tarzan wild man. But damn if Angie doesn't make the experience sound like all that and a bag of chips.

Instead of answering, I look at the time. "I think we'd better get changed and get to the gym before Jordan comes back and hounds us."

Angie looks at me like the lame, mood-killing vice principal who should absolutely *not* be indulging in these conversations with her staff that I am and rolls her eyes.

The gym is its own separate room, though it's still small. It's equipped with two treadmills, two stationary bikes, weights, and yoga mats. Simone, Angie, and I stop when we get to the doorway.

It looks like Roman has taken it upon himself to train

Jordan. He's yelling at (maybe encouraging?) Jordan to finish a weight set. Jordan is standing up, doing his best to lift a good-sized dumbbell with one arm in a bicep curl. Sweat is dripping down his temples, and the strain has caused his face to take on a red hue not often seen in darker tones as he breathes in and out with his mouth.

Roman must have gotten his own workout in already, because he's sweating too. Rather than sweat rolling down his face, it's stuck to his shirt, making the material cling to his muscles.

Angie lets out a gasp and puts her palms together like she's praying. "The Lord is my shepherd; he knows what I want."

"Amen," I can't help but respond.

Angie looks at me and smirks with a hint of pride shining in her eyes, as if to say *well done*.

I quickly avert my gaze, cheeks blazing. There's no forgetting that people are monitoring our every move and conversation, and at the end of the day, when this simulation is over, I'll be going right back to being her vice principal. I can't let Angie, or the whole world, see me drooling over Roman. I can't give an inkling of a hint that I'm wondering what it would take to make Roman loosen a little bit of that quiet restraint he holds close like a secret and see some of those inhibitions slip. Would he growl?

It doesn't matter. None of it does. Not whether or not he growls and not what he meant about being here for me. What matters is winning, and that means stopping Roman from whatever plans I'm sure he has and being able to face my colleagues and the students when I return back to school in a matter of months.

I'm the first to cross the threshold and step into the gym. I go to the bike and turn the resistance up. Can't think about men growling if I'm too busy feeling the burn in my thighs.

BY THE TIME WORKOUTS ARE DONE AND EVERYONE HAS GOTTEN A SEC- ond wind, we all meet in front of the hatch. At this point, it's evident Jordan thinks we're slowing him down. He's so ready to get out there.

Roman pointed out how fixing the antenna will be a multistep process. We convinced Jordan that we need to at least begin the process and chip away at it bit by bit. So we will use this space walk to clean the debris from the antenna and look for the lost rover.

"Remember, the oxygen indicator as well as the monitoring system for our heartbeats will come across with an audible warning if either is too low or too high," Jordan says, pacing back and forth. "If that happens, we need to come in right away."

"Yeah, yeah, we get it," Angie interrupts. "This is the same thing they went over during orientation. Why does it feel like I'm a part of one of those mandatory trainings for school equipment we won't use?"

"It may feel like you're in one of those trainings, but these suits are essential to our survival. The number one reason people get disqualified is because they run out of oxygen. As long as we do our due diligence, we don't have to worry about that," Jordan counters.

While Angie cuts Jordan the stink eye, I glance over at Roman. Maybe I could do something to sabotage his suit to get him disqualified.

As soon as the thought is out, guilt and shame hit me. Who am I? Planning someone's demise? I've never been this mean-spirited before. Then again, I've never had to fight for a library alongside someone who's planning to stop it. Probably. Possibly. *Ugh*. After our conversation, doubts are starting to build up, and a small part of me thinks he might have been telling the truth about wanting to help us. Only a small part.

For now, I'll put off plans that would have him choking on Martian air—metaphorically, of course—and will continue to keep an eye on him.

"All right everyone, let's suit up," Jordan says.

I hold in a sigh. I don't think it would have killed him to throw in a *please*. We're all adults, and I'm sure the others would agree with me and not want to be bossed around. Maybe I'll leave one of my leadership books in his classroom when the new school year starts. But when I look at everyone, they're moving to their suits without any issue, so maybe not.

Camille's words insinuating I'm difficult float in my mind, and I grit my teeth.

We get as much of our suits on as we can by ourselves before turning to one another. I was the last one to grab mine, so I stand by and wait for Simone and Angie to finish helping each other before they can get to me.

"Brianna," Roman says.

He gives me a slow once-over, and I can't believe he's checking me out right here, until he makes a motion with his glove-covered finger for me to turn around. I realize that *look* was actually him inspecting my suit. Of course that's what he was doing. I immediately turn around. There's a tug on my back as Roman adjusts the oxygen tank.

"You're good," he says at my back, so close I force down a shiver.

I turn back around so I can check him out now. *Over*. Check him over. I give his suit a thorough glance then make the motion with my hand for him to spin, and he does so. I look at his oxygen tank, and there's that temptation again to go ahead and sabotage him now. I quash the impulse way down into the tiniest corner of my mind. I won't stoop down to Principal Major's level.

Next we get our helmets on and test the mics.

"Testing, testing, one-two-three," I say.

Everyone else does the same, but when Roman's simple "testing" resounds, the chill I've been suppressing races down my spine.

"Has anyone ever told you that you have a voice for radio, Roman?" Simone says. "It's very soothing."

I couldn't agree more. Roman's voice is deep and smooth. I've always thought it would be perfect for storytelling. Or, I don't know, whispering dirty things.

Jordan's voice says through the headset, "As I'm sure you all remember, our antenna was destroyed by a meteor."

"Yes, Jordan, we do remember the big thing that went boom and scared us half to death," Angie says sarcastically.

Jordan clears his throat. "Right. Well, today it's our mission to gather the scattered pieces and hopefully find the rover!" When he gets to the part about the rover, he can barely contain himself. "I know we can do it. Ready, team? Leggo!"

We stand back as Jordan opens the first door, then we go through the tunnel, unlatch the hatch, and step out onto the Martian terrain.

"This is so cool," Jordan breathes.

Angie sighs. "I could have been in Cancún."

CHAPTER TWELVE

"I. Am. So. Tired," Angie says over the microphone. I can't see her, though I imagine each word mirrors her footsteps.

She's on the opposite side of the Hab, with Simone and Jordan, but she comes over loud and clear in my ear. After hefting as many large pieces of metal and cables from the antenna as we could, most of us were ready to go back inside. However, Jordan wouldn't give up on finding the missing rover.

We spent all morning clearing the debris outside, and we're still not done. While most of the things we picked up weren't heavy, it did take some getting used to, moving around in the space suits and having to see through a helmet. Not to mention, we worked out prior to coming out here.

Now that we're going on our second hour of searching for the robot, I'm not even sure if it's here. We have little handheld scanners that should pick up its signal, yet we've been wandering around like we're searching for the promised land and nothing has popped up.

"Is *anything* showing up on the scanner at all?" I ask Roman, pleading that he says yes. "This is taking forever."

"No." He shakes his head—his whole body, really—then hits the side of the scanner like that will make it work.

"Be careful! If you break that thing, we'll be out here forever looking for the rover."

"I'm not about to break it," he grumbles. "I don't think it's working anyway. We should have found *something* by now."

"I want to go inside," Simone whines.

"Come on, team, let's keep going for a little longer," Jordan encourages. "We're getting close to finding it."

"I am seriously getting sick of this," comes Angie's voice. "Why are we even listening to him? It's four against one. We should be going by majority rules."

This feels like the makings of a mass mutiny. Jordan lets out a deep scream, and I wonder if Angie made some kind of lunge for him.

"Please, guys, just fifteen more minutes," Jordan pleads. "If we don't find it, we'll head back in and try again later. Ahhh! I mean try again tomorrow."

As Jordan fights for his life, I feel a little bad for complaining. We have weeks ahead of us. If our first space walk is already fraught with fighting, the library is doomed.

"Okay," I say with a sigh. "I think we can handle fifteen minutes. But then that's it."

There's a little grumbling (well, a lot from Angie), but everyone agrees.

Roman and I continue our wayward path up a small hill, and for the umpteenth time, I glance at the scanner in his hands. I don't even know how he ended up with it. I should've been the one holding it. That way, if nothing showed up for the rover, at least I would know it wasn't because of *me* sabotaging it. What if Roman did see something on the scanner and simply neglected to say anything? For all I know, we've passed the rover ten times by now and Roman is quietly letting us walk ourselves into exhaustion.

I lean forward so I can look at the scanner with my own eyes. But Roman is holding it in his left hand while I'm on his right side. I'm forced to stretch farther than I normally would to see through the helmet, and then it happens. I don't watch where I'm going and end up tripping over my boots.

As I let out a quick scream, Roman reaches for me, but it's too late. The world starts spinning as I roll down the hill. When I finally come to a stop, I land face up, staring up at the domed panels, which have taken on a butterscotch color.

"Brianna!" Roman says as I hear him making his way down.

The concerned voices of my other crewmates also come through as they try to check up on me.

"I'm fine," I say when I catch my breath. Embarrassed, but alive. "I just fell down a hill. No biggie." I try to get up, but with the suit on I'm like a sad little turtle stuck on its shell.

A second later Roman is looming over me. "Are you okay?" The note of concern in his voice is way too convincing to be fake. "Here, let me help you up."

I reach for his outstretched hand, and he pulls me up. Or at least tries to. Maybe he underestimates how much weight the suit has added to me, or maybe he simply loses his footing in the sand. But in a matter of seconds, we're both on the ground.

I look at Roman's stunned face and giggle. After a few seconds, his laughter joins mine. When we finally stop, tears that I have no way of reaching run down my face, tickling my cheeks, and my face aches from smiling.

"That did not go how I envisioned it in my mind," Roman finally says.

"You mean this wasn't your way of trying to lie up with me?" I tease.

In a flash, his demeanor switches from playful to smoldering. "Naw, your boy's game is a little smoother. If I was trying to lie up with you, it wouldn't be in a pile of dirt," he says, and a rush of heat overtakes me. I'm curious as to what kind of game he's got.

"Just what kind of game are we talking here?" Angie interrupts, reminding me that we're not alone.

I open my mouth to respond, but thankfully Simone distracts everyone when she comments about picking up a signal. I forget too quickly around him when I'm supposed to have all my guards up. I turn away so I'm looking straight up at the ceiling. Roman doesn't say anything, and we lie there a few more moments until he manages to get himself up. When his shadow falls over me this time and he reaches out, his grip is strong and unwavering, allowing him to pull me up all the way.

"Eureka!" Simone yells. "We found the little sucker!"

With the missing rover found, we can finally head back to the Hab.

"Nice going, ladies," I say when we all meet up at the hatch.

Angie opens the hatch and Jordan walks in, carrying the robot like a hard-won trophy.

Before I can follow everyone in, I hear a gasp and turn back around to Roman.

"What's going on?" I ask.

He doesn't say anything, but ominously points up.

I brace myself, prepared to face whatever the simulation has in store for us. I follow the invisible line from

Roman's gloved finger to just above the door and see it—a spider.

A glance from the spider to Roman confirms he's scared. Terrified even. Aww.

"What's the holdup?" Angie asks. "I'm ready to take this suit off and relax."

I open my mouth to tell them about the spider, then reconsider. I don't trust Roman here, but I don't want to embarrass him.

"Hold on, we'll be right there," I say.

Not wanting to scare the others, I can't very well tell Roman that it's a wolf spider and will leave him alone as long as he doesn't mess with it. I reach for the scanner and tug it out of Roman's grip, then tug on his hand. Only then does he tear his gaze away from the spider and look at me.

"Come on," I coax. "Let's catch up with the others. Angie is liable to shut us out if we take too long."

"I'm counting to ten then starting the restabilization process with or without y'all," she says in answer, but I ignore her commentary.

I tug on Roman's hand one more time and he finally jerks forward, not quite at an all-out sprint to get past the spider, but real close. I didn't know someone that big could move so quickly in such a short amount of time.

When we all finally get through the tunnel and out of our space suits, Roman approaches me while the others are busy.

"Just so you know, I wasn't scared of the spider out there," he says, only loud enough so I can hear.

I lift my eyebrows. He's not about to stand here and play in my face. He would probably still be standing there if I hadn't helped. And I don't even know *why* I helped him. I should have let him stand there until his suit ran out of oxygen. Then he would have been gone without me doing any of the dirty work.

A voice in my head says it's because I want him around, and to that I counter that it's simply because I'm a good person.

"Fine," Roman grits out as I keep looking at him with my eyebrows raised. "I hate them, okay?"

"Hate them or are scared of them? It's okay, a lot of people are. You don't have to be ashamed to admit it."

"I'm not ashamed." He looks over his shoulder at the rest of our team and lowers his head even closer to me. "And fine. Yes, I'm scared. Is that what you want to hear?" He clears his throat and stands up straight as he says, "If you tell anyone, I'll deny it," in a deeper voice that's obviously meant to reclaim his rough-and-tough exterior.

I smile sweetly at him and make sure my dimples are at full wattage. "Your secret is safe with me . . . and with any of the thousands of viewers I'm sure are tuning in."

When his eyes widen in realization, I laugh.

———

"I DON'T THINK I SHOULD HAVE COME HERE," SIMONE WHISPERS TO ME as we sit in the common room. "I'm not built for this life. My arms are literally about to fall off."

I'm not sure if she's whispering because she doesn't want anyone else to hear her complain or if she simply lacks the energy needed to summon a louder voice.

In hindsight, we probably should have taken it easy and stuck to cardio instead of involving weights in our workout. But after seeing Roman coaching Jordan, Simone and Angie decided they needed to work on their muscles as well, and despite my desire not to get too close to anyone, I didn't want to be the odd man out. Judging by the ache in my own muscles, that was a mistake.

I try sitting up straighter and encourage Simone. "My arms are killing me too. But at least we're almost done out there, *and* we found the rover. We're one step closer to the grand prize!" I've got to get her to look on the bright side to help keep morale up. It's the only way we'll make it through this.

Simone sighs. "Yeah, you're right. I'm just tired. I guess putting on the space suits and trying to walk through all that sand just solidified how everything is really happening. Man, my kids would have loved it out there today. They probably would have been running all around and would have found the rover long before we did."

I nod. Simone may be tired, but she's likely also homesick. It doesn't matter that we haven't even been here a week. It's not *home*, and we're not a family. It's obvious in her now glassy eyes that she misses her kids.

I briefly hesitate before asking, "Why don't you tell me about your kids?"

Her whole face lights up. "Ashton and Ariana. They're twins, and my whole heart. They're only nine, but you'd swear they're already teenagers with the way they talk and try to make things easier for me."

"They sound great."

"I'm going to use the money I earn here to take them on a trip, and of course put some away for college. Ariana wants to be a nurse, like me. Last time I checked, Ashton wanted to be a filmmaker. He changes his mind every so often though. Do you have any kids?"

"No kids for me. I do have a dog. Which, I know, is not the

same as someone you gave birth to." I shrug one shoulder and feel the pain down in my bones. "But she's my Sheba."

"I am a firm believer that fur babies are real babies. We have two rescue pets, but in their eyes, they're little humans. Hey, when we're done here, we should get our pups together. We can have a doggie playdate at the park while my kids run around."

I consider her invitation. There's my reservation about blurring professional lines, but making some friends for Sheba does sound fun.

"Unless," Simone says, "you don't fraternize with faculty outside of school activities. If that's the case, I get it."

"No, it's not that," I say, even though, yeah, it's exactly that. I can't keep my personal life separate from what's going on at school if I'm hanging with the staff in my free time. Even if the thought of new friends for Sheba is almost too tempting to pass up.

"It was just a thought," Simone says when I don't say anything else. "I'll keep the invitation open in case you change your mind. Now." She whimpers as she pulls herself up. "I'm going to take a note from Angie's book and nap before Jordan thinks up any more torture for us."

"Okay," I say quietly as she walks away. I know it was the right thing not to accept her invitation, but I still feel crappy and like I'm missing out.

I consider taking a nap as well, but even though my body is tired, my mind is too wound up to sleep now that I've got my career on my mind. I look to Jordan, who's tearing through a manual without slowing down to actually digest what it says. Trying to get the rover up and running has got him pressed.

"Do you want some help?" I ask him.

"No," he says stubbornly. "This piece of machinery will not defeat me."

"Well, go, you. Don't forget, Angie is a computer teacher. She may be able to help you." He sets his jaw, so I shrug. "All right. Well, I think I'll just check out the pond in the greenhouse."

Jordan says something, but I'm not sure if he's talking to me or threatening the rover, so I leave him be.

When I walk through the greenhouse's slim sliding door, I'm surprised, and yet not surprised, to see Roman. I can't get away from him for one minute in this place.

"Hey," he says when he looks up and sees me.

He's standing over an open bag of soil. He looks innocent enough, but I look around the rest of the small greenhouse to ensure nothing is out of order.

"What are you doing in here?" I ask, ignoring the dip in my stomach. He needs to stop looking at me like that. He needs to not be here.

Roman rolls his eyes at my suspicious tone and points to the soil. "I'm about to move this in there." He shifts his focus to an empty garden bed. "If you're worried I'm going to ruin anything, you're free to help."

I almost whimper out loud. I'm physically spent. I only came in here to see the tiny pond. But there's no way I'm leaving the gardening under Roman's sole supervision. Getting the dandelions to grow is essential to winning, so I'll power through a little longer.

I force a smile. "I'd love to help."

Roman looks me over, without a doubt noting how raggedy I look, and raises a skeptical eyebrow. "If you say so."

I take in a deep breath to get additional oxygen to my muscles and immediately regret the decision. The moisture-controlled air travels to my throat, and God help me, I can *taste* the rotten eggs. I start coughing, which turns into gagging. When it finally subsides, I wipe at the corners of my eyes.

"You okay there?" Roman asks.

"It's the smell. Or I guess taste. I breathed in too much and it got me." I grimace and wait for the aftertaste to subside. It doesn't.

Roman watches on with his eyebrows slightly raised and lips lifted at the corners.

I glare at him. "It's not funny." It's his fault I'm even in here still.

Cue a full smile stretching across his handsome face and my heart leaping in response. Being away from school, his smiles have come out more and more, and I wonder why that is. What is so special about being here in the Hab that would make him feel free to relax a little?

"Do you need help moving the soil?" I ask. I don't need to focus on his smile or the reasons behind it.

"I got it. Why don't you get the seeds? I don't think that should require additional air intake."

"How chivalrous of you."

Roman hefts up the bag of soil, and instead of standing there to admire the stretch of fabric over his arms, I go to a compact storage box in the corner of the greenhouse. The storage box contains seeds for various plants, gardening gloves, and some handheld tools. I find the labeled seeds for dandelions and grab two pairs of gloves.

"Here you go," I say, passing Roman his gloves. When he reaches out, the tips of our fingers just slightly touch. It's brief, but Roman notices too as our eyes meet for a beat before I drop my gaze.

We both get our gloves on, then face the garden bed and begin planting. As I work on my side, I make sure to watch

Roman from the corner of my eye. He's obviously got experience gardening. He lightly presses the seeds into the soil in tidy rows and correctly spaces everything while I do the same. In some unspoken agreement, we end up trying to outpace each other until it's an all-out race. I finish my side one second behind Roman.

"No fair," I say, crossing my arms. "You must garden at home or something."

"Or, I'm just that good with my hands." He rubs his hands to remove any remaining soil from his gloves and smirks. "I used to garden with my mom and grandma. I guess some skills you just don't forget."

I pout, but wait to see if he'll divulge more. I know about his dad, though I wish I didn't. I'm curious about his mom. I'm curious about a lot of things where he's concerned.

He doesn't offer up any more though. Instead he reaches for my right hand. I know I should pull away, but I'm struck silent as he gently peels the glove off each finger until it slides off. I know there's no excuse for it, but then I allow him to reach for my left hand and tug that glove off as well.

"Do you have a garden at home?" Roman asks me.

I look up from the hand he's still holding to his face. "A what?"

"A garden," he says, laughter in his eyes.

It takes me a few seconds, but I finally remember what a garden is. I also remember the cameras pointing at us, the people witnessing our every interaction.

He keeps a steady gaze as I pull my hand away from his grasp. "I used to have a nice garden, but it's been hard keeping up with everything outside of work." It dawns on me not only how busy and grinding it's been at school but how little I've done at home to relax and refill my well. "I think the only thing I really do for pleasure these days is read."

"Let me guess, you like romance?"

I shrug. "I dabble a bit."

"Do you? I've thought about dabbling myself. What do you suggest? Maybe something with werewolves?"

I know he's teasing, but I feel my eyes go wide and my cheeks heat up. Did I put the book up after Simone gave it back to me or leave it out on the table? I can't remember.

Regardless, I'm not going to back down and keep letting him one-up me. "You know what? If you decide to dabble, I'm happy to lend you a book. Who knows, you might even learn more in one of mine than you would in these manuals you're so fond of."

He tilts his head to the side. "The way Angie talks about them, I have no doubt I should be studying as much as I can. Although, I am a mere man with no extra appendages. I'm not sure if I can measure up to those guys in the books."

So apparently he heard our conversation about Felix and his tentacles. I shouldn't be surprised, considering how small the habitat is as a whole and how loud Angie was.

"Come on, Roman. I'm sure you more than make up in other ways for what you lack in extra appendages."

I can't believe the words tumbling out of my mouth. Judging by the way Roman's eyebrows jump to his hairline, he can't either. My only saving grace is, like our facilitator told us, the microphones don't pick up conversation in here, and the others can't hear me with the door closed.

Before I can backtrack, Roman laughs. It's unguarded, unfiltered, and rumbly and goes straight to my core. All year, I've never seen him laugh, and I immediately realize what a tragedy it is that no one gets to witness this on the regular. I'm so caught up, I can't even feel embarrassed about what I said. In fact, it feels like I've already won the grand prize here.

But then he just keeps on. I wonder, when is he going to stop? Any reasonable person would have sobered up by now. It's not like what I said was *that* funny. Unless he's laughing at me?

I sweep my braids into a bun while waiting for Roman to get ahold of himself. He finally does, and I crook an eyebrow at him. "I don't think what I said was that hilarious."

It looks like he might start again, so I narrow my eyes at him until his face sobers.

"I promise I'm not laughing at you," he says, yet again on the verge of laughing. "I was just caught off guard to hear you say something like that so nonchalantly."

"Why wouldn't I say something like that? It's not like I'm some naive virgin. I know what all sorts of appendages entail." No, I haven't *seen* a lot of appendages, but I'm not a blushing violet. I hate when people assume that just because I'm short and young looking, it makes me inherently more innocent.

Roman sighs and shakes his head. "I never said you didn't. I'm sorry if it feels like I was making fun of you. I promise I wasn't, Bri."

I snap my head back. Oh, so I'm *Bri* now. This coming from the man who refused to call me anything but Vice Principal Rogers two weeks ago. Now here he is, laughing way too hard at my jokes and shortening my name. I don't know what to make of it all. And while the thought of him laughing at me is embarrassing, it's clear he wasn't. He was actually letting loose, and I really like this side of him.

But can I trust it? Is the real Roman finally making an

appearance now that he's outside school grounds? For what has to be the millionth time, I wonder if this is all a ruse.

Roman's tongue flashes along his bottom lip as he looks me up and down. "And for the record, your boy absolutely knows how to use his appendage."

Oh God. I stand corrected. Apparently, I am a blushing violet. Forget blushing. My whole body is a furnace. I'm ready to strip out of this jumpsuit and toss my panties at him.

"You shouldn't say things like that," I say.

"Why not?"

I blink. I actually don't know. Something about boss-employee inappropriateness. Something else having to do with being monitored. I can't form coherent thoughts while he looks at me like that.

He takes a step closer. "Well?"

"It's not nice," I finally get out, my words more breath than sound.

Roman smirks. "I'm not a nice man. My dad made sure of it. But you know what I am? A man who goes after what he wants."

"What you want?" I echo. Before I can process that meaning, Roman takes another determined step forward, almost closing the distance between us. At the same time, my heart jumps into my throat. There's no way he's about to try to kiss me. Not here, out in the open.

I open my mouth to ask what he's doing, when a rush of cool air hits my back as the door opens.

"Hey, guys," Jordan says with a defeated sigh. "I could use some help with the rover out here."

"Where's Angie?" Roman asks. His tone is colored with impatience, while I, for one, am glad for Jordan's interruption.

"I asked her, but she was in the middle of a nap," Jordan says. "So you can guess how that went."

Roman sighs. "I got you." He's back to his normal serious self. How does he do that so quickly?

Roman follows Jordan out of the greenhouse, and I'm left alone with my head spinning. I take in a deep breath, managing not to choke on the smell this time.

When I gather the nerve to come out of the greenhouse, Roman and Jordan have gotten the rover up and running. It's a tiny thing. About a foot wide and as high as my knees. The next time we go outside, it will be released to fill tubes with dirt samples.

"Isn't it cute?" Simone says to me, having gotten up from her nap and now watching the guys. "We should name it."

"It's not cute, and it's not a pet," Jordan says. "It's a tool." Apparently he's decided to hold a grudge against the machine for not bending to his will.

Simone ignores Jordan and speaks to me. "What do you think? We could name it after your dog. How about Sheba Jr.?"

I shake my head. This thing was lost before. It feels like it could be a bad omen if I name it after Sheba, only for us to lose it again. "What about Miles? For the number of miles it will be traveling outside?"

"It's not a pet," Jordan insists again.

"Miles," Roman says. "It's a good, strong name." He pats the top of the rover, and I know he's got to be humoring Simone and me, but it's sweet.

He straightens up and winks at me. I swear, I have no idea who this man is and what he did with the stoic science teacher who used to ration out smiles and soft glances, but I give up for the day. He's too enticing, and the armor I'm supposed to have wrapped around my heart is more like foil than steel, bending easily under his attention.

I shake my head and collapse on the couch.

"HEY, I FOUND THE MUSIC UPLOADED TO THE SYSTEM!" JORDAN AN-nounces a short time later. Since he couldn't figure out *Miles*, he was adamant about learning all there is about our comms system.

"Oh, let's listen to something," Simone says. "We could make it like a ritual or something. Play music when we're winding down."

"Okay," Jordan says. "What do y'all want to hear? There's pop, R & B, jazz, country. It looks like there's a good collection of everything."

"Is there any Isley Brothers?" Simone asks.

"What are you, my grandma?" Angie asks. "I want something I can dance to."

"You can dance to the Isley Brothers," Simone counters.

I sit on the couch watching them. I don't plan on dancing, so I'm staying out of it.

Jordan browses through the music for a minute then nods to himself. "I know the perfect song."

When "Achy Breaky Heart" comes on, Simone, Angie, and I all shout out, "No!"

Jordan cackles, and a few seconds later, "Hey Mr. D.J." by Zhané sounds through the speakers.

Angie stands up. "Nice!" she says, and starts dancing, not caring that she's the only one. Stepping first left, then right, hips swaying in perfect time to the beat. Fluid and smooth. Her arms are raised, hands right in front of her face, as she snaps to the beat with her eyes closed.

Simone joins Angie, her dance moves consisting of smaller

steps from side to side and exaggerated arm movements. They both move with no particular dance routine in mind, just vibes and a drive to combat cabin fever. I guess they've forgotten about their aches and pains from working out.

I look around the room, and my eyes snag on Roman, who's just come from another round in the gym. He works out like he's going to have to take on a horde of aliens by himself. He leans against the wall, looks from me to our dancing teammates, then back to me again. He cocks his head to the side as if to say, *Go on out there with yo' bad self.*

I raise an eyebrow. *Hello, did you forget I'm a vice principal? What would I look like dancing with them?*

He twists his mouth to the side. *You would look like you're having fun. There's no shame in that.*

I tilt my head in their direction. *I'll dance as soon as you get out there.*

He shakes his head and walks toward his room, and I know I've won. That's what I thought. Although I'd love to see what kind of moves he has.

"Come on, Brianna," Simone says.

"I'm good," I tell her, just like I told Roman. I can only imagine the words Superintendent Watts would have for me if I got up and danced with them.

"Suit yourself," Simone says.

When I catch myself tapping my foot to the beat, I get up and go back to our room. Sometimes it sucks trying to keep up boundaries. It sucks, and it's lonely.

CHAPTER THIRTEEN

The next few days are much like the first. After breakfast and a *light* workout, we go back outside to work on clearing the debris again. It still takes up all of our morning, leaving most of us drained, but we do tack on cleaning in the Hab. In the short amount of time we've been here, dust has managed to coat every surface. Because of that, Jordan insists (and I silently gnaw at my cheek to keep from saying something about him asking nicely) that we clean at least twice a day.

On the fifth day, our appointed technical gurus—Angie and Jordan, with Simone there for extra help—begin cleaning the solar panels.

"What about the antenna?" I ask while they're getting into space suits. "I think we need to get it up as soon as possible."

Jordan nods. "You're right, we do. But the solar panels out there are filthy. If we don't clear them today, we might run out of power. Then it won't matter if Mission Control sends us anything."

I didn't think being a subordinate would be the hardest part here for me mentally. But Jordan is our commander, so I let it go again and follow his lead.

"I'll start wiping down the kitchen," Roman says once

our three teammates are outside and he and I are left to take care of cleanup duties.

I nod without directly making eye contact with him and start wiping down the living room. I wipe down the couches and the thirty-two-inch TV no one has used yet. We've been too tired. Next I move to the comms station. It's a large desk with different buttons, all helpfully labeled, and multiple screens that live stream different views from outside. They also connect to cameras on each of our helmets. Since Roman and I are inside, our cameras are off. Lastly, a screen has our names and shows our vitals.

I find the screen showing what Jordan and the ladies are up to. They're facing the solar panels with buckets on the ground and rags in hand. Jordan moves his hand around excitedly, clearly saying something, while Simone is shaking her head and Angie stands with one hand placed on her jutted hip made bulky by the suit. Obviously, getting the panels cleaned is going fantastically.

There have been little gripes here and there, but overall everyone has been getting along. I'm finding it more difficult to stay out of conversations that get a little too personal or not laugh when someone is teasing. Vincent's advice to not hold myself back from my crew comes to mind, and I decide to offer them a little encouragement. When I switch the comms on, I hear an annoyed "Cancún" from Angie, and lean forward into the mic.

"Keep up the good work, guys," I say, upbeat as possible. "Y'all are doing great!"

"And let me guess, after we finish out here, you're going to throw us a pizza party?" Angie deadpans, and surprisingly Jordan snickers.

I laugh awkwardly. "Okay. I'll let y'all get back to it." I click off and bite my lip. Well, that went horribly.

Did they not appreciate the pizza I ordered for them? At intermittent times during the year, I'd have some delivered for the teachers to show appreciation. It wasn't much compared to the amount of work they put in with the students, but I couldn't talk Principal Major into doing anything else. And now I feel silly for thinking I was doing something great.

"Got 'em!" Roman announces.

I turn around to see what he's talking about and bite back a grin. "Roman, I know those aren't . . ."

He grins wickedly. "Found the pizzas."

He's holding up a bag of dehydrated pizza slices.

I break down and laugh. "I'm pretty sure if I try to serve everyone pizzas, they'll chuck me out the door and lock the hatch."

Roman shrugs and places the pizzas back in a lower cabinet. "Their loss. I have it on good authority they taste better than delivery."

"Is that so? By whose authority did you hear that?"

He smiles sheepishly. "Mine. I got hungry while everyone was sleeping last night and made one. Don't tell Jordan though. I don't want to hear him go on about conserving our rations."

"My lips are sealed. But what I want to know is if it was really that good," I say skeptically.

Roman raises his head like he's about to nod, but chuckles and shakes his head no. "It's not. But it is on par with the cafeteria pizza."

I shake my head, touched that Roman managed to turn around what was an otherwise awkward situation that had me feeling like the odd man out.

I offer him one more small smile, then go back to cleaning. I grab the cordless vacuum to tackle the couches again, since wiping them did nothing. But barely one minute into using it, the vacuum stops working.

I frown and turn the switch on and off a couple of times. I know the battery should be charged since we haven't used it much.

I hear a cabinet close behind me, and immediately my suspicions are back in full force. Roman did say he was out here last night while everyone was sleeping. There's no telling what he could have done to the vacuum or anything else. And here I am, getting all weak in the knees over some dumb pizza jokes, unknowingly walking into a false sense of security.

"Do you need some help with that?" Roman asks.

"It just stopped working. I don't know what's wrong with it since it was doing just fine yesterday." I narrow my eyes at him. "Did you happen to tinker with anything while you were out here last night? When everyone was sleeping?"

Roman tightens his jaw and approaches me. "The only thing I touched last night was my pizza. How about I help you with that?"

I hug the vacuum close to my chest and shake my head.

"Bri, I promise you I did not touch that thing. But I *can* help you fix it."

I'm slow to release it, but finally let go when Roman grabs the top and tugs. He flips it around, checking the on-off switch, checking the battery I already inspected and the suction port. After a few more moments, he opens the small flap to the motor and holds the vacuum back out to me.

"Try it now," he says.

I turn it on and am pleased when it whirs to life in my arms. After shutting it back off, I offer Roman a smile that feels more like a grimace. "Thank you for fixing it."

"No problem. Let me show you what I did so you'll know what to do if it goes out again."

Roman pinpoints exactly what he did to make it work, but I can't focus on his words. Not when he's standing this close. He smells so good, which doesn't make sense since we're only allotted two-minute showers, and the image of him stalking toward me in the greenhouse won't leave my mind.

"Don't forget," Roman says beside me. "They warned us that things would break down and that we might run into technical difficulties. It's the nature of this simulation, and I think a lot of this is engineered by design to give us issues. It's one giant puzzle that we have to problem-solve."

Roman's shift in personality—smiling, laughing, joking, staring—now *that's* a puzzle that still doesn't make sense. But this is the first thing he's said that actually does. If the creators of the simulation are going to be giving away big money to teachers, it makes sense they'd throw every obstacle in our path, even those as menial as malfunctioning vacuums. If I hadn't been so wary and suspicious of Roman, I might have figured that part out sooner.

But I didn't, and Roman did. "You really have been reading the manuals to learn," I say, and this time I fully believe it.

He nods. "I told you, I want this mission to be successful just as much as you do."

"But why? Do you need the money? I thought you would have wanted us to fail so you can get a shot at the vice principal job."

He studies my face, lingering on my lips for a few heartbeats before meeting my eyes like he's searching for something. Understanding, maybe? "I'm not out to get your job. I believe the kids deserve a library just as much as you do. And maybe I have other things I'm trying to prove." He drops his gaze before I can ask any more questions. Like what is he trying to prove, and to who? "Now that I've shown you I just want to help everyone, can you please stop looking at me like I'm going to be the one throwing you out the hatch every time something goes wrong?"

I consider the request. So far, all I've had are suspicions and no proof of wrongdoing on his part. He's been more than helpful, actually. He lifts those pleading brown eyes to mine, and I clutch the vacuum closer. What if I agree to a truce, accepting that he's here for benevolent reasons, and it all blows up in my face? I don't want to feel how I did when I found out he'd gone around telling the teachers I was leaving. But I'm tired of second-guessing everything he does.

Holding his gaze, knowing that either I'm about to make the biggest mistake or life in the Hab is about to get a lot less stressful, I nod.

IT TURNS OUT TO BE A PIZZA KIND OF DAY AFTER ALL. ONCE JORDAN, Simone, and Angie come back inside, Roman gives them the same spiel about the pizza slices being better than delivery after they're pumped with water and heated up.

I'm not bitter that the suggestion of pizza is received better coming from Roman than from me, but I also don't hold back my laughter when Angie takes one bite and looks like she's ready to hurl before rushing off to get one of her protein bars. She's going to run out way before the six weeks is up and be forced to eat the food she hates.

After eating, I vacuum again. They brought so much dust inside when they came in, it looks like we'll have to clean the Hab hourly.

With our daily tasks complete, we get the all clear to

take showers. I stay in our room to get some time alone, sitting on my bed, while the others go first. I pick up my journal and flip to the first blank page. I easily fill in the section about the food I've been eating and my overall general mood of feeling satisfied, but after staring at the lines intended for me to fill with my thoughts and blanking on what to write, I put it back on my headboard.

I lie down. I don't want to write out how being here is fine, but thinking about everything I need to do once this is over and I'm back home fills me with an unshakable dread in the pit of my stomach. I can't tell what's causing it. Is it that I don't want to work with Principal Major even if I do win the library? What else would I do? I know for sure I don't want to apply for the school of arts.

Maybe I should have become an astronaut like my brother. Maybe I could be among the first to actually go to Mars. Rather than six weeks, a mission like that would take up years of my life; then I'd have no choice but to stick with it.

With everyone only allotted a few minutes in the shower, my turn comes soon enough, and I put a pause to my existential crisis. I get cleaned up, put on leggings and a crewneck shirt, then join everyone in the common room. They're all fresh and dustless in their similar black loungewear, save for Angie, who is in a hot pink shirt and her robe from Pajama Day. I cannot believe she brought it here. On second thought, yes. Yes, I can believe it.

I keep studying her as I walk closer, trying to figure out what she's doing. Her palm is cupped in front of her face like she's holding something while she moves a finger of the opposite hand in an upward motion, all while laughing. No one else is paying her any attention, even though she's clearly on the verge of losing it.

"So, um, what are you doing?" I ask her as I slowly approach.

"Since we couldn't bring our phones, I have to do something to keep me entertained," she says.

Now I see it. She's pretending to hold a phone in her left hand and using her finger to scroll.

"We have the tablets and TV," I point out helpfully.

"No. I need something with social media. Something like—yass, earwax-cleaning videos." Angie stares intently at her "phone," grimaces, then sighs. "Whew, they got it. These videos always make me feel like I need to see an audiologist. I bet that patient can hear colors now!"

Simone and I make eye contact. I think we both know this situation needs to be handled with care.

"Angie," I say gently. "I'm sure there's something entertaining around here to do. Something that doesn't make us question your sanity?"

She scoffs. "What else should I do? Write in my diary all day like Moesha over there?" She hooks a thumb at Roman.

Simone squeals with laughter.

Roman is sitting at the table, writing in his journal. At Angie's words, his head snaps up and he looks at us like he's wondering how he ended up catching stray insults when he's not bothering anyone.

I cover my mouth to hide my smile. Angie is wrong for that. Funny, but wrong. When Roman looks at me and narrows his eyes like he can hear my thoughts, I let my laugh loose.

I do wonder what he's writing in there. I've done the bare minimum when it comes to my own journal, only answering the daily questions about food and activities. From what I can see, Roman's page is fleshed out. Maybe he's confessing his deep, dark secrets for sabotage. Okay, maybe he wouldn't be so maniacal as to write everything down, but he's writing a lot of *something*, and my curiosity is piqued.

I look from Roman's journal up to his eyes. He uses one hand to cover the page like I'm trying to steal answers from his test. I roll my eyes. *As if.* I was a straight A student. He'd be the one stealing from me. However, he's the one with the Roman Manual I'd love to read through.

Roman watches me and slowly lifts his hand up, like he's inviting me to take that peek I desperately want. It's almost too tempting to ignore.

"Music time!" Simone announces, interrupting our silent conversation, before a beat drops over the speakers.

She hops up from the chair and immediately starts dancing, as has been the ritual this past week. Angie joins her, invisible phone completely forgotten.

"Come on, Brianna!" Simone says. "You've got to come dance with us this time."

Like before, I shake my head no. But unlike before, I feel the pull of the music even more. Simone and Angie are having the time of their lives (as much as one can when stuck in a small enclosure with four other people). And here I am, afraid that by dancing, I'll somehow ruin my career path. What is the harm in letting loose a little?

When Simone beckons again, I stand up before I can talk myself out of it. She smiles and grabs my hands, pulling me even farther so we all make a triangle.

"I knew you had some moves," she says as I begin swinging my shoulders and hips to the beat.

I feel a little stiff at first, but eventually close my eyes and let loose. I dance to the song, feeling the beat from my feet to my chest, eventually spinning around and losing all sense of orientation. When I open my eyes, it's to find Roman looking at me. He's set down his pen and sits there.

I could stop and sit back down, allow my already racing heartbeat to return to normal and my blood, even more heated by his gaze, to cool. Instead, I close my eyes and keep dancing.

CHAPTER FOURTEEN

'**ve** decided to approach this whole simulation from a new angle. I'm not planning on crossing any boundaries, but I am going to try and open myself up more to the team.

Now that I've decided to stop focusing on Roman being a plant, my mind feels free not only to focus on winning the money for the library remodel but also to make this a good experience for everyone. I'm really getting the hang of this whole bond-with-your-crewmates thing. We've got our daily routine established, where we spend the days working then bond in the evening.

"Do y'all want to play a game?" I ask, half expecting to be met with nos.

When they follow me to the couches without any grumbling, I'm so happy I'm tempted to praise them with something like "That's the spirit!" but I'm aware that may not go over too well.

"Why are you cheesin' like that?" Angie asks me.

I immediately drop my smile to spare them from the sight of my gums.

"Aww, don't listen to her," Simone says. "Your smile is cute. Isn't it, Jordan?"

"Uh, yeah," Jordan says, clearly uncomfortable.

I don't know if he's uncomfortable because he doesn't, in fact, think my smile is cute, or if he simply doesn't want to look at his vice principal that way. Either way, I don't care. If Simone really wanted to know what anyone thinks about my smile, she should've asked Roman. I would love to know his answer.

I school my face. "So I was thinking we could play something to help pass the time and bring us all a little closer. As you all know, a team will work better and more cohesively if they can trust one another." At the last bit, I look at Roman and offer a slight smile. Part in acknowledgment that I was stating the truth before and I'm trying not to be so suspicious of him and part in apology. Roman doesn't exactly smile back, but his eyes do soften.

"That's a good idea," Jordan says from beside me. "What did you have in mind?"

"Charades?"

"That sounds like a terrible idea," Angie says.

"No," Simone says. "It sounds fun. Brianna, you go first." She gives me a little nudge. Or at least what I assume was supposed to be a nudge. I almost go flying off the couch and into Roman's lap. But I stand up and think for a second before making any movements.

Once I have it, I start moving my hands, gesturing in the air.

"Three words!" Simone calls out, and I nod, moving on to the next gesture.

"Walking the dog," Angie says, and I shake my head.

"Mopping the floor" is Jordan's guess, which garners another head shake.

"Playing kiddie games when you could be on the warm beaches of Cancún!" Angie says.

I stop and frown at her, holding up three fingers again pointedly.

Angie sighs and slumps in her seat.

I go back to the motion I was doing, slower this time.

"Yeah, you doing it slower is still not making it any easier," Jordan says, sounding on the verge of defeat.

Clearly this idea has backfired, and everyone is not having a good time. It might be time to throw in the towel.

"Icing a cake," Roman says.

I beam, jumping up and down. "You got it!" Now the show is getting started. I point at him. "Your turn." When he looks ready to protest, I shake my head. "I don't make the rules, I just enforce them."

Roman sighs and gets up. He stands in front of us, looking like he'd rather be anywhere else, and I take this opportunity to let my eyes feast on the man. After a few seconds he nods to himself and holds up his hand.

"One word," Jordan says, and Roman nods.

Roman stands still, but his hands keep moving. I'm momentarily hypnotized by their adeptness. How capable they look. Who needs tentacles when you have long fingers like Roman's?

"Reading a book. Drinking coffee. Playing basketball," Jordan calls out, rapid-fire. He really wants to win, but his answers are so off-the-wall and clearly not what Roman is doing.

After a few more wrong guesses from both Jordan and Simone, and Angie not even trying, I finally say, "Typing!"

"Yeah!" Roman says before schooling his features. "You got it."

"Man, that was my next guess," Jordan complains. "Does that mean Brianna gets to go again?"

"Them's the rules!" I say, hopping up again.

As Roman heads back to his seat, we look at each other in passing.

Try to get this one, I say with a lift of my eyebrow.

It's already in the bag, the lift of his smile says.

This time, my category is sports. I suck in a deep breath, spin in a circle, then fling my right arm out.

"Volleyball!" Jordan shouts.

"Darts," says Angie.

"Frisbee throwing?" Simone tries.

I point at her, then put my thumb and index finger close together so she knows she's on the right track. She leans forward with her face set, but all of hers and the others' follow-up answers miss the mark.

"Discus throwing," Roman finally says.

I point at him. "That's it."

"Dang, again? Y'all must be cheating," Angie complains.

Not cheating. Somehow Roman just seems to get me. He catches my eye as we switch positions again, challenging me to guess his word again.

I do. It feels good, like we're on the same team against everyone else to get the most guesses correct, though I'm not keeping score—unless counting how many times Roman lets loose that beautiful smile of his counts (it was eight times).

"Let's play a different game," Simone says after Angie and Jordan give up. "I brought Jenga."

She goes off to the room while we wait. Suddenly, there's a big crash followed by a screaming Simone rushing out. "Spider! Spider!"

Angie gasps and puts a hand to her chest. "They've got spiders on Mars? What the hell kind of planet did you bring me to, Jordan?"

"Simone, it's okay," I try to soothe as she runs around,

swatting at her clothes and hair. "Let me check that there's nothing on you. If there is a spider, I'm sure it's harmless."

"It's in my hair. It's on my back. Get it off!"

I try to help her, but Simone must have been some sort of track star, because she runs around the Hab like she's in the last stretch of a four-hundred-meter sprint. Before I can get to her, Simone opens the door. She blazes through the tunnel, opens the hatch, and sets out into the red sand.

Instantly, red lights flash. Loud warning buzzes sound through the comms speakers. A computer voice screams from the system. With all the chaos of Simone's screaming and all of us yelling at her to come back in, the only thing I'm able to make out from the PA is a detection of loss of oxygen in the Hab and a teammate going out without a helmet. I don't pay it any mind. I'm in the tunnel, five steps away from going out of the Hab to bring Simone back in, when I feel a firm grip on my wrist. I look back to find Roman holding on to me.

"You can't go out there," he says, shaking his head.

I try to pull away from him anyway, but his grip doesn't loosen.

"Simone, come back!" I shout.

```
Warning, oxygen levels critical. Will
become critically low to sustain life in
thirty seconds.
```

I hear the computer loud and clear this time.

"Simone, please come back inside," Jordan says. "We have to close the doors or we'll all lose."

Simone can't hear anything we say. She's too busy fighting for her life out there. With another warning from the computer, Jordan sighs and shuts the hatch. Roman pulls me back through the tunnel and inside the Hab so Jordan can close that door too.

We watch on until finally there is a signal that one of our teammates has perished due to exposure to Martian atmosphere with no protective clothing and no breathable oxygen. Simone's life vitals flash red while everyone else's remain green.

With one last tug, I pull my wrist from Roman's grip and hug myself.

While the chaos of the flashing lights and Simone's departure made my heart go into overdrive, when it comes down to it, the simulation is just that—a simulation. No teachers are harmed in the making of such sweat-inducing performances. A few minutes after Simone's vitals go out, she finally calms down enough to realize there are no spiders on her. We watch through the screen as she looks around her, looking sad and a bit lost, until the workers come from who knows where and escort her out of sight.

"Welp . . . that was anticlimactic," Angie says.

"And then there were four," Jordan tacks on.

I sigh. "I'm going to go to bed. See y'all in the morning."

"Wait!" Angie says. "Did you just forget about there's a whole-ass spider? I, for one, won't be able to sleep knowing it could be crawling around in our room."

"I'll get it," I say, making my way to the room.

I stop at Simone's bed, scanning the sheets for any signs of a spider. I move her bag on the bed, look under the pillow, look around the small nightstand, and don't see anything. My eyes land on the picture of Simone's family, and I can't help the tears that come to the surface.

Simone was going to take her kids on a trip and ensure they had a good start to life with the money she'd earn here. It's not fair.

I wonder if I could have done something differently. Maybe if I hadn't pushed so hard for us to all get along. Logically I know it's not my fault a spider just happened to make an appearance and that Simone is terrified of them, but I can't help but imagine what Superintendent Watts would say: *Did you hear about the vice principal who had a new library for her school within her grasp but then let it slip away? She was part of a simulation, and she got too close with the teachers. She was worrying about their personal lives instead of focusing on the prize.*

"Are you okay?" Roman says.

I didn't realize anyone had followed me in. I quickly blink a few times, trying to get rid of any trace of tears. When that doesn't work, I fake a yawn as I turn around. Lots of people cry when they yawn.

"I'm fine," I say. "Actually, it's been a long day, and I'm beat. But I'm happy to report that there are no signs of any spiders. Or maybe if you're looking at it from Angie's point of view, it's actually not great news." I shrug. "Anyway, I'm going to get some rest."

At the mention of the spider, Roman glances behind me with concern etched onto his handsome face. He tries to play it off, clearing his throat as he continues to study me. "It's okay if you're upset about Simone being eliminated. But there's nothing you could have done. You know that, right?"

No, I don't. For all I know, I could have run outside and pulled Simone back into the Hab before it was too late if Roman hadn't clamped on to my wrist like a vise.

I raise my arm to my chest and place my hand on the spot where Roman grabbed me. Everything happened so fast, I can't even recall what his skin felt like on mine. We've bumped into each other and helped each other with our space suits, but we've never *really* touched. Were his hands warm or cool? They must have been warm. What about his palm? Smooth? Calloused?

Roman's eyes flit to my wrist, like he's making the same realization I have. He works his jaw like he's about to say something, and for some inexplicable reason, something inside of me panics. I drop my arm and fake-yawn again, which turns into a real yawn that has my jaw feeling like it's about to pop out of its socket and I'm sure is probably one of the least attractive things Roman has ever seen.

"Wow, excuse me," I say. "I really am exhausted."

"I better let you get to bed then. I'll see you in the morning." He backs away, pausing at the door with his hand on the doorframe. "For what it's worth, your idea for game night was good." He looks around to make sure no one is near enough to hear him. "I had a lot of fun." And then he's gone.

Before a stupid grin can overtake my face, Angie pokes her head through the doorway, her body nowhere to be seen. "Did you get the spider?"

I walk to my bed and climb in. "Don't worry, Angie. You're safe." My heart? Not so much.

CHAPTER FIFTEEN

The next morning is way more subdued. It's not like the quiet of our first days, when we were exhausted from working out or still trying to acclimate to the new routine. It's a quiet from knowing we failed, and now one of our own is gone.

"This sucks," Angie says.

"Yeah," I agree. "Big-time."

"Now what are we going to do?" she asks, but I have no response.

Roman leans his back against the stove, staring at nothing. Scratch that, he's staring at me. It looks like he's expecting something, though what it is I have no clue.

He sighs, glances at Angie, then looks at me pointedly again. When I still don't get it, he rolls his eyes. "Last I checked, we still had a library on the line," he says.

I sit up at his words. He's proving once again that he's a team player and trying to encourage us. "Roman's right," I say. I was so caught up in my guilt over Simone—letting the personal affect the professional again—I wasn't thinking of why we're here in the first place. "We have to finish our tasks so we can get the money for the school and make Simone proud."

"Okay Mr. and Mrs. Optimistic," Angie says. "I'm pretty

sure Simone would rather have won the money than settle for being proud of us, but I get what you're saying. I guess we just keep going." She gets up and heads for the gym.

Before joining her, I glance at Roman. He watches Angie leave, his face remaining stoic. When he looks at me, there's that small softening of his features, and like a call and response, my pulse speeds up. *Mr. and Mrs. Optimistic.* I really shouldn't like the sound of that as much as I do.

I DON'T BOTHER WITH WEIGHTS IN THE GYM. ROMAN AND I WILL BE going on our expedition to gather rocks. Rather than walking, we'll be driving separate rovers. Since I'm not sure how heavy the rocks will be, I need to conserve what energy I can. From now on, I need to be at the top of my game, doing everything right and smartly to make sure we succeed.

After our workouts, we meet by the space suits. To save time, Angie helps me while Jordan helps Roman. I stand up and face Roman. When we make eye contact, my heart does a little kick. I try to tell myself the nervousness I feel stems from my worry that Angie and Jordan will run into trouble while we're away and *not* that I'm nervous at the thought of being out by myself with Roman. As the girls at school would say, basically I'm being delulu.

Jordan's voice comes over my earpiece. "Okay, I need you two to test your microphones."

"Mic check, mic check, one-two, one-two," Roman says, like he's a real emcee, and I smile at his playfulness.

"Brianna? Can you hear me? I need you to check your mic," Jordan says, snapping me out of my daze from looking at Roman's smile.

I clear my throat. "Testing, one-two-three."

"There we go. Remember, y'all are taking the rovers to

the south to extract twelve pounds of rocks each. The location is already programmed into the navigation. We should be able to communicate the whole time y'all are out," Jordan explains, his voice growing more and more excited as he goes on. I'm fairly certain he gets just as much excitement out of watching us do the task as he would doing it himself. He's content to simply be here.

"Ready?" Roman asks.

"Let's do it," I respond.

"Stand clear. Opening the hatch," Roman says, sounding so official.

We step out of the Hab and make our way to the two rovers. They're able to fit two people apiece, but we'll each take one so the extra weight of the rocks, combined with our own weight, doesn't slow them down.

After removing the heavy tarp placed over each, I'm reminded of the rideable lawnmowers they use to maintain the school grounds. The engines start up easily and smoothly, and map displays show where we'll be heading.

"Nice," Roman comments. He twists half his body to look over at me. "Think you can keep up?"

"Pshh, I've been riding four-wheelers since I was a kid. Let's see if *you* can keep up." I don't wait for his response. I step hard on the gas and take off. And barely move.

My rover doesn't move very fast. In fact, I'm certain we could run at a quicker pace.

"What in the world is this?" I ask.

Roman's answering chuckle in my ear makes me feel like a pet getting the best scratches.

"If we really were on Mars, we'd be traveling a lot farther than the length of a field," he says. "The speed of our rovers are made to account for that."

"Let me guess, you read it in the manual." Ugh.

"God, isn't that cool?" Jordan pipes up. "They thought of everything here."

I huff and relax into my seat, knowing it's going to take a while to get to the expedition spot.

"Should have brought a book to enjoy the downtime," Roman says, and judging by the teasing in his voice, he's not done. "Maybe something adventurous. I think something set in this world, but unlikely soulmates."

I shake my head. I must have left my book out and Roman got to it. "Who knew under all that quiet machismo was the heart of a romantic," I say. "I've figured you out. You may be a science teacher, but you missed your real calling as a literary scholar."

His chuckle is low, but it sends butterflies through my stomach all the same.

"You should be arriving within the next two minutes," Jordan says.

As predicted, we soon arrive at the site. It's on the edge of the large dome, but we can still see the Hab.

As we get off the rovers, Jordan sounds in our ears. "In the toolbox on the back of each of your rovers, you'll find a shovel, which you'll use to fill the box labeled 'specimen' with the rocks. As you fill up the box, the weight will be displayed."

Our race didn't end just because our vehicles are slow. Now that we're stopped, we both rush to get to the field with our boxes and shovels. The ground is tougher, so we have to use the shovels to loosen it and dislodge the rocks we find. We set to work side by side. We're grunting. We're stealing small glances at each other to check the other's progress, looking all the sillier, I'm sure, since we have to move our whole upper bodies. But the work is simple enough that we don't have to put too much thought into it, and it's fun.

By some miracle, I load up my rocks before Roman does and do a victory dance beside my vehicle. "Yes! Take that."

Roman isn't far behind. He sets his materials in the back of his vehicle and shakes his head. "I got way more rocks than you did."

"Excuses, excuses," I say as we get back into our seats. I'm not going to let a technicality taint this win.

"Hey, guys," Jordan says. "Good news. Y'all got the specimens that we need, and once we inspect them, the task is complete."

"If that's the good news, I'm guessing there's something we're not going to like," Roman says.

"Yeah . . ." I can hear Jordan's grimace through the comms unit. "We just received a delayed message from Mission Control. An unexpected dust storm has developed and is heading our way."

That's concerning. What will happen if we're still out here when it hits? How strong will the winds be? Thankfully, with the helmet, my braids won't be full of dust (a vain concern, but water rationing won't allow me to spend more than two minutes washing them), but will there be enough dust flying around to get us lost and off course? Will we get eliminated and have to leave it up to Jordan and Angie to win the library money?

"How long do we have?" I ask.

"About twelve minutes," Jordan replies.

Riding side by side, Roman and I look at each other. I gulp, trying to do some mental calculations in my head. It took us about fifteen minutes to drive out to the spot. We must have been driving for at least ten minutes now. Unfortunately it's been slow going, and with the added weight of the rocks, it feels like we're moving at a crawl.

"What if we just leave the rovers and make a run for it?" Roman asks.

I nod. "Yeah. That sounds good to me. I'm pretty sure we can run to the Hab in half the time it would take to get there on wheels, even in sand and these big suits."

"You can't," Jordan says. "Anything is liable to happen to the rovers and our specimens if left unattended. The dust could cause the wheels to stop working altogether. Or maybe they'd be buried in the dust. Without the rovers we'd have no hope of trying to complete this task again, and it's one of the big four we have to finish. We must get the rovers back to the Hab, then cover them before the storm hits. But don't worry," he tries to soothe. "You two have plenty of time to make it."

I would not put it past whoever was running the simulation to take the rovers out of commission if we left them. I take a deep breath. Okay. Slog over the red ground with an additional twelve pounds of rocks to slow us down, get the rovers covered so the dust doesn't get into all the nooks and crannies and make them stop, then make it back inside the Hab before we get caught up in the dust storm ourselves. No biggie. Mission: *Not* Impossible. We got this.

I tighten my grip on the steering wheel, pushing my shoulders back. No, it doesn't make the rover move faster, but it makes me feel like I'm moving with more purpose. I may have on a large space suit in lieu of some leather pants and kick-ass boots, but I'm a woman on a mission.

"Are you humming the *Mission: Impossible* theme?" Roman asks.

"Uh, what?"

I'm glad I'm not facing him. I forgot he could hear every sound I make. Anyone tuning in to our live stream can. *Why didn't I choose a Beyoncé song to hum?*

"You don't have to stop," Roman says with a slight chuckle, but I ignore him. I don't need the world to know I'm totally and utterly lame.

We finally make it back to the Hab. Roman and I park the rovers. I look around, trying to see if I can tell just when the dust storm will hit and how they'll do it in the dome.

"Jordan, how are we on time?" I ask.

"Y'all are doing great. Three minutes left."

A surge of victory begins welling up in my chest as I grab the box full of rocks and affix the tarp over my rover.

"How about I take that and you get the door?" Roman says as he grabs for my box. Knowing that now is not the time to argue, I give it freely and move to the hatch. I open it, and just as Roman is ten feet away, part of the tarp blows off my rover as if it were never secured.

"Oh no!" I yell. "I need to fix the tarp. I'll be right back." Before Roman can get out anything other than a *What?* I take off back to the rovers. In ten seconds, I manage to get it on, this time ensuring it won't come off.

But when I turn to head back inside, everything goes black.

I don't panic. I blink, my breath sawing in and out, loud to my ears in the confines of my helmet.

"There's something wrong with my helmet," I announce as calmly as I can. "I think the sun visor or whatever is messing up. I can't see anything. I don't know how to make it back to the Hab."

"Roman, can you get her? We're down to one minute," Jordan says.

"I'm already on it," Roman says.

Knowing that this part of the ground has loose rocks, some big and some small, I stand perfectly in place so I don't fall over anything.

I feel cut off from the world. With my helmet so dark, it's hard to tell if my eyes are even open, so I continuously blink. In the space suit, I can't feel any wind blowing against my skin or playing with my braids. I'm not afraid of the dark, haven't been for years, but it's lonely and vulnerable as I stand there.

The last time I was in the dark this long has to have been when I was a little girl. There was a storm, and my parents weren't home. Maybe they were on a date, I can't remember. But it was just me and my siblings at our home in the woods. A storm had come, knocking out all the power, but I wasn't scared. My brothers came to check on Camille and me, my oldest brother, Tay, marching in with a flashlight and shining it on us. Once everyone's good health was confirmed, Tay had the idea to play tag. I loved all my siblings, but I especially looked up to Tay and the way he could turn the worst circumstances around.

I feel a tug on my hand.

"Come on, we need to hurry," Roman says, pulling me along.

I have no choice but to blindly follow, taking smaller steps than normal in case I accidentally slip on a rock. After a few seconds, I feel the shift from the hard ground to the thin flooring of the Hab as Roman directs me with his hand on my back. I hear the clang to let me know the hatch has been shut, and I let out a sigh of relief. Roman removes my helmet, and I look up into his handsome face, which is marred by a slight frown.

"It looks like you've been crying," he says.

I stare at the helmet he still has on. The reflection staring back at me is a melding of his handsome face and my puffy eyes. Even though I wouldn't consider myself a pretty crier, our reflections look good together.

"That's because I have been crying," I say. More often than not, thinking of Tay causes a breach in my already faulty floodgates, even if they're happy memories.

"Were you scared out there?"

"No, I was thinking about my big brother, who passed away a while back. Good memories."

"Maybe you can tell me about him someday." Roman's voice is a soft caress in my ear as it comes across the comm.

"I think I'd like that," I respond, just as softly.

He holds his hand up like he's going to brush the wetness from my face, then looks at his glove, which is caked in red dirt.

He looks from his hand to me, and I recoil slightly, not wanting to get that all over my face. We both laugh, the air grows warmer, and I can't help but marvel at our change in circumstances. In this too-small, peculiar habitat where we could be at each other's throats, there's affection. We planted those dandelion seeds, but it's genuine friendship now blossoming between us.

I don't want to question what I'm feeling too much, but I can't help but wonder, could things stay like this when the simulation is over? When we're back at school, passing each other in the hallway, could Roman's eyes soften when they land on mine? Could our relationship continue to grow and this friendship turn into something more?

I bite my lower lip and shyly look away. These are not the kind of thoughts a vice principal should have for a teacher. They're the kind of thoughts that invite scandal, though, curiously, that word doesn't flash through my mind as sharply as it did before.

Once the pressure has stabilized in the tunnel, the inner door to the Hab swings open and Angie comes rushing out, straight to me.

"Oh my God, you made it!" She wraps her arms around me, hugging tight. "I was so worried you were going to get caught up in the dust storm."

I can't even move my arms because of how tight Angie's grip is. I look over Angie's shoulder to meet the gaze of an amused Roman.

After a few more good squeezes, Angie lets me go and takes a step back. "I'm so glad you made it. I don't think Jordan and I would have lasted long without me killing him. Then I'd be eliminated on principle, and it'd be a whole thing. I mean, I *could* have been in Cancún, but now that I'm here, I may as well get that money, right?"

Without another word, Angie turns to go back in, nodding at Roman and patting him lightly on the shoulder.

"What just happened?" I ask.

"Your best friend just said she was worried about you."

I don't argue the best friend part. I'm touched Angie was so worried about me.

Roman walks to the doorway but stops before he goes in as well. "For the record, she's not the first person you've won over."

And I'm left speechless.

CHAPTER SIXTEEN

T he dust storm brings an unexpected yet welcome calm after the chaos of Roman and me trying to make it back in time. Unfortunately, though it was calm, the dust storm knocked out our power, and the Hab is only running on enough to provide us with life-supporting oxygen. The LED lights are on as well, so we're not in the dark. But that does mean we can't check whether we've received any messages from Mission Control or anyone else. And right now, I'm missing my family.

I miss my parents, my siblings, my niece, and Sheba, and I wish I could call them up and tell them what is going on. I'm sure they're tuning in every chance they get, but it's not the same.

"You doing okay?" Jordan asks. He comes from the kitchen with a cup of water and joins me on the couch.

"I'm fine. Just missing home. Especially my dog. Do you have any pets?"

"A turtle. I don't like dogs."

"I used to judge people who don't like dogs, but I'd like to think I've moved on from that," I say, but can't help but give Jordan the side-eye. Who doesn't like dogs?

Realistically, I know millions of people in the world aren't pet people. But those millions also haven't met Sheba.

Jordan laughs. "Sorry. They scare me. One almost attacked me when I was a kid. Ever since, I start sweating bullets every time I'm near one."

I gasp and lay a hand on his forearm. "You don't need to apologize. I'm the one who's sorry for giving you a hard time." And I feel terrible about it.

"Nah, don't sweat it. You didn't know. It's not like I walk around advertising all my phobias or anything."

"What's going on over here, lovebirds?" Angie says as she walks into the common room.

"Lovebirds?" I say, while at the same time Jordan chokes on his drink. It's all I can do not to move all the way to the kitchen, but I don't want to be dramatic. "Why would you say something like that?"

"Why would I say that? Come on, look at you two," Angie says, wiggling her eyebrows.

I turn my head to look at Jordan. When I realize how close we are, I scoot over.

At that moment, Roman pokes his head out from the computer server closet. "Did the cameras come back up yet?" He's been in there trying to reset the system.

"Not yet," Angie answers. "Roman, back me up here. Don't you think Brianna and Jordan would make the cutest couple? I'm trying to help my girl find some love."

I cover my face with my hands and shake my head. Why does Angie have the worst filter in human history? When I peek through my fingers, I see that Roman's face is blank as he stares at Angie. After a second, he shakes his head and goes back into the room, slamming the door.

"Welp," Angie says. "It looks like Major Pain is in some kind of mood."

"That's probably because he's trying to fix something while you're out here talking nonsense." I look at the door, a sinking feeling in the pit of my stomach. "Angie, listen. I know we're not at school, but I still take my position of vice principal very seriously. I cannot stress enough that there is nothing going on between Jordan and me." I turn to Jordan. "You know you're my people, but I only see you as a friend. I hope my friendliness has never come off as anything other than that."

Jordan looks like he's about to start sweating bullets now as he shakes his head furiously. "Yeah, no, of course it hasn't. I mean, you're great, but I don't see you like that either. Or anyone, really." His cheeks puff out as he lets out a big breath.

I raise my eyebrows and nod. Jordan is simply out here trying to live his best life, not interested in me or anyone else. I commend his honesty and that he doesn't feel the need to justify himself to anyone. I don't know if he means that he wants to be single forever and doesn't have romantic feelings toward anyone, but I know it's not my place to pry. Like I told Angie, we are colleagues, and while I want to be on good terms and feel connected with them while we're here, certain lines have to be maintained.

I turn to Angie. "I appreciate that you're trying to help me find joy." I try to look at it from the angle that Angie wants to help and not pry or stir up workplace drama. "But there is nothing going on between Jordan and me, so please stop."

Angie looks contrite and lets out a long stream of air. "Fine. But don't say I never tried to do anything nice for you."

"You have a heart of gold." I stand up. "Now I need to set the record straight with Roman. I don't need him going back to school and starting any rumors."

I walk to the closet, knocking on the door before opening it without waiting for Roman to invite me in. "Hi." I slide in, realizing just how small the server room is with all the tech equipment as well as the bodies of Roman and me. I have to close the door behind myself to be able to fit all the way inside.

He looks up from his spot on the floor. "Hey. Did you need something?" His tone lacks the warmth I've come to know from our time together.

"I came to see if you needed help. It's a big task we've got you working on."

He holds a small flashlight in his hand and points it at a paper to read the manual he's managed to find. "I think I've got everything squared away. I'm just waiting for it to reboot, and we'll see if that will work. Don't worry, I want the power on just as much as everyone else. I'm not trying to sabotage anything."

"I know you're not," I say honestly. "You being alone in here to mess anything up was the furthest thing from my mind." And now I feel bad that my past actions have caused him to think I'll always be suspicious of his motives. I also feel strangely guilty about what Angie said about Jordan and me. I know I shouldn't. After all, I don't owe Roman any explanations when it comes to my love life. And I'm Roman's superior, so he has no reason to be in the know at this level when it comes to my love life. And yet . . .

"You can go back out there with Angie and your little boyfriend," Roman says, and I lose all feelings of guilt in a flash.

No this man didn't.

I make my back straight and hold my head up high. "Excuse me?"

Roman's jaw flexes in the low light as he meets my gaze, but he doesn't back down either.

Like I do anytime his dad tries to stare me down during the school year, I lift my eyebrow to let him know he needs to come correct. "That was uncalled-for, and you know it."

Finally, Roman proves that he isn't like his dad. He looks away and his shoulders fall a little. "Sorry," he says. "Look, I'm good here. If you want to hang out there and get cozy with Jordan, don't let me stop you."

He was almost there with the apology, and then he had to go and ruin it. Maybe he's trying to get me to back off like the teachers do, but I'm not a teacher and I don't like when people try telling me what to do.

"I was not getting cozy with Jordan," I say.

"No? Angie sure seemed to think so. She thinks y'all would be a cute couple."

Now I know, just *know*, Roman isn't jealous at the thought of me dating Jordan. Maybe the thought of me breaking the school conduct rules brought out his petty side. The thought that I, the person who is in the position he wants, is dating someone I have influence over. *That* I can see.

But as I watch the tenseness in Roman's jaw, the way his shoulders are wound up tight . . . Well, I'll be damned.

"It doesn't matter what Angie thinks. I'm not interested in dating Jordan."

Roman's eyes snap to mine and my heartbeat picks up. "No? Why not?"

I lick my suddenly dry lips. This conversation is taking a turn I was not expecting. We're veering into dangerous territory and I need to put a stop to it. "Because I don't date colleagues."

At my words, he goes silent. He searches my eyes, then something changes in his face. He looks a little hurt and disappointed. "Why not?" he asks quietly. Almost too quietly in this space where the fans not only act like a white noise track but also ensure no one overhears our conversation.

"You mean, why don't I date my colleagues? Because it would be unethical. Because of the power imbalance that comes along with me dating someone who reports to me. Because I value my job." Because Superintendent Watts would surely skewer me over the same greasy ovens used to make the god-awful school pizzas before withdrawing her mentorship, and I'd forever be floundering through life without a purpose. "Take your pick."

He rubs at his temples and sighs.

"Roman, why are you asking me this? Is it because of Jordan, or because . . ." I don't bother finishing the question. It's not worth the embarrassment if I've once again inflated our connection in my mind and he says no.

He reaches forward and grabs my hand. "I'm asking because yes, I want to date you. I don't like thinking about you being with Jordan or any other dudes because I like you."

He caresses my knuckles with his thumb. His hand is warm, his skin soft. It serves as a distraction as I try to think of a response to his confession, but all I can do is focus on his skin against mine.

"When I said you are amazing, I meant every word," he says.

"Roman," I finally say. "We can't."

"Why not?"

"I already told you. My job. Your job too. We can't date."

"But you want to." He doesn't state it presumptuously. Just matter-of-factly, with all the confidence in the world, and he's so right.

I do want to date him. I want to learn all about his life and, in turn, tell him about mine. I want to see what we have in common, what opinions we share and what things he's wrong about. But learning all there is to know about Roman won't change the fact that at the end of the day, I'm the vice principal and he's a teacher who reports to me. I can't cross that line.

"You did it, Roman!" Jordan says through a crack in the door. He isn't able to open it any wider with me there, and I'm not about to step back into Roman's personal space to let him. "The monitors are back up and working."

"Thanks," Roman says, not taking his eyes off me.

Jordan walks away from the door, and I know I need to get out of here.

"Well, great job," I say. "You just, um, keep reading those manuals."

I take a small step forward, waiting to see if Roman will move. He doesn't. "Excuse me, I'm just going to squeeze right on out." I finally manage to pass between him and the door, but not without having my whole backside push against his front.

When I'm out in the common room, I school my features and hope the conversation that just transpired between Roman and me isn't written all over my face.

"Come look at this mess we've got going on," Angie says to me from her spot at the comms station.

I mentally shake the remaining warm-and-fuzzies out of my head and walk to them. "Where did they even get all of this dust from?" I wonder aloud. Dust fills the screens, and we can only intermittently make out the ground.

"This shit better not be full of asbestos," Angie says, and all I can think of are lawyers' commercials about getting my claim in.

"That's going to be hell to clean up later," Roman says. He's appeared behind me, and it's obvious that he's done it on purpose.

I bite down on my lip as he leans forward, his body caging me in, and one of his hands rests on the desk and the other one on the chair while he watches the storm.

I turn my head and find Angie looking at us with speculation. Oh God. Angie must know something happened in that closet. I do my best to hold stock-still, not react. Maybe if I act like I'm not aware that every breath I take is filled with Roman's scent, Angie will let it go.

Angie does not let it go.

"I have a teeny, tiny, innocent little question for you," Angie says when we're in our room later.

I hesitantly put down my book and stick my head out of my pod. "Yes?"

"So, are you not worried about Roman being the principal's son?"

"What do you mean? Why should that bother me?"

Angie narrows her eyes at me. "If you like living dangerously, then I love that for you. Really. Just watch out. Roman typically hates just about everyone, and I'd hate to see you get your feelings hurt."

I automatically want to correct her. Roman doesn't hate everyone. He gets along with Kareem and Raven, with the students. And here, me. But she's already too deep in my personal business.

"I appreciate the concern, but I'm fine. The same way I told you nothing is going on between Jordan and me earlier, it holds true for Roman." I lean back in my bed before she can detect any lies.

I WAKE UP THE NEXT MORNING IN A STATE OF DISBELIEF AND ELATION.
I can't believe Roman said he wants to date me. *Roman* wants to date *me*. Brianna with the too-gummy smile. Bri-

anna with the word vomit whenever I get around him. Rather than being on another planet, it's like I'm in an alternate reality.

With a sigh, I flop on my back, let my smile fall, and look up at the ceiling of my pod. Once I get out of this bed, I need to put thoughts of getting to know Roman better behind me. I made my stance on dating teachers crystal clear to him yesterday, and I need to make sure I hold on to my word.

Will I have to tell him we can't be friends as well? Before I left the server room yesterday, it didn't seem like he was ready to back down. In such a short period of time I've grown used to the way he smiles just for me. I don't want to have to lose that. But I know getting closer to him would be a mistake.

I finally get out of bed. Jordan is at the experiment station, looking at something with a magnifying glass. I'm surprised to see Angie up and eating oatmeal rather than a protein bar. I'm proud of her for branching out.

"Good morning," I say, eyeing her. "You're up early."

Angie takes in a deep breath. "Yesterday, I was really worried I was going to lose you and be stuck here with Jordan. I've come to accept that this is my life. It's not Cancún, and it smells like the pits of hell, but I'm here." Even though I like it, I'm thrown by her air of calm acceptance. Maybe she did yoga this morning or something. "So I'm going to help us win, get that teacher bonus, and use it to go to Jamaica, bay-bay!"

That's more like it. I shake my head and walk to the cabinets to make some tea. I pour hot water in the pot and add tea leaves. While waiting for the tea to steep, I turn and lean my back against the counter, looking around inconspicuously.

"Looking for someone?" Angie asks.

"No," I quickly respond, fiddling with my shirt. "But I am wondering what everyone is up to this morning. What is Jordan looking at?"

"It's the samples from the rocks you and Roman brought back."

"I see. And Roman, where is he?" I mean, Angie was the one who brought him up to begin with.

Angie smiles like she's satisfied. "He's in the greenhouse. Said he was going to check on the plants since nothing shows signs of sprouting yet."

I nod. Then I mess with my shirt some more. Then my foot starts tapping. I want to go speak to Roman. I need to reiterate to him that we can't date. But if I do, Angie will think I want to spend time with him.

"Well." Angie stands up from her stool. "I'm going to get some cardio in. You'll come join me after you eat?"

"Yes, of course," I answer quickly. Maybe a little too quickly, as I'm eager for Angie to leave the room, but hopefully she won't notice.

"Well, okay then." Angie walks away, smiling at me one more time before she's out of sight.

I take the pot off the stove so it won't burn and start a fire, and head for the greenhouse. I don't worry about Jordan thinking anything is up. He's still engrossed with the magnifying glass.

Once I'm in the greenhouse, I immediately spot Roman. He's inspecting the sprinklers. He turns in my direction as I walk in and close the door.

"Hey," he says.

"Morning." I walk toward him, stopping before I can get too close. But I don't stop so far away that I don't notice the bags under his eyes and the overall worn-down look he has. "Are you okay? You don't look so good." I hope he's not getting sick.

His smile is tight. "I'm fine. I just woke up with a headache."

"Have you taken any medicine?"

"Yeah." He puts his hand on his head, pushing his hair back in the opposite direction of his waves. "I'm not putting too much faith in it working. Once a migraine starts, it's too late for medicine."

I grimace. He must not be feeling well at all if he's messing up his hair. I want to reach up and smooth it back down. Massage his temples to help him feel better. But I don't dare. I clasp my fingers together behind my back.

"I didn't know that you get migraines." It feels like it's something I should be aware of. But I can't think of a day when he's missed school or it seemed like he was in pain.

"I don't get them often, and they're usually not debilitating, just annoying, which can cause me to get irritated quickly . . . or act like a pain." He looks at me and cocks an eyebrow.

I instantly feel bad, realizing he must be aware that the teachers call his dad Major Pain and him Major Pain Jr. While his dad one thousand percent deserves the nickname, I hate that Roman is aware of it, and even more that I haven't put a stop to it. If I was aware that the teachers had some joke about my name, who knows what I'd do. Actually, I do know. I'd cry about it.

"You're not a pain," I say emphatically. "If you hear anyone calling you that, let me know, and I'll put a stop to it right away." That might have come off a little more feral than intended, but I try to tell myself that I would be just as protective of anyone who I thought might be getting their feelings hurt.

Roman salutes me. "Yes, ma'am."

I smile and nod, confident he'll take me up on the offer and assured in my capability to put a stop to the nasty name. I look around at the plants and sprinklers, then at the dandelion plot. We haven't yielded any sprouts yet, and I'm beginning to get antsy. There is one lone dandelion from the old plot that has already lost its flower, with nothing left save for the wispy spores. I walk closer.

"How are we going to get these to grow?" I ask.

Roman stops next to me and plucks the old dandelion from the soil. It's a straggler from what the crew before us had planted.

"Hey, don't!" I begin, but it's too late.

He holds it out to me. "Here. Make a wish."

"I can't. We're supposed to keep whatever we can grow or put it with the compost. I heard Jordan say he wanted to make dandelion soup at some point." Roman's flat look tells me exactly what he thinks of dandelion soup. I shrug. "Look, those are his dreams, not mine."

"It's one dandelion," Roman dismisses. "And if it makes you feel better, I'll keep the stem when you're done."

"Jordan would kill us if he knew we were about to send more than a hundred seeds into the Hab."

Roman looks very serious as he says, "If Jordan tries anything, let me know, and I'll put a stop to it right away." The half smile he lets slip is pure, unadulterated charm.

He holds the dandelion under my nose, waiting for me to comply. Finally, I suck in a deep breath and make a wish. Surprisingly, it's not about my career or even the library—I wish for real, honest connections. I'm tired of being lonely.

I blow a stream of air directed toward the center, and about a hundred seeds fly out, swirling around Roman and floating in the air around us. I smile as I hold my hand out for any of the seeds to land in. I catch two, lift my palm to show Roman, and freeze. As in awe as I am with the magic of this moment, he seems to be in awe of me.

My pulse speeds up and my stomach is a jumbled mess. Especially when his eyes land on my lips.

Never mind that just a few minutes ago I came in here to tell him directly, once again, that we can't date. The Brianna who thought up that horrible idea was out of her mind. Because why can't we? Why shouldn't we?

Because you're colleagues, you're on camera, and the man clearly isn't feeling well. I want to plug my ears, but that won't drown out the voice of reason in my head.

"You need to stop looking at me like that," I finally say.

"Like what?"

I swallow past my own desires to get the words out of my mouth. "Like you want to kiss me. We can't date, and we certainly can't kiss."

"We're not at school, and we're both adults," he says, and I have to admit he makes an excellent point. "And most importantly," he continues, "I want to. I haven't wanted anything like this in a long, long time."

As I open my mouth to do something—repeat myself until I believe it, tell him to pucker up, who knows—an alarm begins blaring throughout the Hab. I initially think the people in charge of the simulation *can* actually hear us in here. That they've been watching and, after deciding we've crossed a big line, are now calling us on it. But then I realize that loud hitting sounds can be heard. Are we being attacked? Roman and I look at each other with wild, surprised eyes before taking off out of the greenhouse.

CHAPTER SEVENTEEN

liens! Oh lawd, we're being attacked by aliens!"

It's a cacophony of alarms blaring, robotic warnings of imminent doom (or at least that's what I think; who can tell with all the other chaos?), what sounds like hail raining down, and over it all, Angie's voice reigns supreme with her shouts of aliens.

I stop in the middle of the Hab, looking around wildly as I stand in the doorway of the gym, from Angie to the comms and cameras that are showing nothing but dust and finally to Roman, who's wincing while shielding his eyes. All this noise can't be good for his headache.

Jordan comes barreling from his and Roman's bedroom. "Meteor shower!" he exclaims, almost out of breath. "There's a meteor shower, and the meteors are coming through the ceiling."

Angie stops yelling about aliens, and we all run to the bedroom. Sure enough, the ceiling now sports dozens of little holes where the artificial sunlight breaks through. I stand back, not wanting to get pelted by anything. "Jordan, what do we do?" I shout, loud enough to be heard over the warning system.

But Jordan doesn't say anything. He stands in the middle of the room, frozen as he takes in the destruction. I try to think of the different emergency scenarios and procedures we went over in training, but I can't think through all the noise. It's too much. There's something about all the noise and the assault on my senses that makes my mind equally as jumbled and ready for flight, even though I know this is not real. It's just a test. I've always been good at tests, but this is something else. This is hard and cold failure. As we all stand around, not knowing what to do, I see that everything we've been working toward so hard is about to end. I'll have to go home and actually think about what I want to do as far as my career goes. Either that or face Principal Major and his smug face and the kids who won't get their library. I want to cover my ears and run away.

"Listen up, everyone," Roman shouts. "We need to cover the holes. Angie, Brianna, find as much duct tape as you can. Jordan, we'll get the ladders."

Normally, direct orders make me bristle, but something about the no-nonsense, authoritative command in Roman's voice does the exact opposite. It makes everything in me stand at attention. It sends chills down my spine and makes my heart race. *This better not awaken anything in me.*

"Let's move, people!" he insists. Given purpose, we scramble to work on our tasks, and I place a hand on my stomach. It's like all the dandelion seeds I blew earlier found their way right to my stomach and are floating around.

How much duct tape can a Hab store? As it turns out, a lot. There's certainly enough to stock a small grocery store. I can't imagine it will take more than a few rolls to patch the holes, so Angie and I each grab two, which will allow everyone to have one.

When we get back to their room, Roman and Jordan are coming in with arms full of ladders and step stools. The alarms are still blaring, but now it doesn't seem so jarring, like the end of the world is looming. We set to work, standing on ladders to reach the ceiling. Using teeth and fingers to rip pieces of the duct tape off, I work on the sides, leaving the highest parts of the ceiling for Roman and Jordan. Still, by the time we're done, my arms ache from reaching up for so long.

"We did it," Jordan says after a thorough glance around confirms all the holes have been sealed.

I smile. I want to clap and cheer, let everyone know how great of a job we did, but I don't want to jinx anything. We can celebrate after we've all caught our breath.

As we're folding up the ladders and preparing to put up the tape, the alarms finally stop. At that, I let out a deep sigh. "I think this calls for a celebration," I say to Roman, smiling. "Pizza?"

Roman looks down at me. He looks tired, worn down by the past half hour's chaos, but he manages his signature half smile. "You read my mind."

"You guys can get started on the pizzas," Jordan says. "I need to clean up the meteors. I'll save some to study too. Who knows, they might have put some interesting materials in them."

On the heels of Jordan's words, a large crash rocks the Hab, shaking it from floor to ceiling. More alarms blaring, more computerized voices shouting at us about a loss of oxygen.

We look through the guys' bedroom door and find a gaping hole in the previously repaired ceiling. In the middle of the floor, a burning rock the size of a chair is impacted into the ground.

"You're going to need a bigger broom!" Angie shouts.

We all know there's no repairing this one. I slide the

duct tape rolls off my arms and start passing them out again. "Looks like we'll have to seal the room off."

The guys run inside to get their bags and whatever else they can grab from their beds in thirty seconds, then we work to seal the top, bottom, and sides of the door. Once complete, Jordan moves to the comms system and is somehow able to shut off oxygen and power to that particular room. Finally, the blaring stops.

I take a deep breath before speaking, but Angie beats me to it. "*Do not even* say good job. For all we know, a meteorite will come through our bedroom next, and we'll be left to sleep out here on the couches."

Fair enough.

I shrug sheepishly. I'm definitely not jinxing it this time.

Roman lets out a pained grunt, and I turn to see him grimacing and holding his head.

"I think you need to lie down," I say, moving to his side. "Can I take your bag?"

He shakes his head, and I fight not to bare my teeth. Stupid men and their inability to look weak even for a second. "Come on."

I lead him to my and Angie's room, which is now everybody's room.

"You can use the empty bed over there." I point straight ahead, but when I look behind me, Roman is gone, having already climbed into the first bed he could find. Mine.

What's most important is for him to get rest now. I'll have him move later.

"Can I get you anything?" I ask in a low tone once he's under the covers. "Water? More medicine?"

He speaks into the pillow, and it sounds like he wants me to stay with him. My heart lurches and I imagine climbing into bed, massaging his temples and neck.

Before I can do anything foolish, I lean closer. "I'm sorry, what was that?"

This time his answer in the negative is easier to make out.

"Okay," I say. "I'll close the pod and turn off the lights. I'll be back to check on you later."

I begin to reach for his back, but think better of it and stop. I'm already imagining doing dirty things to him while he's under the weather. Now is the time to keep my hands to myself.

I close the screen on his pod, and though my mind fights each step I take, I close the door and leave him alone in the room.

"How's your man doing?" Angie asks as I walk out of the room.

"Angie, he's not my man. We're just colleagues."

"I didn't say *your* man. I said *our* man."

"Oh." My guilty overactive imagination had me hearing things that weren't even said. Again. My imagination is doing too much when it comes to Roman. "He's okay. He just needs quiet and rest."

And I need to get my heart and libido under control.

THERE REALLY AREN'T ENOUGH THINGS TO DO HERE TO KEEP US OCCU-
pied. I can only vacuum so much, read so many manuals, and give the plants so much water before my mind reverts back to Roman. The man, no, menace, won't leave my mind. Why did he have to be so sexy when he took charge during the meteor shower? Maybe that migraine of his was a blessing in disguise, because Lord knows what I would have done if he'd used that same tone when he said he wanted to kiss me.

Thinking of his migraine, I look toward the bedroom

door and wonder if I should check on him again. Angie is sitting next to me at the table. She's finally given up her imaginary phone and is playing on one of the tablets. Since she seems engrossed enough, I begin sliding off my stool. Her spidey senses pick up and she turns to me. "Where are you going?"

Now that she's decided she's all in on this simulation, suddenly my every move is under her scrutiny. Though the scrutiny may also stem from the fact that I've checked on Roman four times already.

"I'm just getting a tablet," I say, playing it off. "I want to see if any messages are coming through yet."

She watches me as I grab a tablet then continue past the bedroom door. I continue on into the greenhouse so I can be alone.

I power on my tablet and check whether there are any messages from my family. The power is back up, but nothing has come in. I wonder if it's because of the antenna.

I consider drafting individual messages to everyone that will send when the reception is fully up and running, but my thoughts are as blank as the email draft I pull up. What should I say? My parents' and Vincent's messages would be easy updates. But I feel like I should say more to Camille. If she's been keeping track of what's going on, she must have picked up that something is going on between Roman and me by now. Her reply would say I'm causing more trouble and confusion for myself, knowing that any relationship between us is doomed. But after realizing Roman isn't a villain out to steal my job like I thought he was, I don't want to hear any words of caution Camille has on the matter. Does it make me delulu? Maybe. But I'm delulu and happy.

In the end, I send a message addressed to everyone

saying that I miss them and to give Zara and Sheba kisses for me. They'll get it at some point.

Jordan is frowning at one of the screens at the comms station when I go to return the tablet.

"What's going on?" I ask.

"This right here." He points to a screen with a black background and green letters. "It monitors how we're doing on the tasks. Timelines and such. We've been doing good with the physical exercises and maintaining the Hab and have completed two of the major tasks. It all looks good, except for this metric." He points to the one dark orange row. "We were supposed to have the antenna up by now. We're still receiving communications from Mission Control, but it's been delaying by hours." He grabs a fistful of locs then drags a hand over his face. "If we had fixed it first thing, you and Roman wouldn't have almost gotten caught out there, and we would have known about the meteor shower."

If only someone had mentioned fixing the antenna first. That's right, I did, and Jordan wanted to play around with other things.

I don't vocalize my thoughts. It's enough to know that I'm right. But seeing Jordan overwhelmed, I do go into fix-it mode. "This is a concern, but it's not unfixable. As soon as this dust storm is over, we'll get out there and repair the damage."

Jordan has a faraway look in his eyes, and I know his mind must be whirring with different possibilities. "No, we can't wait that long. The storm is forecasted to last another thirty-six hours. If we wait for it to end, we might miss even more critical information, or the thing will break completely, and we'll be out of luck."

"Or likely both," I say. Given how it's been one catastrophe after another, I wouldn't put it past the organizers to cause tragedy to strike twice in the same day. When did I become this jaded creature? "So what are you proposing we do?"

"We need to fix the antenna as soon as possible. Today if we can. I've been watching the camera feeds, and the dust isn't always pouring down like this. There are stretches of time when it's more like a passing mist. That's when we go."

Jordan is right. There are moments when the dust lets up. If we want the simulation to succeed, that will be the best time to go.

"Okay," I agree. "We continue to monitor, then go when visibility is best. What will we be doing out there? How do we fix it? I want to be prepared."

Before, Jordan had Angie and Simone to help him. With Simone gone, I assume I'll be taking her place.

"About that," Jordan begins. "The last part of fixing the antenna involves replacing some hardware. It's kind of high up there. We'd probably need someone with some good arm reach. You know, someone with a long torso. We'll need someone with long legs, too."

"I get it," I cut in. "I'm too short. Guess I'll be inside during the mission."

"Hey, don't look so glum. Every member of this team is valuable. You'll provide much-needed support over comms."

I nod, knowing Jordan is right. Each part we play serves a critical role. Just like at school. "You're right. I'll be glad to cheer y'all on and provide support from in here." At least I won't have to worry about going out in the dust.

"That's the spirit. I just hope Roman will feel better by the time the dust slows down."

I hear an old record scratch in my mind and frown. "Roman won't be in any condition to go out there." Jordan's eyes widen and he leans away from me looking a little scared. I attempt to dial down the overprotectiveness so I don't scare him—like the dog from his childhood—and clear my throat, saying in a softer tone, "What I mean is, Roman was in pretty bad shape when he went down. I think he'll need at least a couple of days to recover. Maybe we shouldn't count on him to be able to help out there?" I say the last bit as a question, but it is most undeniably a command. Roman needs someone to look out for his well-being, and apparently it's going to be me.

"Yeah, I guess you're right. He did look worse for wear." Jordan sighs. "I guess all we can do now is wait out the storm and move quickly if we get the chance." He stands up. "I need to debrief Angie so she'll be ready to move when it's time."

CHAPTER EIGHTEEN

I quietly open the bedroom door and slip in. Once it closes behind me, I wait for my eyes to adjust to the low light. I walk to my bed—Roman's temporary bed—and begin to pull the screen up.

"Hey," I whisper. "I came to check on you, and I brought you some wat—"

Lord. Have. Mercy.

There is a stranger in my bed. Gone is the poor, pitiful, in-desperate-need-of-rest Roman that I left here alone. That man is gone. *Gone.* In his place is a masterpiece. It's shirtless Roman, which, in my book, equates to the same thing—a masterpiece.

He's still conked out, lying on his back with his hands supporting his head. I study the smooth skin on his chest and abs. Look at his arms. He's got tattoos running along them, which I did not see coming. With who his dad is and with how serious Roman appears, I wonder what's the story with the ink. Who is this man I'm learning more and more about? And why does he always hide this man away? Why always the long-sleeve shirts? What is the reason? Well, I *know* the reason. If he, a tall Black man, were to show up to school displaying his beautiful ink, he'd get middle school girls falling all over him since that would surely cause a hormonal awakening (and nobody wants the girls to become even more scheming than they already are), and parents would be even warier of him teaching their kids, thinking that the way his skin looks, which is a totally artistic way to express himself, says something negative about his personality. They'd judge a book by its cover.

I study him longer than what is probably considered appropriate, but no one is around to catch me, so . . . My eyes roam up his neck and to his face, and I'm surprised to see his eyes open when I get to them.

I jump. "Oh!" Caught red-handed, and honestly, it's what I get. I can only hope Roman's eyes haven't been open for long. "I, uh, didn't know you were awake. Anyway, I came to see if you needed some water. You've been sleeping for a while. I wasn't sure how long you should go without water. So if you want to go back to sleep, that's fine. I can come back later."

Noooo. Stop talking, Brianna. Just stop.

"Bri," he says. I snap my eyes to his, blinking rapidly. "Breathe."

I suck in a gulp of air, holding it in for a few seconds before letting it go. "Sorry."

"It's cool. You don't need to apologize." He hauls himself up so that he's leaning against the headboard. "You said that water's for me?"

"Here." I all but shove it his way, surprised it doesn't spill on the sheets.

"Thank you." Roman takes the cup, his fingers brushing mine.

When he's done, I hold my hand out to take the cup back to the kitchen. I nod at him and begin to back away. Before I can take more than a step, Roman speaks up. "Wait."

I look at him with raised eyebrows.

"Can you stay for a few minutes?" he asks.

I bite down on my lower lip, unsure. Staying, with him looking like that, does not seem like the best idea.

"It feels like I've been sleeping the day away and missed everything. Can you catch me up?"

He looks hopeful, and if I'm honest with myself, I want to stay, no matter my vow to pull back. "Okay. A few minutes," I say, placing the now-empty cup on the headboard.

"You can sit. I won't bite." He scoots over to leave more room in the bed's edge for me. Then he seems to take in his surroundings fully, his eyes landing on the picture of me holding Sheba when she was a puppy before he looks back at me. "This is your bed, isn't it?"

"Yeah. You kind of gravitated toward it and I didn't have the heart to tell you to move."

"I must have been really out of it. How long was I sleeping?"

"Six hours," I say without having to do any further math in my head. I've been keeping track. I go on to tell him about the need to fix the antenna and the plan for Jordan and Angie to go out once conditions allow for it.

"Okay." He nods determinedly. "If we get the chance, let me know and I'll help."

"Absolutely not," I say, crossing my arms over my chest. Roman looks taken aback, so I spell it out for him. "I don't get migraines, but I know enough about them. I know it was most likely brought on by all the stressors of this simulation, the way we've had to ration water and food, and the loud warnings from this morning. Unless you want to be laid out for longer, I don't think we can allow you to do anything with the antenna while you're still recovering."

Roman squints at me for a few seconds then shakes his head. "You're kind of bossy, you know."

"I'm not bossy."

"No? First you threaten to come down on anyone who calls me Major Pain. Now you threaten *me* if I help out with the antenna."

"I didn't threaten you. I'm just saying. Our nurse isn't here, so maintaining the mental stability and physical health of everyone has fallen to me." It's something I decided just now. "You're my number one patient, Roman, being that you're my only patient."

"Well, good. It makes me feel special."

The way he looks at me, even in the low light, or most especially in the low light, makes me nervous. My stomach is swirling with butterflies, and I'm sure my pulse is off the charts. I lick my lips. "So how are you feeling? Is your headache gone?"

"Not all the way, but I'm recovering. It's a lot better than it was earlier."

I nod. I should probably leave now. He's not back to one hundred percent yet, so he could use more rest.

"I like your tattoos," I say instead of walking out. "I must admit, I was surprised when I found you here without a shirt. In my bed. With everything on full display."

"Does it make you uncomfortable?" he asks.

Uncomfortable? No. Ravenous? Yes. "No. I grew up with two older brothers. I'm used to seeing men walk around without shirts on."

"Then why won't you look at me?"

I grip a handful of the sheets. What do I say to that? It's not like I can admit to wanting to get up close and personal with every part of him and that I'm just barely holding myself back. "I just didn't want to make *you* uncomfortable."

"You won't. I like when you look at me."

"Roman!" I exclaim, falling speechless. How can he just say these things to me? Like these are normal, everyday conversations we've been having forever. "Why do you keep saying things like that?" I finally ask. If he's going to be blunt, so will I.

"I thought yesterday I made it pretty clear. I like you, Bri. Is that plain enough?"

I shake my head. "Where is this coming from? I don't get it."

"It's been here. I couldn't do anything about it at school. But we're not at school now. Here, you're not Vice Principal Rogers. I'm not Mr. Major. We're just Brianna and Roman."

Have any names ever sounded so sweet together?

He moves from his spot against the headboard, scooting closer to me. If I simply move my shoulder, I'll touch him. And maybe that's what he wants.

"I want to get to know you more. I like spending time around you. I think you're funny, smart, beautiful. I like all the different hairstyles you wear." He tucks a braid behind my ear.

"In the library at school you said I was amazing . . ." I'm fishing for compliments, but he's the one who started reeling them out.

"Yes, you're amazing. And sexy. You're my dream girl." His words are music to my ears. "But, if you don't feel the same . . ."

"I do," I say quickly. I shouldn't admit it, but there it is.

Roman is encouraged by my answer and moves in even closer so that his legs bracket me on the bed. His hand drops from my ear to my shoulder and down my arm, then he picks up my hand and interlaces our fingers.

"I just . . . I don't know if this is a good idea," I say.

"Maybe it's not." He shrugs. "But we're here now. We might as well make this happen while we're in the present."

I like that way of thinking. I need to stay in the present.

I'm not at school. I'm not even out in the common room, where cameras are everywhere. I'm holding hands with my literal dream man.

I nod. "Okay. While we're here in the simulation, when we're behind closed doors and it's just the two of us, we can get to know each other better."

He lets out a satisfied sigh. "I'll take you however I can have you. In here, where it's just us. Out there, in front of everybody. I'll follow your lead."

"Okay," I say, but inside I'm shouting. I get three weeks with him.

"You say okay, but you're all stiff. Relax, Bri. Touch me if you want to."

This man has no idea what kind of pass he's giving me. "If I touch you," I say, "I don't think I'll ever be able to stop."

"Sounds like a plan to me."

I bring my free hand up and run it along his forearm, up to his bicep and shoulder, then back down again. His skin is so hot, muscles hard. I explore his chest and stomach, letting my hands linger leisurely. Now that I've gotten started, he might possibly have to bind my wrists together to get me to stop.

I turn so I'm fully facing him, untangling our fingers so I can use both hands. Roman tilts his head back and closes his eyes, letting me get my fill, and I love that he gets how much I needed his permission to simply take my time. Then I hear the door start to open. I tear myself away from Roman, jumping off the bed.

"Why are the lights off?" I hear Angie say two seconds before the light is switched on.

Roman lets out a grunt and shields his eyes with his arm.

"Angie, the light is too bright for Roman," I tell her.

"Sorry, I forgot about the migraine. I'll . . ." She trails off and I look behind me to see what's going on. Angie is staring open-mouthed at Roman. Her eyes go from him to the ceiling, and she raises one hand in the air. "Mine eyes have seen glory!"

"Angie!" I admonish. Hey, I get it. Roman is glorious indeed, more so now that the lights are on. But it's too bright for him. This won't help his recovery. "The lights, please."

"Oops." Angie turns the lights off then smirks at me. "You know what? I'm not even going to ask what you two were doing alone in the dark. It's either something boring, like you were checking up on him, or it's something juicy, like y'all were about to get down. I'll let my imagination do the work."

I absolutely cannot with her. "Did you need something?"

"The storm has calmed down. Jordan wants to go ahead and fix the antenna while we can. We're about to get dressed in our space suits."

"Okay. I'll be right there," I say. Once Angie is out the door, I turn back to Roman. "I better go help. You stay here and rest."

He salutes me and gets situated back against the headboard.

Before leaving, I give his arm one more squeeze. Then, because I can't help it and because apparently I'm allowed to, I bend over and kiss him on the cheek. "Get some rest so you can feel better."

He watches me with soft eyes as I back up and turn for the door.

I leave the room and meet Jordan and Angie as they're getting their space suits on. I make sure their oxygen is securely in place, then see them out the door.

I get set up at the comms station, getting connected with a headset as I spot Jordan and Angie on the screen. I also keep an eye on the screen monitoring the weather, and they immediately set out to work on the antenna.

The dust is coming down like drizzle, coating the two in red. I watch them work, my leg bouncing like crazy to get out some nervous energy.

They get the first part complete, and I know there's still quite a long ways to go.

"I don't know how visibility is for y'all, but from here it looks like it's picking up," I say.

"Yeah," Jordan says, breathing hard. "I noticed."

"Okay, how much longer do you think it will be?"

"Maybe ten minutes? We have to connect more of the cables, but they're hard to stretch."

I hate feeling so helpless while they do all the work. I put my braids into a ponytail, then take them out again. As the seconds tick by, the visibility gets worse, and the winds pick up.

"Guys, I'm going to be real; I'm really getting worried. It's getting harder and harder to see y'all. Maybe wrap it up now and try to finish again later?"

"We're almost"—Jordan passes something to Angie—"done."

Staring at the screen is giving me too much anxiety, so I start pacing again. I really want them to be able to fix the antenna, but not if it means they get stuck out there. This may have been too big of a risk.

I close my eyes and channel positive thoughts their way.

"Swear to God, your humming is not helping," Angie says. "I promise I'll move faster if you just stop."

"Sorry," I say. I didn't realize I was humming again.

I turn back to the cameras and freeze. I can't see Jordan or Angie. It looks like a blizzard. Where did we even get all this dust? It seems excessive.

"Guys, just let me know when you're heading back. I can't see you at all," I say.

"We're done!" Jordan says in triumph.

"Great going, guys," I say, only breathing half a breath of relief. "Come on back to the Hab. Hurry."

On the heels of my words, a large gust of wind shakes the Hab, and I look up, afraid the dome might cave in.

"I can't see anything!" Angie screams.

Jordan lets out a very uncharacteristic curse that has me raising my eyebrows.

"Guys, please don't panic," I plead. I have to think. What can we do? "Can you see each other?"

"I can't see anything," Angie grits out. "As soon as I wipe my visor with my hand, it's covered in more of this red dust."

"You need to find each other. Then get back to the Hab. I know you can't see, but y'all are only, what, fifty feet away? If you can find each other, you can make it back here."

"Angie," Jordan says, "stay where you are, and I'll find you."

I wipe the sweat off my upper lip while I continue to stare at the monitors. If Angie and Jordan don't find each other and make it back to the Hab, they'll run out of oxygen and be eliminated. "Come on, guys, you can do it," I say under my breath.

The silent encouragement doesn't work. Jordan can't find Angie. Angie is screaming because she can't see and is upset that Jordan can't find her. I wish the dust could let up for just a moment. Long enough for them to see and get the lay of the land to know where they need to go. But seconds tick by, then minutes, and the dust continues to cascade down.

A warning flashes from one of the monitors, and my

stomach sinks. Jordan and Angie have been out there too long. Their oxygen is critical.

"Okay, new game plan," I say. "You are likely to run out of oxygen before you can find each other. Just try to make your way back to the Hab. Crawl on the ground and put your hands out as feelers if you have to."

If only I could go out there and help.

Angie and Jordan are still lost out there. I wonder if they're even in the vicinity, or has not being able to see led them toward the hills and craters? If they fall and get hurt, it will be my fault for telling them to try and find their way back by any means.

The monitor with everyone's health and statistics begins flashing red for Angie's and Jordan's names.

"I have a confession," Angie says quietly and quite solemnly. "I wasn't planning on going on vacation to Cancún simply for some fun. I was going to chase after Carlos. We met during ballroom dancing. He was a good man." Angie sniffs. "He has family there, and I was going to go win him back. I can admit why it didn't work out. I was the problem. I knew there weren't going to be any football players here, but I came anyway so I could forget him. But I can't."

My mouth is wide open by the time Angie is done talking. But I'm proud of her.

"I have a confession too," Jordan announces. "I didn't come here just for the adventure. My family members don't believe in me. My asshole older brother says I always freeze up when it counts and I'm a living embarrassment. I was going to use this opportunity to show him how wrong he is." He breathes heavily into his mic. "But he was right."

"No," I grit out. It breaks my heart to hear him so defeated. He's a great teacher, he was integral in getting us here, and he reminds me so much of how I feel in comparison to my siblings. "Jordan, your brother was wrong. You're not an embarrassment. You're amazing. And who cares that you didn't come here for the adventure? None of us did." I sniff as tears begin streaking down my face. "And Angie . . . yeah, you might be the problem, but the first step is admitting it. If things don't work out with Carlos, you'll find someone even better. Someone who can handle you in all your glory. You two are amazing. Now find your way back to the Hab so I can tell you in person and throw you a pizza party!"

Jordan chuckles, but it's sad. "No, Bri, you're the amazing one. You're the only one here for good motivations. The kids. We don't deserve you here, and we don't deserve you at the school."

"Stop talking like this is over. It's not over yet," I say through clenched teeth.

"We're out of oxygen," Angie says, and I look to the monitor to confirm it's true. Now a countdown displays how long they have left to breathe before they expire.

"Remember me, and all the laughs we had together," Jordan says.

It's ridiculous and melodramatic and unnecessary, given that I'll see them again when the new school year begins, but I can't help but feel like I'm really losing them.

When the monitor finally shows that they've expired, I continue staring, hoping for one more glimpse of my friends so I can say goodbye, but all there is to see is a blizzard of dust.

I remove my headphones and place them on the desk. I walk to the bedroom, and when I get to my bed, Roman is sleeping. I briefly hesitate, then slide my shoes off and begin to climb in.

Roman stirs from his sleep, blinking me into focus. "It looks like you've been crying," he says.

"That's because I have. Angie and Jordan were eliminated. They ran out of oxygen after fixing the antenna."

Roman opens up his arms, and I crawl under the covers, lying so I'm tucked against his chest as he rubs my back.

"I'm sorry," he says, voice gravelly with sleep.

I nod. It's just Roman and me left. I hope we can make it through with no more issues.

CHAPTER NINETEEN

Waking up in my bed, in Roman's arms, is . . . strange. A good strange.

Roman's hand caresses my back, and I smile to myself. Everything in this simulation has gone haywire, but in an unbelievable turn of events, here I am, with him.

He's shirtless, he's warm, and he emits a sense of peace. But I can't help but think of what drove me to his arms last night—losing Angie and Jordan—and all the wind is sucked from my sails.

"How are you feeling?" Roman asks.

"I think that's supposed to be my line." I rub his arm. "But I'll answer anyway. I'm sad about Jordan and Angie. And I'm wondering how we're going to get through the rest of the simulation with just the two of us. But I know it could always be worse. I could be stuck here with our rover, Miles, all by myself."

"So I'm slightly better than a robot. Good to know." Roman sounds wounded, but I know he's only joking.

"Well, you are slightly handier. You can reach the teas for me, after all. I don't think Miles can help with that. Even if I were to stand on him and—" I cut off with a shriek as Roman tickles my side.

I fight to get free of him, turning over in the bed until

my legs are tangled in the sheets and I'm out of breath. Roman stops, and I open my eyes to find I'm face-to-face with him. Nose to nose. All our moving in the bed brought us so much closer.

"Hi," I say.

"Hey," he answers back.

"How is your migraine?"

"It's gone."

I swallow. I can't figure out why I'm breathing so hard. That's right, Roman just tried to tickle me to death. Because I've been sharing a bed with him for the past who knows how many hours. And I still can't get over it.

As he looks at me, I bite down on my lip, and his eyes zero in on the movement. I thought my heart rate should be going down now that I'm lying still, but under Roman's scrutiny, it only increases. I wish he'd kiss me already.

He runs a thumb over my hip. "I started feeling a lot better when you came in the room."

I frown. What were we talking about? Oh yeah, Roman's migraine.

"I'm glad I could help," I say, my voice nearly breaking when he goes from rubbing my hip to gripping it. The touch lights my body up like a match set against tinder. I want him. But it's too soon, isn't it? It's not like we're really together, even if in my mind we've gotten married, had fifty million babies, and retired on a private beach in the Caribbean.

Come back down to Earth, girl, I tell myself. Still, I can't help but ask him, "Are you sure the migraine is gone? I hear kissing is good for headaches. The deep breaths you take help with the airflow to your head."

Roman hums low in his throat, slips his hand under my

shirt, and settles it on my lower back. I arch into his touch, which causes my chest to push up into his, and our wild heartbeats become impossibly closer. "You know," he whispers right above my lips, "my head does hurt a little. Maybe we should test your theory."

His lips feel perfect against mine. Warm and soft, tender yet insistent that our mouths keep moving. He moves his hand up from my lower back to cup the side of my face before migrating to the back of my neck and gripping my braids. I guess it's still not enough, because his hand is on the move again, back to my hip, where his fingers dig in.

I let out a soft moan, loving how he barely seems to be restraining himself. If we were making love right now, I think I could get him to lose control. At the thought, I throw my leg over his and tilt my hips so I can feel where he's hard. He tangles his tongue with mine in response, matching the pace of our grinding bodies.

When I hear a loud alarm blare through the speakers, I freeze in Roman's arms, then butt my head against his chest, shaking my head back and forth. "No. No more. No more disasters or warnings of imminent doom. Just give us one calm day."

This isn't a simulation for life on Mars. It's testing for psychological warfare.

"It's all good," Roman soothes. "You hear that? It's coming from the comms. You said Jordan and Angie got the antenna up, right? We're probably just getting messages in from Mission Control."

I feel no shame over the fact that I was ready to punch the air over the thought of another crisis. I let out a deep breath as my body staves off the bit of adrenaline that was ready to help me act in fight-or-flight mode. It takes a few more breaths before my pulse is steady. I think my body has developed PTSD from everything I've been through so far.

"If that's a message from Mission Control, I guess we better get up," I say grudgingly, pulling away and sliding to the edge of the bed. Roman lets me go with a sigh, worming his way into my heart that much more as I see he's as reluctant as I am to end our morning cuddle session.

After having been laid up for so long, the first thing Roman wants to do is take a shower. Before leaving the room, he crooks an eyebrow, inviting me to join him. I laugh. I would absolutely love to see him in all his glory, but we're not there quite yet, and the shower stall is too small.

As he goes on, I change out of the day-old jumpsuit I've been wearing and put on a fresh one. A shower will have to wait for later.

I leave the bedroom and enter the common room. My first stop is the comms station. The monitors show that outside, everything is clear. No dust storm. And while of course I knew there wouldn't be, there's no sign of Angie and Jordan either. Just the quiet of nothing, save for the steady hum of fans and computers. I glance at the monitor showing each teammate's health status, now only showing Roman's and mine, and my heart breaks a little knowing that we lost the other three. Even if they're all alive and well outside the simulation, we came in together, and I had planned on us all leaving together. Well, except Roman. But how was I supposed to guess that his motivations were true? I had no idea he'd be the one I'd end up depending on to complete the tasks or that we'd grow so close.

The message from Mission Control is short. They congratulate us on getting the antenna back up.

By the time I've taken stock of the remaining tasks, Roman is coming out of the shower. He's freshly washed and groomed in his jumpsuit. Not only is his body clean, but he's also trimmed his beard and mustache, and his waves are back. The only thing I don't like—a tiny gripe, really— is that he's no longer shirtless. I wonder if he goes to sleep like that every night or if last night was a deviation because of his migraine. I guess I'll find out later tonight.

I force my eyes away from him and back to my work. I take stock of how much water we have left. With three teammates gone, there's plenty of water for Roman and me to survive on. I can even take a longer shower. Instead of our previously allotted two minutes, maybe I'll go crazy and bump it to five. It's the small wins that count.

"Did you eat breakfast yet?" Roman asks from the kitchen.

Busy looking at the charts Jordan was filling out for us about the daily maintenance of the Hab, I respond with a distracted "Not yet."

"Breakfast is ready," Roman says a few minutes later.

"What?" I look back to the kitchen to find two bowls set out. I close out of the data and walk to the kitchen. My heart melts when I see Roman has set out some oatmeal and tea. "I thought the oatmeal was all gone. I was looking for it yesterday."

"Nope. It was just where you couldn't reach." At my glare, he starts cheesing and I shake my head. "How's everything looking?"

"Honestly, it's looking really good. We knew the antenna was going to be the hardest part, and Jordan and Angie were able to knock it out before they were eliminated. All that's left is to keep up with our physical activities, straighten up outside, keep it clean in here, and grow dandelions. I almost feel bad with how easy we're going to have it in the next few weeks."

Then again, if it's easy sailing from here task-wise, that will leave plenty of opportunities for Roman and me to make the most of the remaining weeks we have together. Roman looks at me, his eyes holding secrets from the camera only I can see, and I'm positive we're on the same wavelength. I touch the soil where the dandelions should be sprouting by now and frown.

After some light fitness that consisted of jogging on the treadmill for me and looking good while strength training for Roman, we went our separate ways to tackle the daily tasks. Roman, seemingly completely over his migraine, set about completing the first round of dusting and vacuuming while I came to the greenhouse to inspect the crops.

Standing at the garden bed now, I look at the built-in sprinklers. I don't get it. Nothing seems to be malfunctioning or leaking, and yet the soil is way too wet. I sigh. If we can't get this figured out, it may just be best to get rid of the soil and the seeds already planted and start over fresh. It will be a waste that could potentially affect our bottom line of resources and what is carried over for the next group, but it's either that or we lose because we can't grow what essentially amount to the easiest weeds that pop up all over America.

After checking the lettuce and potatoes, both of which have started growing but aren't counted toward our big tasks, I leave the greenhouse.

I see Roman dusting the comms station and fight back a smile. He's laser focused on wiping away every speck of dust, running the cloth along each surface meticulously.

"How's it looking?" he asks when he glances my way.

"Mighty fine indeed."

"Are the dandelions finally starting to come in?"

"Huh? Ohhh. No, not yet. The soil is drenched. I think we need to toss it and start over."

Roman stops what he's doing. He stands up straight and puts the cloth he's been using over his shoulder and heads toward me. "What did you think I was asking about?"

I blink rapidly while heat overtakes my face. He looks way too sexy strutting toward me like that. I won't even try to convince him I was talking about the greenhouse. That would be a bald-faced lie, and he'd see straight through. I take the path where the least amount of embarrassment lies and shrug.

Roman's mouth tips up in a sexy smirk as he stops in front of me. "You don't know, huh?" Roman didn't come to play. His voice has dropped an octave, sexy and low; the smolder he's directing at me is doing its thang and smoldering, affecting me in every which way, just as he intended. "Maybe you saw something you liked? Something not in the greenhouse?"

"Maybe I did," I concede. I'm heartbeats away from jumping him but know I can't. Not out here where the cameras are on and rolling, anyway.

I let out a slow breath. I need to keep my head in the game. At least during working hours. I may have found myself in some sort of . . . situationship with Roman, but that needs to remain behind closed doors.

Maybe I can consider our time here a test. If I can keep my hands to myself while we get tasks done and not let on that we are anything other than partners, but use our private time to do more fun things like make out, then maybe things between us don't have to end when the new school year starts.

I take a small step back and make a show of looking

around the Hab, trying to convey to Roman that Big Brother is watching and we need to be careful of what we do. It looks like Roman wants to laugh at me, his eyes lighting up, but clearly he reads me loud and clear and backs up as well. When he does, I fight the urge to step back into his personal space. I'm a mess.

Later, his eyes declare, and I feel a pulse of heat.

"Sounds like we got another message from Mission Control," Roman says. "Let's check it out."

We move over to the comms station, where a message is waiting for us.

We see that the antenna has come back
online, and we are able to send you messages
once again. We are sorry for the casualties
you have sustained along the way. Rest
assured, we knew this mission would be a
tough one, but you two are living proof that
mankind can prevail in the toughest of
circumstances. Following this message, you
will receive two messages from your
families, who miss you on Earth.

I feel my spirit lighten as I read the message from Mission Control. Finally, some contact from my family.

I don't have to wait long. The first video to show 100 percent loaded is addressed to me, and I immediately press play.

My family comes on the screen, huddled on Camille's cream couch. They all give warm greetings. They tell me how great a job I'm doing, with Vincent giving me some special advice on how to best move in the space suit to see with the helmet on.

"*And someone else wants to say hi,*" Camille says. She gives Zara to Lance and pats her lap. "*Say 'Hi, Mommy!'*"

My eyes get misty as Sheba stretches on Camille's lap. She's so long, her chest is on Camille, while her paws extend across Lance. Once they say their goodbyes and the video cuts out, I swallow the lump in my throat.

"I miss them so much," I say wistfully.

"It seems like you and your family are close," Roman comments from beside me. For a moment, I forgot I had an audience and immediately begin dabbing at my eyes. Roman stops my hand, brushing my cheek with his thumb. "It's beautiful."

I smile, leaning into his touch. "Yeah, they are. We've had our share of ups and downs, and we're not perfect. No family is. But anytime I'm away from them for too long, I get the most intense homesickness that doesn't go away until we're all back together. Sometimes I'll go through these phases where I start avoiding them, but once I come back around, it makes me realize how foolish I can be."

"Why would you avoid them?"

I turn my head to the monitors to dodge Roman's inquisitive stare and shrug. I don't want to tell him I've been indecisive about my career, and being around my successful brother and sister makes me feel like I don't measure up. Instead I give a half-truth. "It can be hard when you're always comparing yourself to the Black excellence that is my astronaut brother and his entrepreneur fiancée and my doctor sister and her ex-Navy husband. Then, there's little ol' me. And what do I have? Sheba." Okay, so I got a little more truthful than I meant to. What is it about Roman that always has me saying too much?

"'Little ol' you'? Nah, Bri. You're amazing."

I didn't know I'd fall in love with hearing that word

from his lips, but there it is again—*amazing*. My heart trips over itself, and my breath hitches. The honesty and conviction. "Th-thank you, Roman," I stammer. Then, because I just can't take it anymore, I blurt out, "Do you want to see something in the room?" And by *see something*, I mean *kiss*. I want to kiss him. So bad.

Roman's eyebrows shoot straight up to his hairline at my question. Before he can answer, two chimes sound in succession and we both turn to the monitors.

"It looks like your video came through. Do you want to watch it?" I ask.

"I'll check it out later," he dismisses. "There's another one addressed to the both of us. I wonder what this is."

Roman clicks play, and I immediately recognize our school cafeteria. The librarian, Mrs. Yates, is there, as well as Principal Major, looking like he's putting up with everything, along with Superintendent Watts and various students.

"*Vice Principal Rogers. Mr. Major. We are so proud of how well you two are representing your school, our district, and this community!*" Superintendent Watts says. "*We know it's hard there, working alone, by yourselves, but your dedication to your goals is inspiring to us all. Keep focused on the grand prize. We're counting on you!*"

I know it's all lip service, that the optics look great for the school. That's all I should care about, but I didn't miss the hidden meaning behind every word Superintendent Watts said. She's warning me about Roman, again.

I glance at Roman. He turns his head to me and smiles reassuringly, though it doesn't fully reach his eyes. He must be feeling the pressure too. It's just the two of us and we've got to see the rest of this simulation through. We're committed, and I'm also committed to seeing this thing between Roman and me through. I'll just have to be careful and not get caught.

ROMAN AND I DON'T GO TO THE ROOM AND MAKE OUT. INSTEAD WE SUIT up and head outside.

I look around. Nothing but red and rocks and red mountains against a fake red sky. How long has it been since I've seen the actual sun? Felt its rays kiss my skin or had to shade my eyes from the brightness? I miss the feel of the wind stirring through my braids. Hell, I even miss Houston's humidity that's always sure to swell my hair to twice its normal volume when I don't have braids in.

I shake my head. This place is starting to get to me. If I can just push through a little longer, I'll make it to the other side.

"I guess we better get to it," Roman's voice says in my ear.

I nod and we start moving toward the field. Like our first task, our goal now is to clean the mess the dust storm left. We pick up debris sticking out of the sand. Some of it I don't even recognize, and I wonder if the organizers just threw additional stuff out here for shits and giggles.

"I found Miles!" Roman says, and I look in his direction. Roman has just pulled the rover out of a hill of dust and is gently cleaning it off with his gloved hand.

I run over and sink to my knees beside Roman. "Oh, you poor thing. We left you out here all alone."

Roman wipes off a little more dust and ensures the rover won't tip over. "I think that'll do it. But how come it's not turning back on?"

"*Him.* Don't be disrespectful. You'll hurt his feelings. How do we turn him back on?"

Roman sighs in his mic and continues looking Miles over. "I see. It's solar powered, but its little battery—*his* little battery," he corrects himself when I clear my throat, "must have gotten knocked loose in the storm."

I look around again. There's no way we'll be able to find a small battery in all this dust and sand. "Another one bites the dust," I say with a sigh, stroking Miles. Will this simulation ever let us live in peace?

"What do you mean, 'another one bites the dust'? We didn't even look for the battery."

"Yeah, but look at everything we'd have to dig through. Finding the battery would be like finding a needle in a haystack. Time-consuming and pointless. And I'm tired and sweaty and hungry. And I'm tired of all this stupid red and the stupid dust!" I punctuate my frustration by grabbing a fistful of sand and tossing it away from me. And I know it's finally happened. I've cracked. The simulation has finally broken me.

I'm breathing so hard I can't hear anything else, and the mist from my breath is fogging up my helmet. I keep my head bent and eyes facing my lap, afraid that if I glance up, Roman will be looking at me like I've lost my mind. And he would be correct.

As I clap my hands together, trying to get the remaining dust off my gloves, Roman's voice comes through my comms. But he's not speaking. He's humming. I sit in stupefied silence as I realize he's humming the theme song to *Mission: Impossible*. His voice is low and in perfect pitch. If I weren't in such a bad mood, I'd ask him to really sing so I could know what his voice sounds like.

"Don't give up, Bri," he says when he pauses. "You're not here alone. I'm here, and we can find the battery if we do it together. We can do anything together."

I know that in the grand scheme of things, not being able to power up Miles is a nonproblem. Keeping him operating isn't a requirement of the task, only finding him was. But damned if I won't let Roman's enthusiasm and belief in me—in us as a team—be wasted.

"Okay," I say. "Let's find Miles's battery."

Roman is the first to stand up, pulling me to my feet. As I stare up into his face behind the glass barriers of our helmets, he starts humming again. This time I join in.

We keep searching through piles of sand and under rocks. Even as we go separate ways, with me on one side and Roman on the other, Roman's baritone continues to carry the tune, so I harmonize with the alto notes.

Finally, after who knows how long, I see it. A small rectangle under a group of rocks. I lunge for it, picking the battery up and waving it in the air in victory. "Got it! I got it!" I yell.

Roman runs over to me and I throw myself in his arms, laughing as he spins me around.

We get back to where we left Miles on the ground. "Would you like to do the honors?" Roman asks.

I nod and attach the battery where it goes, right on top of his head. Or what passes for a head. Within seconds, lights flicker as he begins coming to life, and I clap.

"We did it," I say with a sigh as the energy begins draining from me. I don't know how long we were out here cleaning or how long we looked for Miles, but I'm beat. And happy. I turn to Roman. "Thank you for not letting me give up."

"I knew it was important to you. All you needed was a little push. And don't worry, when I'm right here by your side, I won't let you give up." He squeezes my thigh briefly. "I think we're pretty much done out here. Ready to go inside?"

I nod, and we head back inside the Hab.

"What do you miss from the outside world?" I ask Roman while we eat rectangles of fried rice. The food isn't bad, but

I can't help but wish for more. "I'll tell you what. I would kill for some fried crab rangoon and egg drop soup to go on the side."

Roman thinks for a minute. "I could go for some wings or burgers."

"Do you cook?"

He looks at me like I've lost my mind. "Cook? Girl, I throw down. They don't call me the master of the pit for nothing."

"Who? Who calls you that?"

He chuckles. "I do. But it's true. You'll see one day."

I smile down into my food and scoop another bite.

"What else?" he asks. At my blank look he continues, "What else do you miss from the outside world besides food?"

"Everything. Sheba. My bed. Colors. Ugh, I am so tired of red." I throw my hands out. I don't have to point to anything in particular, because it's all red. "My brother said I should bring some paints or something. I should have listened to him."

Roman finishes eating and gets up. "I have an idea. Don't go anywhere."

I don't know what Roman has in mind, but he's all over the place. He grabs cups from the kitchen and fills them with our water rations. He moves to our tiny lab and takes some of the dirt samples. He rushes to the greenhouse then comes back out with a small handful of leaves. He even grabs blue and black pens from our supplies, opens them with all the focus of a trained surgeon, and dumps the ink into two cups.

When he goes to the drawer with the manuals, he regards me. "Vacuum or dishwasher?"

"Um, dishwasher?"

He nods, flipping through the pages and tearing two out.

"What are you doing?" I finally ask.

"You said you miss colors. Now you've got some primary and then some."

I inspect the cups. He made black and blue with the pens, green with the leaves, red with the dirt, and yellow with packets of mustard, all mixed with water.

The way I want to kiss him right now. But to do that, we'd have to go to our room, and all his hard work would go to waste.

"The only things we don't have are brushes," he says. "We'll have to use our fingers."

I dip my finger into the cup of diluted mustard, testing the consistency, and think of what to paint. When I have an idea, I pull the paper toward me and begin. Roman starts on his own, and we work in silence with the cups of paint set between us as a makeshift barrier so we don't see what the other is doing. It goes without saying that this is absolutely a competition and we will be seeing who has the best picture when we're done.

"Anything else you miss from the outside?" Roman asks.

I like how he's turned this into a therapeutic session for me to paint and complain.

"I know this is bad, so don't come at me, but I miss gossip." At his taken aback look I laugh. "Before I was vice principal, I used to gossip with the teachers at my old school all the time. Well, *I* didn't gossip. Just listened. But it's different as a vice principal. Everyone keeps all the juicy stuff to themselves so they don't get in trouble, I guess."

"For what it's worth, they don't gossip around me either," Roman says, and I instantly feel ridiculous for complaining. Of course the teachers wouldn't gossip around him. They'd think he'd tell his dad everything.

"I'm sorry, that was inconsiderate."

He goes on, ignoring the apology. "But I still pick up on

things. For example, I have it on good authority that a certain teacher who raps and another teacher who likes birds have been dancing around each other all year."

I gasp, loving the juicy tidbit. He's talking about his friends Kareem and Raven. I had no idea there was something simmering between them.

Roman wipes his finger on a damp cloth he brought over for us. "All done. Let me see what you made."

"Wait! I need more info on the teachers first. Do you think either of them will make a move?" I am fully invested.

Roman shrugs, but he knows I'm hanging on his every word and is loving it. "I heard a very cool, very handsome science teacher tried to get one of them to make the first move and offered up date ideas, but nobody wants to listen to him. Let me see your picture."

"Hold on. What date ideas did the science teacher suggest? Maybe they were bad."

He levels his gaze at me. "Not only is the science teacher very cool and handsome, he's also a romantic."

"Hmm, what are the chances that someone who calls themselves a romantic actually is one?"

"This science teacher is the real deal. One of the dates he suggested to Karee—um, the teacher who likes rap—was dinner and painting. You can't tell me, or the science teacher, the ladies don't love that."

I look at our table with its paints again, and my heart melts. "You know, you—make that the science teacher—may have a point."

"Yup. Now quit stalling and show me your picture."

When he uses that tone, how can I resist? I lift my picture to him, and Roman's eyes widen.

"Wow, Brianna. That looks just like me."

It's no masterpiece, but I was able to vaguely land his

skin tone by mixing red, yellow, and blue. The waves of his hair came out great.

"I'm a little rusty," I say, "but I used to paint all the time when I was younger. I almost went to school for art but changed my major at the last minute. I always told myself I'd get back into it. I just need to find the time. And I guess motivation. Let me see what you did."

Roman looks almost pained as he holds his picture up.

"Who is that?" I ask. His picture is, for lack of a better word, bad. It's a person. A girl, certainly, but that's about as much as I can make out. "Who is that?" I ask again.

"I didn't know I was going up against Picasso," he grumbles. He shakes his head, looking thoroughly embarrassed.

"You know what, I was going to help you clean up, but now I feel like I need to look in a mirror. There might be something I'm not seeing."

I rise from the table, but I do take a few of the cups of paint with me, one in particular.

I walk back to the table and stop in front of Roman. "I'm going to call it an early night." I wipe some of the mustard on his cheek. I had to get back at him for the awful painting somehow, and I hope he takes the bait.

HE TAKES THE BAIT.

Half an hour after I get to the room, Roman follows. I look up from the book I was reading and watch him close the door behind himself and stalk toward me.

He stops by the bed and looks at me a second before barking, "Book down."

My back goes straight, but the desire to see where this is headed is stronger than my natural urge to ignore any commands. I bite my lip and set the book down.

"Stand up," he orders next.

I stand up and tilt my head back to look at him. I want to reach out and latch on to him, but I know I need to practice patience in at least some areas of my life.

Roman steps forward, bringing us impossibly close. "I've been waiting to do this all day," he says before capturing my mouth with his.

The waiting definitely paid off. I kiss him back, trying not to be so awestruck that this is happening—*again*. Not only is it happening again, but it's so good. I work on committing to memory the taste of him, sweet and addictive, as I suck on his bottom lip then open my mouth as his tongue sweeps in.

If this is going to end at some point, I need to have one hell of a memory to recall. My hands are interlaced behind his neck. I slide one down to his zipper. He's got a black shirt under his jumpsuit, so I reach for the hem of his shirt and tug it up. Roman does the same for me, pulling my shirt over my head and off as we momentarily break apart.

His eyebrows lift in clear appreciation as his eyes trace my chest, making me feel powerful and desired.

He meets my eyes again, smiling slightly before tugging me back to him. This time, it's nearly skin on skin, save for my bra, as we go back to devouring each other's lips. I trail my hands over Roman's biceps to his chest and down his stomach. Not allowing my mind to second-guess, I let my fingers go exactly where they desire. Roman is rock-hard in my hand as it closes over him through his boxer briefs. It's still not enough. I manage to get one hand in his boxers and stroke up and down. Roman rocks his hips in time with my strokes.

"I want you," I say against his lips, knowing closed

mouths don't get fed. I didn't intend for this to go any further than a kiss, but I also never intended to come to depend on Roman as a partner when I arrived in this simulation, let alone kiss him. It's way past time to readjust my expectations.

"You got me," Roman responds, voice only halfway audible and fully carried by lust.

I shake my head. "More."

We fall onto the bed, and he slides my pants and underwear down in one tug. His hand goes to my core, rubbing me in a way that makes my back arch. Then he slides one finger inside. I gasp at the sensation, but still say, "More," and he works another finger in.

It feels good, but I'm not able to concentrate on so many things at once. I tear my lips away from Roman while riding his hand and continuing to stroke him. With his lips no longer occupied, Roman is free to trail kisses along my neck. His fingers are magic. My body tightens, but he keeps his finger thrusts steady until I finally let go and I'm falling over the edge. At the same time, he gives a deep groan before he too comes undone, all over my stomach.

Once we both catch our breath, I look up to find Roman looking at me. "You good?" he asks.

I bite down on my lower lip, swollen from Roman's kisses, and smile. "I'm good. I'm . . . great."

ROMAN CLOSES THE BATHROOM DOOR BEHIND HIM. AS HE TAKES ME IN with lazy eyes, I can't help but notice how relaxed he looks. Mere weeks ago, I thought I'd have given anything to see him look at me the way he looked at his friend Raven, but now I see how wrong I was. His eyes now feel like a caress to my soul as his gaze sweeps me from topknot bun to black socks. Those beautiful brown eyes, soft and open. This is a kind of gaze I never even imagined.

"Ready to hit the hay?" Roman asks, gesturing to the bed.

What was mine is now ours. In this tiny habitat that has been our home for the past three weeks, we are the last two standing, but I feel like this isn't it. For the first time, I'm not only letting myself imagine what it would be like to take our relationship out of this simulation, but I'm hoping for it. The seed has been planted in my mind and in my heart, and I'm going to see it through. Roman may shoot me down, but I've at least got to take a shot.

I move to the bed first, climbing in and moving to the far left side so Roman can get in. He lies down and faces me, and we both stare at each other until we start laughing.

"Okay," I say. "This is awkward. Are we just supposed to fall asleep, or . . ." If Roman suggests more kissing, I won't turn him down.

Humor is still alight in his eyes as he snakes his hand out and rests it on my hip. "We can go to sleep. We can talk."

Say kiss.

"Whatever you want to do," he finishes.

He didn't *not* say kiss. I'm about to make the suggestion, but Roman beats me by saying, "Did you always want to be an administrator?"

Oh, he wants to talk about school. I shouldn't be surprised. Or disappointed. It's the one big thing we have in common.

I stifle a sigh before answering. "Actually, no. I wanted to be a librarian, then an artist. I went to school with a focus in business, which wasn't my forte, so I went into teaching. I got a teaching degree, but I was also interested in psychology, so when I started teaching, I was simultaneously going to night school for psychology."

"That's a lot. What grade did you start teaching?"

"Elementary. That was . . . a mistake, I think. I love kids. Love them. But being a full-time teacher wasn't it for me. I wanted to help kids some other way. After I got my psychology degree, I was able to be a guidance counselor. I felt like I was getting closer, but it still didn't seem like the right fit. Then the vice principal position came up, and I thought, 'Yes. That's what I need to be doing. That's how I can help both kids and teachers.'"

"How's the VP role playing out?"

I look at him while biting my lower lip. I think about the past year and all the strife from his dad, how I feel obligated to keep the teachers at arm's length, how lonely and how hard it's been, and how the one thing I want to do—leaving a mark on the school by getting the library built—has been such a battle.

"I'm still adjusting. I'm hoping it will get better next year. But that answer probably doesn't make you too happy," I say.

"Why would you say that?"

"Because being vice principal is what you wanted, right? I'm the one in the position you went for, and I'm probably doing a million things different from what you would have."

"Bri, you are a great vice principal." His hand moves from my hip to the dip at my waist, stroking my side. Lighting a fire in my stomach. I lift one of my hands to his chest. His muscles under my palm flex in time with the movement of his hand.

"And who says I want the job of VP?" he continues.

My gaze jumps from his chest to his eyes, and I raise my eyebrows. "Don't you? Isn't that the whole reason your dad has been such a pain in my ass? Why you were so rude to me the whole school year?"

Thinking about Principal Major's attitude and Roman's aloofness has me setting my jaw. I almost take my hand off his chest. But I don't. I don't need to be petty when we've moved beyond that.

"Hey." Roman squeezes my side, which has the added effect of bringing my body closer to his. "I'm sorry that I came off rude. I've had the biggest crush on you all year. That's what it was. I thought once you realized who my dad was, you'd want nothing to do with me. I guess it was easier to just shut down when I was around you."

"Is that what the other teachers do when they realize who your dad is? Write you off?"

Roman runs his hand up and down my back and makes an affirmative humming sound. "Pretty much, yeah. But I've gotten used to it."

I hate how resigned he is and that the teachers can be so judgmental without trying to get to know him. "It still sucks," I say. "That's not something you should have to get used to. People shouldn't judge you based on your dad."

"It doesn't bother *you* that my dad is the principal?" Roman asks me. "You of all people have the right to hold a grudge."

"Have there been times I thought you were on your dad's side in all of this and become a little sus? Yes. But even knowing who your dad is hasn't been enough for me to stay away. You two aren't the same. So no, it doesn't bother me. I just wish everyone else could look past it as well."

He kisses the top of my head. "People are going to think what they want and assume what they want anyway. My energy is best used being a good teacher and role model for the kids."

"That's true." For those really worth Roman's time, it won't matter who his dad is. "Did you always want to be a teacher? And did you decide to follow after your dad's footsteps?"

"No, I didn't. I actually hated school as a kid. I guess elementary school was cool. But my parents separated when I was in middle school, and my mom wanted to be closer to her family. She took me with her right in the middle of the year. You know how hard it can be for kids to adjust when they're new and everyone else has friends. At first I didn't fit in, and then I started hanging with the wrong crowd. When I got in a fight and was suspended my freshman year of high school, my mom decided it was best for me to be raised with my dad."

"I promise you I am taking this so seriously, but I have a question. Are you by chance from Bel-Air?"

He squeezes me tight as he laughs, and I love the sound. "Thank you for that laugh. And no, I'm no Fresh Prince. When I moved in with my dad in Houston, he was strict and overall unimpressed by anything I did. I still didn't care about school until I had one teacher who wouldn't give up on me. His name was Mr. Calloway, and he's the reason I decided to become a teacher. When I got my degree, something flipped in my dad though. He had this vision of us running the school together. I fed into it at first, just glad he was proud of me, but being the vice principal of his school isn't what I want. I've told him that, and, well, you know how he doesn't listen."

"But didn't you interview for the position?"

"Yeah, and I bombed on purpose. I hoped it would get him off my back about it, but he wants me to interview again."

"I never realized you two had a tumultuous relationship. I always thought you wanted my job."

I mull over everything. It's a relief to know Roman doesn't actually want to be the vice principal. But that only makes Principal Major's actions with the library and the football field that much more ridiculous. The man needs to stop trying to control everything.

"I—" Roman starts, then takes a deep breath. "I want to tell you something."

A yawn escapes me. "Hold that thought. Before you say anything else, can you take your shirt off?" The sleepier I get, the harder it is to keep my mind from veering to all the naughty things I want to do with and to Roman.

He chuckles but sits up and obliges.

"Mmm," I say as he lies down, and I snuggle back into his chest. His bare, warm chest. "It feels so good being here with you."

Roman's arms tighten against my back, and I don't mind the nonverbal response. His body language lets me know I'm safe expressing my feelings to him. I don't know if he feels the same or if I'm moving too fast, but Roman makes me feel like I'm moving at the right speed. I'm safe to say whatever it is I want and safe to feel whatever it is I feel. I can only hope he feels that same sense of openness and acceptance from me.

"Was there something you wanted to tell me?" I ask, barely able to keep my eyes open and not sure if my words came out clearly.

"I'll tell you tomorrow," he says with a sigh. "Let's go to sleep. There's no telling what they've got in store for us next."

Roman turns the light off above us, and I'm sleeping within seconds.

CHAPTER TWENTY

Roman and I are playing a game.

It started while we were cleaning the kitchen. We haven't turned the music on since Simone was eliminated, so Roman suggested we take turns picking songs. He went first, putting on a song by Usher, followed by Ne-Yo, then he took it way back with "Adore" by Prince.

"This must be more of that romantic side of yours showing out," I said quietly when we passed each other at the stove. Roman smirked on his way to pick another song, "I Like Me Better" by Lauv. He looked at me meaningfully, tilting his head as if to say, *Do you get it yet?* And I swooned right there once I realized he was directing the songs at me. Who knows what I would have done if the cameras weren't on.

Now that I understand, before his song is over, I put one in the queue to play next. When "Hello" by Beyoncé comes on, I see Roman smile as he goes on to dust around our tiny lab. And so we go, back and forth, flirting through song choice.

"Really?" I choke out when "Candy Shop" by 50 Cent comes on. I can't believe they even loaded the song into the system.

"What?" Roman asks. "He's talking about candy, right?"

When his song is over, I'm tempted to play "My Neck, My Back" but chicken out at the last second. What if students are watching us right now and the explicit version of the song plays? That would be an interesting conversation during the school year. *Miss Rogers, why was that one song telling players to get on their knees?* Yeah, I think not. I keep it safe and go with Brandy.

Roman and I finally meet at the living room area of the Hab after making our way around and begin dusting together. He starts bobbing his head to the beat as Brandy sings about full moons. Then he's behind me.

"Let's dance," he whispers.

His nearness sends goose bumps down my arms, but I shake my head. "The cameras." Did he forget? Or . . .

"So what? It's just dancing, like what you did with Simone and Angie."

It's not the same and he knows it. For one, Simone and Angie never made my blood sing with their mere presence, and two, I never made out with them.

I shake my head *no* again, wishing we were somewhere I could dance out in the open with him.

Roman backs up, but I see his reflection in the TV screen. He's moving his head to the beat and I end up stopping what I'm doing to stare. He meets my gaze through the screen and that familiar glint is in his eyes, daring me to live a little. *It's just dancing.*

It starts like it did with Simone and Angie. Me easing in by swaying my hips to the beat. I see Roman is nonchalantly making his way back to me, giving me plenty of time to put a stop to this dance session. But I don't. I turn around, he comes up to me, and we're mirroring each other's movements.

"I think Angie's got some competition on her hands," I say, slightly breathless. "I didn't know you had all that rhythm."

"I'm not at her level yet, but give me time."

I know my smile is way too big, but I can't help it around him, and it hits me how doing this with Roman feels like home. I can see us fitting right in with my family as one of our get-togethers ends with the inevitable slow dance. It always starts with Dad playing his and Mom's song, "Always." After a minute Camille and Lance join in, then Vincent and Amerie. I'm always on the outside looking in, but how amazing would it be if I didn't have to be? If Roman was there with me? If our relationship wasn't temporary?

Neither of us are there to man the music anymore, so it auto-plays. When a slow jam starts, Roman puts his hands at my waist and leaves plenty of room between us, which I quickly erase. I wrap my arms around his shoulders, hands resting at his neck, and he caresses my back.

Technically, we're still dancing, but it feels like so much more. Like we're on the verge of making love. Chest to chest, when I breathe, I breathe him in. Warm, sweet, spicy. Decadent. I don't know if he moves closer or I do, but our legs are practically entwined.

"We shouldn't be dancing like this," I have enough sense to say, but I make no move to stop.

"No, we shouldn't," Roman agrees. But neither of us puts a stop to it.

Roman pulls back just enough so he can look down at me as the lyrics float in the air and say all the things we can't say out in the open. I don't know what's on my face, but I know I feel utterly smitten by him. I know I want his lips on mine. Maybe that's what he reads on my face. His eyes travel down to my mouth, but as soon as he angles his chin down, I panic.

I stop our dance. Pull out of his embrace and blink hard, trying to get everything back in focus. The cameras. Everyone watching. My career.

"Sorry," Roman says.

I look up at him, sure he can now read the conflict on my face as clear as I can read his disappointment and hurt.

He swallows and turns around, going to clean the comms, though we already went over that area.

I don't call after him. I close my eyes again and take in a deep breath. This is all getting too complicated. I don't want what's going on between Roman and me to affect my career, but I don't want to hurt him.

While the music continues to auto-play now that our game is surely over, I go back over the kitchen.

"I'M SORRY," I TELL ROMAN WHEN WE'RE IN THE ROOM THAT NIGHT.

We were able to continue working, though the vibe between us felt stilted for the rest of the day.

"Sorry for what?" Roman asks. His hand is around my waist as we lie in bed, so I know he's not mad at me, but that doesn't mean he isn't hurt.

"For pushing you away while we were dancing," I say.

"I'm the one who broke the rules though. I'm the one who got greedy and wanted to kiss you so bad I didn't care who saw in that moment."

"Stop," I plead, shaking my head against his chest.

"Why?"

"Because when you say all these sweet things I just . . . I

get butterflies." I press a hand to my stomach and blow out a breath.

"You think you're the only one?"

"Um. Yes?"

He chuckles. "No. Do you remember the very first time we met?"

While my favorite memory of Roman from the past school year is when we were looking at each other across the gym, I do remember our very first interaction. It happened during staff development week when the teachers were getting their classes ready at the start of the year. I had just parked my car and happened to get out of it at the same time that Roman, who was parked next to me, got out of his. Our car doors slammed shut at the same time, creating a funny echo effect, and we glanced over at each other.

"Do you mean when we closed our doors at the same time? I remember laughing while you just stood there," I say. The laughter was because I was nervous. There was the most gorgeous man I'd ever seen, tall, dark, and handsome with the most kissable lips, and I was laughing in front of him like a fool because we'd just happened to close our doors at the same time.

"I stood there because I was struck dumb. When you laughed and smiled at me, it took my breath away. It became impossible not to want to look for it every time I saw you. Whether it was in the teachers' lounge or when you came to observe my classroom or if I saw you walking down the hall. Shoot, even at those boring staff development days. Butterflies, every single time."

God, just why? Why is he so perfect?

Every second I spend with Roman is like nourishment

to my soul. A soul that's been starved of love and affection. But the time I spend with him also complicates the future I've seen for myself that much more.

I know I'm fast approaching some hard decisions, but those decisions don't have to be made today.

CHAPTER TWENTY-ONE

D oes it feel like we're waiting for the other shoe to drop?"
I ask Roman as we sit at the lab table.

It's a small desk, really meant for one, but we've managed to squeeze in two chairs. Roman inspects a specimen under a microscope and answers questions about its properties on a form provided, while a magnifying glass sits forgotten in front of me. This busywork is boring, and I find my mind drifting all too easily.

Roman and I have found a good rhythm, so most of the past week has become boring and stagnant. We wake up, exercise, clean the dust off the solar panels, come inside, clean the dust off the furniture, perform any number of experiments with rocks, check the crops in the greenhouse, then call it a day.

I'm always counting down the hours until we can get away from the cameras and microphones and just *be* without worrying about being seen or overheard.

"I'm hoping the other shoe *doesn't* drop," Roman says.

"But things have been so quiet and boring."

When it's quiet in the Hab, it's too loud in my mind. There are too many hours in the day I spend thinking about After. How will it be going back to school. If—when—Roman and I end things after this, how am I going to act normal around him? I know too much about him now. I know his taste buds aren't picky in the least. Food for him really is just fuel, though he's partial to meat. I know his drawing skills are trash. I know his body heats up like an inferno at night, but it's still the perfect temperature to snuggle up against. I'm not likely to forget it either.

So yeah, I need something here to break up the quiet so I'm not going out of my mind and beginning to imagine a life that includes Roman in the After.

"It's boring by design," Roman says. "Life on Mars won't always be about managing one crisis after another. There will be long stretches of time when nothing happens but routine. We're showing them how people will handle it."

"Why do you have to make so much sense?" I blow out a breath and pick my magnifying glass back up.

My worksheet is asking about the layers of the rock. I lean forward to inspect it, but my unbound braids fall in my face, blocking out the light coming from the lamp above us. I push my braids back, but they don't stay in place when I lean forward again.

I jump when I feel Roman's fingers brush my shoulders and my neck as he gathers the braids and acts as my hair holder.

"Thank you," I say, able to find the pattern in the rock without the hindrance of shadows. It's not until after I put my findings to paper that Roman releases my hair.

Instead of verbalizing a *You're welcome*, Roman moves his hand under the table, where the cameras can't see, and squeezes my thigh. I'm only too pleased when he leaves it there as we complete our work.

After we're done, when it's too early and would look too suspicious if we both went to the bedroom, Roman sits at the kitchen table, writing in his journal. I haven't cracked mine open in days, but I love that he uses his.

"What are you writing about in there?" I ask, trying to be nosy but not really expecting an answer.

He looks up and smirks. "You."

"Sure. And let me guess, it says, 'The nerdy vice principal won't stop complaining about being bored.'"

"Nope." He clears his throat. "The nerdy vice principal kept me awake with her snoring again."

I know it's all in good fun, and while I love who I am, something about hearing Roman call me a nerd is a huge prick to my ego. And like so many things, it goes back to feeling like I'm not measuring up somehow. Does he *really* like this nerd, or does he only seem into me because we're conveniently trapped here together?

"Ha ha," I say, trying to save face. I rise from the table. "Well, I'll let you get back to it. I'm going to go check on the greenhouse again."

I leave before he has a chance to respond or before I can do anything lame like let any tears escape. I haven't had a good cry in what seems like weeks, and I'm clearly due for one.

But before I can make it more than five steps inside the greenhouse, Roman is there.

"Brianna, wait," he says.

I glance at him over my shoulder but keep walking, going straight for the dandelions. Seeing that the things still won't grow adds more frustration, and I know I'm reaching a tipping point.

Roman joins me at the plot, our shoulders nearly touching.

"What is wrong with these? Why won't they grow?" I ask, hating the telltale quiver in my voice. "I think they gave us some bad seeds."

"I don't. Just because they're taking a while doesn't mean they won't sprout and grow."

If the dandelions are anything like me, they can have thirty years and still not do anything.

I sigh. If I'm comparing my life to that of a weed, I'm taking this pity party too far.

"I didn't get to finish telling you about my journal entry," Roman says.

"If you have more to say about my quirky personality, can you tell me about it later?"

"It also says that you're my perfect match."

I pause, sure I didn't hear him right. "What?"

"Did you think you were the only nerd here?"

"Um. Yes?"

"Do you know who Roderick Hall is? The seventh grader who got detention at least five times for doing *Avatar: The Last Airbender* moves in the cafeteria?" At my bemused nod, Roman continues. "Well, that used to be me, but with *DBZ*."

"*DBZ*?"

He looks down at me with wide eyes. "*Dragon Ball Z*. Brianna, please tell me you're joking."

I smile. "I grew up with two brothers, of course I know *DBZ*."

"Who's your favorite character?"

"Piccolo, duh!"

Roman lets out a relieved breath. "See what I mean? Perfect match," he says softly. "And I really want to kiss you right now."

His eyes entrap me, making it impossible for me to look away. Though, to be honest, I'm a more-than-willing captive. I stare into his eyes, seeing my face reflecting back from his beautiful irises, and I'm not falling for Roman—

I'm flying. Ready to go to another plane of existence with this man as long as he keeps looking at me like this. I don't think this level of willingness is healthy.

"Don't talk about it," I say. "Be about it."

"Are we just going to ignore the cameras? Not that having an audience would stop *me*. But your job . . ."

I blink, then my eyes open wide in realization. I forgot we were under surveillance—that's what being around Roman does to me. Here in the greenhouse, they can't hear us, but they can see us well enough. Just out in the open for anyone to see me getting cozy with Roman. For any of my colleagues to think I could cross lines and play favorites. For Principal Major to have even more of a reason to be hard on me.

A voice in my mind screams, *So the hell what? We're consenting adults. What we do outside of school hours is no one's business but ours.* But full-out and open PDA could have consequences that would derail everything I'm working for. Everything Roman has worked for as well.

But I want him. No, I *need* him.

"Tonight then," I say. "After we eat."

He smiles. "You want to schedule kissing after dinner?"

I bite my lip and shake my head. "Not just kissing. I want you."

Roman swallows and his nostrils flare, and my muscles tighten knowing he wants me too. "After dinner."

I HAVE NEVER BEEN LESS INTERESTED IN EATING A MEAL IN MY LIFE. I was prepared to eat some beef jerky and call it a night, but Roman insisted on sustenance, so now we're wasting time at the table.

Roman sets his slice of pizza down and wipes any sauce

against a cloth napkin before turning the page of my once-lost-but-now-found book, *That Time I Got Drunk and Yeeted a Love Potion at a Werewolf.* I don't know what part he's on, but the looks he gives me when glancing up let me know there's got to be something spicy going on.

"Stop playing and eat your food," I say under my breath.

His response is to turn the page again and make an interested humming sound in the back of his throat. I try to ignore him by focusing on my own food, but he keeps bumping his knee into mine or reaching over me to get the salt I know he's not going to use on his pizza. Anything to get my attention back on him.

He's insufferable, and I love it.

"I'll walk around to make sure the lights are off and everything is powered down," Roman volunteers after we've both finished eating. He grabs my plate and takes it with his to the sink. "You can go hang out in our room."

I don't need him to tell me twice.

When I get to the bedroom, I glance around the space looking for . . . what? I don't know. I spot the candle Simone left behind. I grab it and set it on my footboard for added ambiance. Next I look at Angie's bed. I put her box of condoms in her bag after she left, and now I'm pulling it back out and feeling guilty. These aren't mine. Angie won't be using them, but still. And what if I read Roman wrong and we were having two totally different conversations? I think we're about to make sweet, sweet love, and he's under the impression we're going to play some board games? I heave a sigh and open the box, grabbing one, then run to my bed and slip it under a pillow. It's there if we need it. If not, no harm done.

By the time Roman enters the room, I'm a ball of nerves. The door clicks shut behind him, and my breathing is in full erratic mode when he glances at me standing in the middle of the room.

He frowns and my stomach drops. Yup, I knew I read him wrong. He wasn't planning on doing anything tonight but relaxing after a hard day.

"I thought you'd have on less clothes," Roman says.

Oh.

I don't waste time. I unzip my jumpsuit and let it pool on the floor, exposing me in nothing but my bra and panties. I quickly think over whether I should let my braids down from the bun or keep it up, and decide to keep it up and out of my face.

Roman's eyebrows shoot up at my eagerness, but nonetheless, his eyes hungrily devour my body. After getting his fill, he reaches for his zipper and pulls it down. He's broader than I am, so he has to help the jumpsuit off his shoulders, down his torso, and past his slim hips as it finally falls on the floor.

I suck in a deep breath once Roman stands straight. Now only in his boxer briefs, he's beautiful. So gorgeous I could weep. Now, however, is not the time for tears. Now is the time to commit everything about Roman to memory. Every muscle, every tattoo, every faded scar. I want to remember so that when I finally, *finally* get back to making art, Roman standing there will be the first thing my pen will put to paper.

He takes the first step, and I move to meet him in the middle, both of us stopping before we collide. As eager as I am, I take the pause to get my bearings. This isn't a line I've crossed with many men, and there's no going back after this. We won't be simple colleagues. I will have known how it feels to have him moving inside me. He'll know what I look like naked.

Roman cups my jaw, lifting my head to meet his eyes. "Are you sure about this?"

If there's one thing in this life I'm sure of, it's that I want Roman. Have wanted him since the moment I saw him. Maybe our relationship won't pan out, maybe my heart is too open when it comes to him, but I'm standing with the literal man of my dreams and I'm not letting all the what-ifs hold me back.

"I'm sure," I breathe, turning my head in his hand to kiss his palm.

I wrap my arm around Roman's back as he leans down and brings his other hand up to cup my face and take my lips with his. It's another unhurried kiss like before. Like we have forever to stand here and learn each other's mouths and tastes. To learn each other's rhythm and tempo. I suck on Roman's full bottom lip, running my tongue along the bottom crease, and something about having my lips on his is akin to sensory overload. All we're doing is kissing, but behind my closed eyelids I sees bursts of colors. Blues, greens, yellows. More color than I've seen in weeks.

Roman moves from kissing my lips to laying pecks on my cheek, lifting up my head so he can get to the crook of my neck, which is a special spot that makes shivers race down my spine. His hands travel lower and grasp my ass, bringing my body even closer to his. More sensory overload. His hot skin. He's just so hard everywhere. More colors. Pink, purple, neon. I thought he was kissing me like we had all day, but no, he's kissing like he's on a mission to take my soul. Not that it's not his by now.

Breathing hard, I move to hike one leg around Roman's waist. He gets the message, slipping his hands under my thighs and lifting me up. He strides to the bed as I lay kisses on his throat. After he sets me down on the bed, I look up to meet his darkened gaze and see an inkling of doubt. Before he can fix his lips to ask me if I'm sure again, I unhook my bra. I reach for Roman's boxers next, slipping my fingers under the band and lowering them down his legs. I moan softly as my inner muscles clench at the sight of him.

Roman crawls on the bed, settling his warm body right over mine. He leans over me on his elbows, and I lift my hips to close the small space between our bodies.

"I don't have a condom," he says with a tinge of panic.

I reach under my pillow and pull the one from earlier out, biting my lip sheepishly. "I've got one."

"But how?" he says in absolute amazement.

I shake my head. "You don't want to know."

Roman looks like he's holding in a laugh but takes the packet from my fingers and sits back so he can slide the condom on.

He leans back over me, and I can't help but hold in my own laugh at the audacity it took for me to go through Angie's things and take a condom. It's all seemed to work for my good though. Roman kisses me while my lips are still in a smile. "You're beautiful when you smile."

I'm taken aback by the honesty in his eyes as they lock with mine. I know some men don't like to be called beautiful, but I can't find it in me to keep my thoughts to myself. "You're beautiful always." The most beautiful man I've ever laid eyes on.

A smile ghosts his lips before he leans down to kiss me again. This kiss quickly turns hungry as he grinds against me, the friction of our bodies causing pulses of pleasure to radiate throughout. He lines up at my entrance, pushing and stretching me in the most delicious way until he's fully seated. Little sparks of pleasure radiate from my whole body as he moves in and out, grabbing hold of one of my hips for leverage as I meet his every thrust. "You okay, Bri?" he asks, his voice labored and restrained.

But I don't want labored and restrained from him. I want wild and out of control. "More," I say in his ear. Maybe it's the word or the way I say it, but either way, something snaps in him. He lets out a sound from deep in the back of his throat before he starts moving harder and faster. I hang on, silently applauding how I'm able to match his thrusts. And when the pleasure builds so much I'm ready to burst, I don't try to delay it. I let it wash over me as I throw my head back in bliss and a sea of colors, feeling Roman shudder over me.

We both collapse in a heap on the bed. Roman picks his head up, eyes bleary and lips looking thoroughly kissed. He looks me over, no doubt seeing evidence of the lone tear of happiness that made a trail down my cheek and into my hairline. I close my eyes and contentedly smile when he kisses my cheek.

CHAPTER TWENTY-TWO

I wake up to a nudging at my shoulder and roll over, blinking sleep out of my eyes, to find Roman holding two cups of oatmeal. I sit up, leaning against the headboard as I smile at him.

"For the nourishment of your body," he says, handing the bowl out to me. "May it keep you going and going and going."

I roll my eyes as I take the proffered bowl in hand and set it in my lap. As Roman sits beside me, I briefly wonder if anyone saw him make the two bowls on camera and subsequently walk back to the room and out of eyesight. There may be a few raised eyebrows, if not outright suspicion, but surprisingly I can't bring myself to care. After what we shared last night and how close we've gotten over the past few weeks, my heart won't let me put anyone else above my desires.

Now, to figure out if Roman feels the same way.

"So," I start, stirring my oatmeal and blowing on it to cool it down. "Just two more weeks until the simulation is over. A few more weeks to recoup. Then we're back to school. Back to good ol' schoolio."

Roman settles against the headboard next to me. "Summers always go by too fast."

"They sure do. Once the fall semester starts, I'm already looking forward to summer again." I take a bite of my oatmeal. "You know, the other breaks throughout the year are nice too. But if I had to rank them in order of importance, it would go: summer, Christmas break, spring break, and then the extra day off we get for MLK Day. I mean, I personally don't think his dream was for teachers and the like to struggle as much as we do, but the day to lift up the king is nice."

I stuff a large spoonful into my mouth this time so I'll stop talking.

Roman looks at me with raised eyebrows then smiles and nods in agreement. "I feel you on that MLK Day. He one hundred percent did not intend for us teachers to have to struggle as much as we do."

My oatmeal goes down smoothly as my chest lightens. I love how he just gets me. Accepts my quirks when anyone else would write me off. It makes sense; he said we're a perfect match.

We eat in a comfortable silence while I turn the words over in my head to ask Roman about what comes after the simulation. To ask about *more*. More time with him. More hugs and kisses. More mind-blowing nights spent wrapped in each other's arms. Maybe this is another one of my impulsive decisions like joining the simulation was, but look where that got me—eating breakfast with Roman after spending the previous night making love.

I turn my body to face him. "Roman, have you considered what happens after?"

"After?"

"Yeah. What if we don't end? After the simulation, what if we just keep seeing each other? I know it was my idea to keep this limited, so if you want to stick to our original terms I get it. But if you want to take a chance to see where this relationship can really go . . ." I trail off, my heart hammering inside my chest with the hope he isn't about to rip it into shreds.

"You really want to keep seeing me?" he asks like he's surprised.

Is Martian dust red? "Of course I do."

Roman doesn't answer, but he does crush his lips to mine, which I guess is all the answer I need. When this is over, I get to keep him.

When our kiss ends, our foreheads still press against each other. "Roman, I want you to know, I want to be with you, but I also want to protect both of our reputations. I'm not ashamed to be with you, but we wouldn't be able to flaunt our relationship at school. Is that something you can accept?"

"I would never put your career in jeopardy. And I can't say much right now, but school may not even be an issue. I'm not sure if I'll be back in my position when school starts again."

I back up so I can get a good look at him. "Wait, what? What are you planning to do?"

"I still have options I'm considering, and nothing is set in stone. But either way, you and me are good. We're more than good, Bri. Always believe that."

I want all the details, but at the thought of the freedom we'd have if Roman and I no longer worked at the same school, my heart flies that much higher. Am I really about to have it all—the career *and* the man? I lean in and kiss Roman again, unable to keep my hands off him even knowing we need to get the day started.

Roman grabs the forgotten bowl from my lap and places it by his on the headboard then leans back into me.

"We need to go out and start the day," I attempt to say. Most of my words are swallowed up by his mouth against mine, but I'm certain he gets the bulk of my message.

Roman pulls away from me, but not off the bed. Rising to his knees, he takes off the shirt he put on to go to the kitchen. "See, that's the thing. An important part of this whole simulation is the human element and bonding, right?"

Bonding was mostly important at the beginning stages of the simulation. We've moved way beyond that, though I'm not about to contradict him now that he's taken off his shirt.

He takes my silence as encouragement to keep going and smirks. "In the name of team bonding, I can't very well have you start the day without an orgasm. What kind of teammate would that make me?"

He's back to using *that* tone. The one that causes students to rush to vacate the halls when they're out loitering. The one he used to take charge when the meteorites were crashing through his and Jordan's bedroom, even though he was in pain. The one teachers like to call his Major Pain tone. But the only pain I feel is the mental pain of him not being inside me right now.

Obviously fed up with my lack of response, Roman narrows his eyes and leans in closer. "I'm waiting for an answer. What kind of teammate would I be if I let you start your day without an orgasm?"

"A bad one," I get out of my throat, which is thickened with lust.

He licks his lips. "That's right. Now, throw off that sheet and open your legs."

What if, after the simulation is over, rather than go back to work, I just . . . don't? What if I stay in bed all day every day, waiting for Roman to come home and repeat these exact words?

He lifts an eyebrow when, once again, I'm too dumbstruck by him to respond. But dumbstruck does not equal noncompliant. I fling off the sheet and open my legs.

TWO DAYS LATER, I'M WASHING OUR TWO BOWLS CLEAN FROM BREAK-fast while humming "Cater 2 U" by Destiny's Child. It was fun imagining waiting for Roman to come home after a long day at work while I wait in bed for him, but around the twentieth iteration of my daydream, I started to feel a little selfish. In a relationship there needs to be both give and take to make it work. I shifted my imagination to thoughts of me welcoming him home with a nice smooch on the mouth before I help him take off his jacket and shoes and lead him to the bedroom I've so painstakingly prepared for a peaceful homecoming. Where I then proceed to lay it down.

What does it say that my daydreams don't have me working, and certainly not being vice principal?

Nothing, I decide. Just because I daydream of not being vice principal doesn't mean that's what I really want. Daydreams are fun, but in the end, they're just for fun. And of course, I can't help but daydream about spending every waking moment I'm able to getting my fill of Roman. *My* Roman.

"What are you smiling over there for?" Roman asks.

I blink away images of him losing control in our future shared bed and look at the real-life version of Roman dusting the comms station. "Oh, nothing," I answer, grateful my skin is too dark to show any blushing.

As I dry the bowls, a notification sound comes from the

comms system. As has become habit born of PTSD from our first few weeks of calamity, my heart jolts at the sound. Roman's quick "It's just an incoming message" puts me at ease.

"Anything we need to be worried about?" I ask, hoping it's a simple, friendly check-in from Mission Control.

"Nah," Roman says, and I breathe easier until he continues. "It's another round of video messages from our families and friends."

Well, that is almost worse. Not that I don't want to hear from my family. But since being here, I've gone against every single warning Camille gave me. Hell, I stopped avoiding touching Roman in sight of the cameras after our night together. We haven't been doing any obvious PDA like kissing when we're out in the open, but there have been some lingering touches on my end, presses of his hand against the small of my back that I've leaned into, and the way we sat together on the couch when we finally decided to turn on the TV because Roman agreed to watch *Hamilton* with me.

While I'm ready to move forward in my relationship with Roman, I'm not ready to face Camille or anyone else commenting on how cozy the two of us are together.

I make my voice sound nonchalant. "I'm glad it's only the messages. I'll check on mine later. I want to see how the dandelions are doing first. Are you going to check your messages?"

Roman is silent for a beat before answering. "I don't have any. I'll keep cleaning."

Something about his tone seems off. Could it be that he's disappointed his dad still hasn't sent a message? I know their relationship isn't what I thought it was, and maybe Roman is upset. Before I go to the greenhouse, I walk by Roman and squeeze his bicep. "Okay. Maybe after we're both done with the morning chores, we can hang out in the greenhouse by the rock pond."

Roman bends down and kisses my cheek. It's my most reckless move by far, but it's not like I'll be his vice principal for long anyway. "It's a date," he says.

I interlock my fingers so I won't look totally whipped by covering my heart with my hand as I walk away.

It's those damned dandelions again. There is something wrong with the pipes. No matter what kind of adjustments we make, the soil remains wet. I mentioned to Roman that I thought we should dump the soil and start fresh, but he said we should give it a couple more days to see if he could fix it. As much as he's read the manuals and has been able to fix everything else that had broken down, it must have been a matter of pride that he can't nail down what the issue with the pipes is.

I feel the soil, and my finger comes away with bits of moist dirt stuck to it. We're running out of time. Roman may want to avoid the hassle of switching everything out, but it's the only way if we're going to complete this task in time. It's the last big one we need.

Decided on the best course of action, I test the heavy planter to see if I can empty it myself. I grunt as I try to heft it up, but it doesn't budge. Time to bring in the muscles.

I open the door to get Roman and stop when I hear a voice that isn't Roman's; I immediately recognize Principal Major's voice. Odd. I thought he didn't send Roman anything. Or maybe it's a message with the teachers and superintendent included again. I walk forward to see who all is in the message, but the words playing halt me in my steps.

"*You've been doing a good job getting close to her and*

gaining her trust. I know this isn't something you wanted to do, but it's best for the school . . ."

I don't hear anything else. I can't. For the last few weeks, I've been flying in the clouds, and gravity has finally caught up. I'm falling back to reality, and I see everything so clearly. Roman didn't come here with the intent to help us win and get the library remodeled. The exact opposite, actually. And everything we've shared, the feelings he proclaims to have for me, are as fake as this simulation.

I don't know how long I stand there putting all the pieces together until Roman is standing in front of me. Eyebrows pinched as he gazes at me, he looks worried. More, he looks guilty. And I hope, above all other emotions he may portray, that the guilt is real. That he feels it in his soul. Here I was, thinking we had something special and making plans for the future, and all the while, Roman had his own set of plans.

"You heard everything?" he asks.

I sniff, because *of course* my emotions wouldn't miss their time to shine, and swallow the knot of heartache down. "I heard enough."

"I can explain."

Do I want to hear his explanation? I was at the top of my graduating class. I've pretty much got it figured out. Got him and his motivations figured out.

But I've also got a soft heart. Too soft for my own good where Roman is concerned. And part of me wants him to prove me wrong. Maybe Principal Major wants to turn Roman as heartless and cutthroat as he is, but Roman isn't his dad. The red haze is fading, no doubt aided by the release of tears, and I nod. "I'm waiting." I won't make this easy.

"Can we go somewhere private?" He gestures to the bedroom, and I stride ahead without a word.

If I open my mouth, I'm not sure if what comes out will be a simple acquiescence to hear him out or if I'll act out of character and end up cussing out Roman *and* his daddy.

We make it to the room and I sit on the bed, leaving no space for Roman. I fold my arms across my chest and raise my eyebrows. I'm pretty sure Roman's got the hint—*let me hear what you have to say, and it better be good.*

He clears his throat and begins. "I'm not going to try and gaslight you. You heard my dad talking about me ruining the mission here."

At the revelation I knew was coming, I close my eyes. Yes, I knew it was coming, but I can't even stand to look at Roman as he confirms that my suspicions were correct from the very beginning.

"He really doesn't want that library built," Roman continues. "When he found out you were joining the simulation to get the money for the library anyway, he wanted me to come in and make sure it wasn't successful. *You* weren't successful."

"And, what? You just went along with it?" How could I have allowed myself to believe him? I knew what his motives were from the jump. But my stupid—because there is absolutely no other word for it—crush on him had me behaving like a hormonal preteen, glad the cool and sexy kid was showing me attention.

"I let him think I was going along with it."

I don't hold his gaze. And I don't believe him.

"Bri," he pleads. "You've got to believe that the only one I was fooling was my dad."

I explode from the bed. "Here's what I know, *Mr. Major*. From the very beginning, I asked why you were here. I knew it was because of your dad, and yet you denied it." I hold up my pointer finger and begin ticking off his offenses. "I know we've had mysterious breakdowns like, I don't know, the damn sprinklers overwatering the dandelions. Maybe it's a coincidence, maybe it's by design. I know that on one of our most crucial tasks, getting the antenna fixed, you happened to come down with a migraine and couldn't help. Funny how you didn't have one all school year. And I know"—my voice breaks as I pop a third finger up—"all school year you've done nothing but ignore me. But suddenly we're here, where the stakes are as high as can be, and your dad has sent you on a mission to derail everything. Well, what better way to get me distracted than to pretend to be into me." My chin is trembling, and hot, angry, ugly tears are falling down my cheeks, but I don't care. My heart is breaking and I need to let it out now so it doesn't suffocate me later. Roman might have been raised by a parent who taught him to be callous and aloof, and it's clear he wants to honor that. If these tears make him uncomfortable or make me look weak, then so be it.

"It's not like that, Brianna," Roman says softly. His tone is so heartbreakingly sad, it gets through the haze. "I know all those things you mentioned make me seem suspect. I won't try to explain any of it away. But the one thing I will fight until you hear me is that I did not try to get close to you to distract you. My intentions with you have always been to make you mine. Even knowing you're everything that's good in this world, Earth, and especially Mars, and I don't deserve to be with you, let alone breathe the same air as you do."

With each word he utters, my heart grows softer and softer. I'm quickly losing the will to fight against him. What if I put on my space suit and ran for the highest hill? Would that be enough distance to keep his words from penetrating my heart? If I actually went to Mars, would that do it?

"I want to be with you, Brianna. If you don't believe anything else, believe that. Everything I feel for you, everything you feel for me, it's all real."

I want to clamp my hands over my ears and shake my head no. I don't want to hear these pretty words. But at the same time, I want to bathe in them. Luxuriate in every syllable, every consonant, and let them be a balm to my stinging heart.

"Roman," I plead. I need him to stop talking before I do something stupid like forgive him.

But he doesn't. He gets right in my personal space and cups my cheeks in his hands. "Everything between us is real." He repeats it over and over, trying to make me believe him. Trying to make me trust him again.

It takes effort, but I back out of his hold and put some much-needed space between us. I'm able to think a little clearer without the distraction of his touch.

I've been built up then let down by him three times now. When I found out he'd been telling the teachers I was leaving. When he blindsided me by showing up as part of our team. And now that I've found out he's been lying about his purpose here. Three strikes, you're out. He may be saying all the right things, but I would be dumb to let this go and not expect to be hurt again.

I shake my head. "This isn't something I can just forgive and forget. You should have told me from the very beginning about your dad's plans, especially when I asked you point-blank. Now I don't know if I can trust you." I swallow and take a deep breath. "I need time. By myself."

Roman watches silently as I climb into the bed and close the screen, leaving him on the other side. Our day isn't even close to done, but I can't be near him right now.

After a few moments, I hear his footsteps move farther away, and the door opens and shuts as he leaves the bedroom.

CHAPTER TWENTY-THREE

I stay in my bed all day and try to distract myself from Principal Major's voice replaying in my mind, and Roman's confession. My hours are spent alternating between reading the same pages in one of my books and staring at the lights that line the bed.

Some time later, Roman comes back in the room. I hold my breath when I hear his footsteps pause beside my bed, then let it out when I hear him climb into a different one. When the day is over and I should be sleeping, there's an ever-revolving door of questions and doubts running through my head.

Was Roman really telling the truth when he said his dad was the one he was lying to, or was he trying to save face? Did he read every manual he could to know how to fix the various gadgets, or was it to learn each machine inside and out so that on our last day here everything would fail with no possible way to fix it all?

I huff out a breath, hating the doubts flowing through my mind and how my imagination is coming up with all sorts of diabolical things I was certain Roman wouldn't do. Or would he?

"Are you awake?" Roman asks from the other side of the screen. His voice sounds clear and devoid of the sexy raspiness he normally has when he wakes up, confirming that he didn't sleep either.

"I'm awake," I say, and lift the screen. I've hidden long enough, and now it's time to face the new day.

When I slide out of the bed and stand up, it's a punch to my chest when I see Roman waiting a few feet away. He looks horrible, with dark bags under his eyes and a small frown tugging at his lips. I *feel* horrible, like my heart's been ripped out and stomped on. I get the sense everything that happened yesterday could melt away if I reached out to him and made contact. My hand itches to grab hold of his, give us both some kind of assurance everything will be fine, but self-preservation keeps my arms locked to my sides.

He opens his mouth, and with my emotions so topsy-turvy, I know I'm not in the mental state to hear more apologies or explanations.

"I guess we better go out there and get started," I say before he has the chance to utter any words.

His shoulders lift on a sigh and he nods. "Yeah. Okay."

I stop in the bathroom to get cleaned up while Roman continues on to the common room. Unsurprisingly, the image that greets me in the mirror is horrendous. My face is puffy and the tip of my nose is red from crying last night. I'll still have to go out there and work with Roman, but I don't need to look like I'm falling apart.

I soak a small hand towel in water and let it sit on my face for a few minutes while I try rebuilding my battered emotional barriers. I need to tap into Vice Principal Rogers and bring forth the superpowers I use at school when someone is testing me, despite the fact that I feel very unsuper right now. When I take the towel off and glance in the mirror, at least I don't look as run-down.

When I come out of the bathroom, Roman is at the

stove making breakfast, so I go to the comms station to do a visual scan of the outside cameras. The conditions look perfect. No dust storms, no debris, and the antenna is up and functional. I even see our rover, Miles, slowly moving around in the sand.

There's a light indicating we still have unopened messages, and for a second I'm physically sick, like my stomach is about to take another free fall, as Principal Major's voice replays in my head.

"Food is ready," Roman says to me, and I'm only too happy to turn away and go to the table.

"What is this?" I ask as I take the seat across from him but avoid direct eye contact.

"Eggs and Spam. I would have made this sooner if I knew we had it. Earth, Mars. I don't think it matters where you are, it'll taste the same."

I break a piece of the Spam off with my fork and sniff. "Is it real meat?"

"Yes, it's real meat," he says with a slight chuckle.

I take a tentative bite, surprised by how flavorful it is. Crispy on the outside, since Roman fried it, and soft on the inside.

"What do you think?" he asks after I take a few more bites.

"It's not bad." I know the response is short and clipped, and even though I hate this subdued air surrounding us like fog that's hard to see through, I don't have it in me to keep giving more of myself.

Roman finishes his food first and waits for me. Instead of allowing him to take my plate, I cover it as I slip off my stool.

"I'll do the dishes since you cooked," I say, and without waiting for him, take my plate and his to the sink.

I'm positive the vibe I'm giving out screams "I want to be left alone," but Roman follows me to the sink. At first it's easy to ignore him as he leans with his back against the small counter and his arms crossed over his chest. I focus on making sure each particle of food disappears. But when I grab the pan and begin washing, my barriers start weakening.

I see the pan and the dish towel in my hand, but I also see the softness in Roman's eyes when he brought me breakfast in bed and hear his sweet baritone when he began humming the *Mission: Impossible* song so I wouldn't give up on finding Miles's battery. When it comes down to it, I want to believe what he felt for me is as real as what I've always felt for him.

I set the pan down. Roman's still right beside me, stubbornly waiting for me to acknowledge him. I close my eyes and let my head fall against his arm, and we stand together as the minutes pass by.

When I tilt my head up to finally meet his gaze, I know that no matter what plans he did or didn't make with his dad, my heart belongs to him. He rests his hand on my hip, and while I have plenty of time to move away, knowing full well the cameras are right on us, I stay in place as he bends down and kisses me. It's tender and sweet, and every bit the reassurance of his feelings I need.

"We good?" he asks, his grip tightening slightly at my hip like he can't bear to let me go.

"Yeah," I say. "We're good."

He finally releases me, and it's really time to get the day started.

Roman pulls out his journal, and I start dusting. When I'm back at the comms station, the blinking for the unread message annoys me so much I decide to just see what it's about.

It's another message from the school. This time from a group of students, probably those enrolled in summer school. They're all cheering on Roman and me, excited for the library remodel. It's evident that to their minds, winning the money is pretty much a done deal.

"What do we need to do today?" Roman asks, coming up behind me.

I exit out of the message and rub at my temples as they begin to throb. Too much stress and not enough sleep.

"We need to clean the solar panels," I say.

"How about I take care of those, and you rest today," Roman says, scanning my face. "And don't argue. You had me rest when I had a migraine, and you're not looking all that great right now."

I could be offended, but even after using the cool water to get rid of some of the puffiness, I know I must look bad. I feel it too.

"Fine," I say. "But you'll still need help getting the suit on."

While helping Roman get ready to go outside, my head throbs and I can't get the students' faces out of my mind. It would be such a tragedy for their hopeful smiles to disappear if we didn't walk out of here with money for the library.

Roman strokes my hair with his big, gloved hand. "As soon as I get back in, you need to go lie down."

"Yes, Mr. Major," I say before helping him with the helmet.

He turns around so I can attach the oxygen. In the second it takes me to reach up and secure the tank, the intrusive thoughts hit me at full force. I think of my boyfriend from college and how he made different plans that left me and my heart in the dust. I think about Principal Major changing the plans for the library and trying to pit Roman against me. I'm still not positive if Roman's actions throughout our time here have worked to help or hinder the outcome. And ultimately, I think I can't take the risk of him not being one hundred percent in this.

I bring my arm back down before completely attaching his oxygen tank and step back. "Okay, good to go."

Roman walks out of the Hab, going through the tunnel to open the hatch, then steps outside. As soon as he's far enough, I hit a button that allows me to control the hatch's lock, knowing Roman won't be able to unlock it from outside.

As he approaches the solar panels, an alert plays over the comms as well as his headpiece, alerting us that his oxygen is depleting quickly from a leak. He turns back to the Hab and tries to open the hatch. "What the—? Bri, can you open the door?"

My heart pumps wildly in my chest as I watch him through the screen.

"Brianna?" He pulls at the hatch again, but it doesn't budge.

Think of the kids. Think of the kids. I ball my fists, battling with myself not to let him in.

Roman must finally catch on that the predicament he's in is my doing. He shakes his head and hangs it low. Before I can act on my second thoughts, he removes his helmet.

"I'm sorry," he whispers through the microphone, looking up into the camera above the door. He takes in a deep breath. "Ugh, it smells like rotten eggs." He lets out a sad chuckle. It's a sadness I feel in every ounce of my soul.

Within seconds, the alert switches from warning about

Roman's oxygen leak to blaring his imminent demise. It feels like the least I can do is stay and watch as my deception fully unfolds, but I don't have it in me. I turn away and head back to the bedroom. I slip into my bed and close the screen even though no one is here that I would need the extra privacy from.

Eventually, the alerts over the speakers become silent. And my heart is broken. Or rather, I'm broken. I know it because there are no tears. Just me and the empty stillness as I sit with what I've done.

IT'S QUIET WHEN I GET UP THE NEXT MORNING. QUIET AND LONELY. Quiet, lonely, and *wrong*. I wasn't supposed to be the only one left standing. Simone, Angie, Jordan—we came in as a team. Roman . . . I'm still not sure about his motives. But it felt like he was part of our team as well. And now it's just me.

I lie in the bed I was sharing with Roman just days ago. Not just sharing, but smiling, laughing, loving. If I knew the kiss we shared yesterday morning was going to be our last, I'd have made it count.

But with so many kids counting on me, with their futures on the line, I couldn't take the risk Roman wasn't one hundred percent on board. And now that probably means there's no future for *us*.

As I roll out of bed and stand in the empty room, I wonder what it says about me that even after all this, my feelings have not dissipated in the least. I still want a future with him. My heart felt like it was torn into a million pieces and scattered among the dust when I finally got the courage to check the cameras last night before going to bed and saw that he was well and truly gone. And I'm the one who sent him away.

There is a comfort to be found in following a routine. I guess it's why experts push the practice so much for kids. I do what I've done the past five weeks. I eat breakfast, clean my bowl, dust the furniture and comms, check on the cameras and Miles, and look over the rock samples. It's tough getting into my space suit with no one to help, but I manage it and go clean the solar panels. Finally, I get to checking in on the greenhouse.

Today I'm ready to finally switch out the soil and plant new seeds. I'm hoping something will sprout in the time I have left. I might even pray over them.

I walk in, expecting everything to be just as I left it yesterday, but as I approach the dandelion plot, I think my eyes are playing tricks on me. I get close, so close my nose touches the soil, and I realize I'm not seeing things. There are sprouts—multiple!

I cover my mouth with my hands so I don't scream but realize no one is here anyway. I can absolutely scream, so that's just what I do. We did it. We completed all the tasks. We're going to get the money for the school, Superintendent Watts is going to approve the library remodel, and Principal Major is going to have to deal with my intolerable happiness for the next year.

I close my eyes and take a deep breath as Roman's handsome face crosses my mind, and his look of acceptance after removing his helmet pierces my heart. He really didn't try to sabotage the dandelions.

Why couldn't these have sprouted one day sooner?

CHAPTER TWENTY-FOUR

Leaving the Hab and riding back home should be enough to bring me to tears.

I'm breathing in clean, fresh air. The stench of rotten eggs and sulfur is no longer embedded in my pores. I'm surrounded by colors. From the black tires of the shuttle to the greens and browns of the trees we drive by to the beautiful blue sky marking my homecoming. It's so bright today that when I first left the Hab I had to cover my eyes and put on the sunglasses the facilitator handed me.

Speaking of—the facilitator. It's the same woman who dropped our group off on the first day. Only today, she's way less chatty and a whole lot more awkward. I wish she would just come out and ask me what's clearly on her mind—why did you lock your teammate out? The more I think of my actions that day, the more I'm sure that's what I'll be remembered for. Not for helping the school get the new library, but for being the reason there was only one person to complete the challenge instead of two.

At least I'm no longer the forgotten Rogers sibling.

I sigh and stare out the window at the passing Texas landscape of green pastures with roaming cattle and horses. We pass a silver minivan on the right and come up on a dusty eighteen-wheeler with the words "Wash Me" written in the dirt across its back.

"So," I begin. I need some assurance I haven't turned myself into some sort of social pariah. "I bet that's the first time someone has intentionally locked one of their teammates out during one of these simulations, huh?"

The facilitator shakes her head. "You'd think so, but it's actually not. A couple of cycles ago, the whole team worked together to drag one of their crew members outside the Hab without a helmet or space suit. He wouldn't stop singing 'Despacito.' Literally. He didn't know the words or Spanish. He'd only say, 'despacito,' and mumble the chorus. Unfortunately, he happened to be their only IT guru, and the whole mission fell apart shortly after. At least you waited until the major tasks were complete."

I offer a small smile before turning back to the window. Now we're passing a rest stop. I don't find comfort in knowing I'm not the first person to kick someone off. There is no comfort when I'm plagued with what-ifs. What if I had trusted Roman fully? What if the dandelions had sprouted sooner? What if I'd never heard Principal Major's message? Would Roman be here with me right now? Would we be making plans to move forward with our relationship no matter what anyone had to say?

"Do you mind if I roll the window down?" I ask.

"Go for it."

I press the button for the window to go down automatically and sit with my head against the headrest, enjoying the feel of fresh air washing over my face and stirring my braids, while trying not to think.

The facilitator takes me back to the Space Center for debriefing and final paperwork. By the time everything is over and done with, Lance is waiting in the parking lot for me. I almost lose it when I see his familiar face.

"Hey, little sis," he says, engulfing me in a hug. He clears his throat. "That is, Astronaut Rogers."

I roll my eyes and hand over my bag. "I am not an astronaut."

"Does your momma know that? The way she's been lamenting these past two months, she'd swear up and down that you really did go to Mars."

"I'm sure that's an exaggeration. She has plenty of other things to focus on to forget about me and my adventures."

Lance shakes his head. "Tell that to her. She thinks Vincent's need for thrills can spread to us like a virus, and she's worried you'll try to become a real astronaut now that you've gotten a taste of it. She made Zara promise to stay away from all things space."

"But Zara is only three months. Actually, I guess going on five months now. But still, my point remains."

Lance shakes his head with a beleaguered sigh. "I know," he says, and gets into the driver's seat of his Subaru.

As I get in and sink into the leather seat, I inhale deeply. It smells so good.

"You know, your mom was worried about you, but she's also proud of you," Lance says.

"I know," I say automatically, then go back to taking deep drags of air.

"Like, *really* proud of you. Camille wanted to throw a barbecue this past Fourth of July. Your mom insisted we buy an inflatable projector to watch the live stream of you and the simulation. Then she went on at least a five-minute spiel telling everyone she talked to about your degrees and everything you've done to help kids."

"Wow. That's . . . wow."

I always knew Mom was proud of me, just not *as* proud as she is of Vincent and Camille. But to hear about her pride from Lance's perspective, the little girl in me can't help but smile.

"Thank you for sharing that with me," I say. "Now"—I lift up my sunglasses so Lance can get the full effect of my glare—"imagine my surprise when I began unpacking my bag and found a book in there I'm sure I didn't buy. I wonder who could have left that little gem, hmm?"

Lance tries unsuccessfully to hold in his laugh as we speed down the highway. "That was all Camille."

LANCE PULLS UP TO HIS AND CAMILLE'S HOUSE. I GET OUT AND FOLLOW him to the front door and inside. As I step into their spacious house, I see Zara batting at the colorful toys hanging from her walker. My heart swells, full of love and bittersweetness at how much she's grown in just six weeks. Before I know it, she'll be asking me to take her to the mall, like any good aunty would, so she can spend all my money.

"Cami, I got our space cadet home safe and sound!" Lance shouts.

As we step farther into the house from the foyer, Lance goes to pick up Zara from her walker, peppering her with kisses as she giggles in his arms.

"Aww." I place a hand over my heart. "She found her laugh."

I hear the slight but indistinguishable pitter-patter of steps before Sheba comes into view. I was worried that my pup would forget about me or decide she wanted to live with Camille and Lance or that she'd be mad and ignore me altogether. But Sheba pauses two seconds max before realizing it's me. Her head goes back as she prepares her body for launch, though it takes another two seconds for Sheba to gain enough traction on the marble floor when her feet move too quickly. Once her body is in accord with physics, she lurches forward like a rocket.

Laughing, I bend down, hugging her to me. Soon enough, my laughter turns into gut-wrenching sobs as all the emotions I've been repressing come bursting through. I haven't allowed myself to cry since sabotaging Roman, and now I can't stop. I let all my feelings spill out: guilt, love, foolishness, and now, with Sheba back at my side, happiness.

"You didn't forget me," I sob into Sheba's fur.

"Of course she didn't forget you," Camille says behind us. "You're her favorite person. That was a silly thought."

If there's one thing Camille is going to do, it's act like she knows everything. But since in this instance she is clearly right, I won't say anything.

I pull my head back from Sheba's soft fur—though I'm still scratching behind her ears as she whines and her wagging tail causes her whole body to sway—and look back at Camille. "Well, I missed you too."

Camille's eyes study my face before she declares, "I'll get us some wine."

After more pets for Sheba, I finally stand up. I say hi to Zara, who is now being fed a bottle by Lance, then go outside, where Camille is waiting for me. She even has a box of tissues in my usual spot.

Camille watches me and takes a sip of her water with cucumber before starting. "You did the exact opposite of what I told you to do."

I throw my head back and close my eyes. "I know," I whisper.

"You may as well tell me about it. About *him*. And don't worry, when you go through that box, I've got plenty more."

I go on to recount my past six weeks. The first day in the Hab, all the games we played and how we got to know each other, my initial suspicions of Roman and deciding I could trust him, subsequently falling even harder for him, and my line of thinking when I messed up his oxygen line. And finally the realization that he wasn't trying to ruin the dandelions after all.

At some point in the tale, Camille's glass gets stuck halfway to her mouth. When I'm done, she brings it up to take another sip, then shakes her head. "That is a lot. And really, I can't say that I blame you. You knew Principal Major didn't want you to succeed. It's logical that he'd send his son to make sure you didn't. Who could have guessed his son would have plans of his own? And who could have guessed that things would get even more complicated by you falling for him?" Camille pauses and raises one finger. "Actually, I did call that one."

"Can you not? For once?"

Camille sighs. "Fine. Just this once. But for what it's worth, from the footage I did watch, he looked equally smitten with you."

My hand stills on Sheba's head. Even though we're outside, instead of sniffing around and exploring, Sheba has opted to stay right next to me, probably worried I'll disappear again. "You thought he looked smitten with me? What would make you say that?" I need her to be very specific.

Camille shrugs. "You could just tell. From the beginning, his body language seemed more open with you than with anyone else. And it was like every week he cared less and less that there were cameras and that you two are *work colleagues.*" She stresses the last point. "Everyone was talking about that painting date he set up for you."

I smile, thinking about the horrendous picture he made of me. "You don't think he was faking?" I ask, and immediately hold my breath while Camille contemplates her answer.

"No, I don't. I think his dad made a shitty and highly inappropriate, not to mention unprofessional, request, and he was in a bad situation. Now, that's not to say that he's off the hook. He should have told you what his dad was up to from the beginning. If I were you, I would have sabotaged his butt too. And I hope you're going to finally write that letter to your school board." Camille huffs, getting herself worked up. "As a matter of fact, I've got a few things I want to get off my chest about that principal, so I may just go ahead and write the letter myself."

"Camille."

"What?"

I shake my head. "Never mind." I was going to tell her she was doing too much, but I actually like when my big sister tries to look out for me.

"So what are you going to do about your situation with Roman?"

"I don't know. I really don't."

"Well, things at school are going to be *awkward*," she sings.

"Maybe not. I think . . . I think I'm going to quit."

Camille's eyebrows shoot up as my words tumble out, surprising even myself.

"All these years I've been trying to find that one thing that can make me happy and fulfilled. I love making a difference in children's lives, but since the beginning, it's been an uphill battle. Well, I won the money for staying in the simulation for the full six weeks, and I've got a sizable savings, not to mention my retirement funds if worse comes to worst, but I think I could really do this."

"What?" Camille interrupts. "You could really do what?"

"Start a foundation. I want to help kids all over the world access books and reading. Of course, I'll start right here in the city, but in time, I think I could grow it into something big. What do you think?" I ask hesitantly.

Camille smiles. "I think you've found your calling."

I nod. This decision feels good and solid. For the first time in my life, I know what I truly want. And it's not to be an astronaut like my big brother or a doctor like my big sister. It took me a while, but I'm finally seeing a path of my own that is clear.

"You know," I begin, "for so long, I've wanted what you and Vincent have. To be sure that I'm in the right career. All my life it's felt like I've been playing catch-up to you. You've always seemed to have it all together."

She smiles softly. "Yeah, I was watching when you told Roman you didn't live up to the Rogers name. I'm so sorry you ever felt that way, but Bri, I told you I don't have it all together. To be honest, there are times when I'm barely keeping my head above water." I look at her in disbelief and Camille nods emphatically. "I'm so serious. My life has never been perfect, and having Zara has really thrown me for a loop. My emotions are all over the place. I want to stay with her and get all the cuddles I can while she's this small. But I need to go to work and take care of my patients. But if I'm at work too long, I'm neglecting my family and missing so much. The guilt is never-ending, and it always feels like I'm the one playing catch-up in my own life." She sighs. "You know I like to control things, but I have to constantly let Lance hold down the fort here at home and rely on my colleagues at work to fill in the gaps that I can't. Mom made everything look so easy, and I always thought if I ever had kids, I'd be able to follow in her footsteps. But it's so hard."

"I'm sure it was hard on Mom too. But there was also so much love and fun for us that we probably black out most of the hard parts and can't remember the hell we must have raised."

"Speak for yourself. You were the little hellion. Always causing the most trouble out of all of us."

"No, I wasn't. That was all Vince."

Camille shakes her head no. "Vince didn't start until he was accepted into NASA's training program. You've been a handful since you were a kid. Remind me, who was it that decided to steal the peaches from Old Man Willie's yard again?"

We both laugh, and when it dies down, I reach over to pat Camille's hand. "You are a great mom. You're a super mom. Super sister and super woman as well. I said I've always felt like I had to play catch-up to you, but that's because I admire you so much. You are a great role model."

Camille squeezes my hand and sniffs. "Oh my God, what is this?" She reaches for a tissue and quickly dabs her eyes. "Not me out here choking on my feelings. Ew." Camille has always been the calm and composed one, the least likely of my siblings to cry. I count it as a win that I've gotten my sister to show her softer emotions.

"That's right, let it all out," I say. "Feel those feelings. Let them surround you with the warm-and-fuzzies. Because you want to know what else? Zara loves you so much. She thinks you're the best momma in the whole world."

"Stop!"

"And that husband of yours was made just for you. It's

like you two are pieces of a puzzle that just fit, and it's more than evident that he knows it too. You are his queen!"

"Ahhh!"

We laugh and cry so hard that we don't hear our mom step outside until she's standing between us. "What is going on out here?"

At the sound of my mom's voice, I instantly hop out of my chair. "Momma!"

She throws her arms around me and squeezes tight, going on and on about her baby being home and how if I ever think of going to Mars for real, it'll be over her dead body. I just let her rattle on as I hug her back.

After always thinking that I had to play catch-up with my siblings and feeling like I was the last and least important of us to my mom, I realize how wrong I've been. And if I've been wrong about the fundamental truths that have shaped my adult years, could I be wrong in other areas of my life? Like, maybe I was wrong when I thought it was over between Roman and me.

Maybe.

"Camille," Mom says when she finally releases me and looks to Camille, "have you been crying?"

CHAPTER TWENTY-FIVE

I walk into my office and close the door with my back before leaning against it and taking a deep breath. While all the teachers are coming back to prepare for the students' return in the new school year, I'm packing up my office to leave.

With the school year fast approaching, I hated to leave without giving enough notice and time to find someone else to step up, but now that I know in my heart what I want to do, I can't stay. In the immortal words of Cookie from *Empire*, I gotta put me first.

Someone knocks at my door, sending vibrations through my back. I quickly move away from the door and to my desk so I won't get hit. "Come in," I call.

The door opens to reveal Angie. She's got a manila folder trapped between her arm and chest, a slice of pizza in one hand, and a wide smile stretched across her face. "Guess whose new chair came in today? I'll give you a hint—mine!"

I smile as I lean against my desk.

"I'm going to assume you were the one to approve it."

I shrug. "I heard there was a boost to the budget and some extra funds that needed to be allocated somewhere."

I'm leaving, but I couldn't help but check and see what

the school budget was going to look like for the new year. Once I saw that Principal Major had vastly overstated how much the new football field would be, I made the executive decision that the teachers deserved a real treat. I felt a little like Oprah as I placed the order. *You get a chair! And you get a chair!* For all they do for the students, it's the least they deserve. Chairs, and I've scheduled for pizzas from Big Lou's to be delivered to the staff all week as they move back into their classrooms.

"Thank you, Brianna," Angie says, her words heartfelt. "And I really am going to miss you. It was great working with you last year and at the Hab."

I swallow the lump in my throat.

When I arrived at the school, I worried that I'd be shunned after I sabotaged Roman to get him out of the Hab. But that hasn't been the case. Every teacher I've come across has greeted me with a wide smile and open arms, congratulating me on a job well done. It's the most welcoming they've ever been to me, which makes my leaving all the more bittersweet.

When Simone heard I was leaving, I immediately handed her my phone so she could plug her number in, then she added me across every social media platform while we were standing there and making plans to meet for coffee. I was and am touched beyond words to be leaving this season in my life with at least a friend, if not love.

And throughout all the congratulations and well wishes in my next endeavor, no one has said a thing about Roman. Not one teacher has mentioned how close we seemed, the kiss we shared on camera, or how I locked him out of the hatch. If I weren't there, I might wonder if it actually happened. But the Roman-sized hole in my heart proves that yes, it did. It's more likely the teachers all agreed to *not* talk about him in advance. I both appreciate and lament their consideration. I haven't seen Roman since coming back to wrap everything up, and I'm dying to know what he's up to and how he's doing. Does he still care about me, or did he consider everything we shared in the Hab a wash after he left?

I clear my throat, focusing back on Angie and trying to take my mind off Roman. "I'll miss you too. Maybe we can meet up for coffee sometime."

"Coffee sounds good. Or a book club. I think you and Simone will absolutely love the first book I have in mind."

"More growling men?" I ask.

"No. In this one, he hates everyone but her." Angie wiggles her brows. "Sounds good, right? I'll call you so we can set it up!" And with that, she turns and struts away.

I smile to myself. If she doesn't call me, then I'm calling her. That book sounds delightful.

"Knock knock," I hear a deep voice say, and stiffen.

I turn around to find Principal Major in the doorway. I have to immediately tamp down my anger and resentment and the urge I've had all week to yell at him. To call him a black hole who not only ruined the chance of happiness I had with Roman but also sucks all the joy out of the school and teachers. But again, I know I would start crying, and he's just not worth it.

"Principal Major," I say.

"Miss Rogers. I wanted to make sure you have everything or see if there was anything you needed."

"Coming to make sure I'm actually packing up to get out of here, you mean?" I won't cuss him out, but I also won't act like he hasn't been a thorn in my side. We are not parting ways like besties. "Don't worry, I'm good."

He nods, probably satisfied that there are no pretenses

between us. He looks around my office like he's seeing it for the first time. Now that I think about it, he never actually came here during the whole school year. He just assigned me a place to park and summoned me to him when it was necessary for us to talk in person.

"There's not much space in here, is there?" he comments. He's not even inside fully, and for that I'm thankful. This space isn't big enough for all my boxes and his insufferable presence.

As he continues looking around—at what, I'm not sure since there's only so much one can see when peering into a shoebox—I can't help but notice that he looks a little . . . ashamed? And what is this feeling trying to get into me now . . . the stirrings of forgiveness?

After all, I won't have to deal with him any longer after this. I feel sorry that he's so stuck in his old ways. It's not that he's a bad principal. At least, he's not the worst. He does want the school and the kids to succeed. And I know he was dragged upside down and inside out after Roman listened to his message in the simulation congratulating Roman for doing a good job at gaining my trust. However, since he never outright said the word *sabotage*, I can only guess that's how he managed not to get fired. Camille couldn't believe even her strongly worded letter didn't do the job.

I can only hope he does better for the next vice principal. Whether it be Roman or someone else.

"I'm all good here," I say. "I'll have the rest of these boxes out by the end of the day."

Principal Major nods. For a second I contemplate asking about Roman. If anyone knows what he's up to, surely it would be his father. But as quickly as the urge pops up, it's gone. Principal Major and I will never have the kind of relationship where I can ask after his son. Maybe if this were an alternate reality or if we were able to show each other grace instead of battling to press our will on the other.

Once Principal Major leaves, I start moving boxes from my office to my car. I don't have many since there was only so much I could add in there without cluttering it up. The last thing I grab is my painting. I still have yet to pick up a pencil and some paper. I felt inspired while in the Hab, but now I realize that inspiration was in large part due to Roman. How can I even think of trying to draw, knowing memories of our dinner-and-drawing date would likely assault me if I tried?

I suck in a deep breath. When will I ever be able to stop thinking about him? That's a pointless question. Never. That's the answer. I'll never stop thinking about him. And I'll forever mourn that we didn't have a real shot at a love out here in the real world.

When I close my eyes, I'll forever hear his voice saying my name, the way he said it when he thought I was being silly or when we were lying in bed and he held me with so much tenderness and love.

"Brianna."

Great. Not only do I hear it when my eyes are closed, I apparently hear it when I'm out and about trying to live a normal life too.

"Brianna."

I gasp and stop. I'm not hearing things. I turn around, and there he is. Facing me as he stands in the middle of the parking lot.

Roman is here. After seeing him in nothing but the jumpsuit for six straight weeks, he looks like a new man in fitted jeans and a dark gray polo with actual short sleeves. The colors he wears are muted compared to the yellow compact and blue SUV near us and the sun in the sky, but I can't think of a more beautiful sight my eyes have seen.

We stare at each other for what feels like eons. Roman's eyes rake over me, but I don't take my gaze off his face in case he disappears. He's freshly groomed. Goatee trimmed, perfect edge-up and waves. If I hadn't gotten used to looking in those beautiful brown eyes every day over the course of five weeks, I might have believed he was the same unaffected and aloof teacher waiting for me to stop talking to him.

But I did spend those weeks with him. Studying him like it was my life's greatest work, so I know there is nothing aloof in the way he's looking at me. He's nervous. It takes everything in me not to throw myself at him, but I don't know where we stand. For all I know, he could be here to yell at me because of how things ended at the Hab. To clear the air and get everything off his chest now, while he has the chance, before I leave the school for good.

I blink, breaking the spell Roman had on me, and take in a gulp of air. "What are you doing here?" I bite my bottom lip. What a dumb question. He's obviously here to get ready for school. "I mean, I haven't seen you all week. I'm surprised to see you now. Not that I think you've been slacking or anything," I rush to add. "I know that being prepared is important to you and all." I squeeze the frame of the picture until the pain of it digging into my hands is finally enough to get me to stop talking. "You know what," I say once I compose myself, "ignore everything. What are you doing here?"

Roman's eyes soften, and for a second it looks like he might smile. But he sobers again and takes a deep breath. "I heard that you decided to resign. I wanted to get it from the source this time to make sure it's true."

"Oh." I hope the disappointment isn't evident in my tone. "Yeah. This time it's true. I've given it a lot of thought, and I think this is what's best for me. On the plus side, there's an open position for vice principal if you know anyone capable of fulfilling the role. If I know my former principal, he's already got someone in mind."

"What are you going to do?"

"I'm starting a foundation to help spread literacy and provide books for school-aged children." Each time I say it, a thrill runs through me as something in me shouts, *Yes! This is the right path.*

Roman nods. "I think you'll do phenomenally, Bri. I really do."

"Thank you. That means a lot."

As we stand in another round of awkward silence, a weight begins to press on my chest. It's so hard to stand in front of him and have all these memories of good times we shared ruined by our last days together. For probably the hundredth time, I want to go yell at Principal Major.

This time Roman is the one to break eye contact as his gaze shifts away from me and he blinks. He clears his throat. "I, um, wanted to give you something."

He takes a few steps forward, closing the distance between us, and my stomach does a flip-flop at his nearness. He's not close enough for me to touch, but I can smell his fresh cologne.

He hands me a notebook I recognize.

"Is this your journal?" I look at the orange notebook in my hand.

"I know that it was messed up how everything went down and that this won't absolve me of anything, but, well, I guess I'm hoping . . . Damn, I don't know what I'm hoping for. But I want you to have this. Is that okay?"

He looks so lost that I'm at a loss for words and all I can do is nod.

"Okay. Good." Roman nods once and takes a step back, away from me. Finally, he turns around, and I see him head inside the school.

I go to my car. Instead of driving away after starting the engine, I look at the outside of Roman's journal, weighing it in my hands. Even though curiosity ate at me for weeks, wondering what thoughts or secrets he was revealing in here, after kicking him out of the Hab I couldn't bring myself to then intrude on his privacy. But now he's given me explicit permission. The need for self-restraint is gone. Still in my seat with the AC blasting, I open the journal and start reading the entries.

By the time I'm done, my hands are shaking. Roman was telling the truth the whole time. He never planned on doing his dad's bidding. He was really there because he believed in my vision. He believed in me. I look at his last entry, the one he wrote after I heard the message from his dad. While all the entries say something about me—seriously, every single entry mentions me in some capacity—the last one is for me.

Brianna,

I'm so sorry I didn't tell you about my dad's plan. I know it might be too little too late and that tomorrow when you wake up in the morning, you might decide you don't want to talk to me ever again. If that's the case, it's what I deserve. But I have all these thoughts running in my mind and need to get them out because you know what I've realized in five weeks? I'm still learning about myself.

That sounds weird, right? But it's true. For example, my favorite color used to be black. Now it's blue.

Why blue? It's just superior. If you don't believe me, put your coveralls on and look in the mirror. Have you ever noticed how good the color looks on you? Or maybe it looks good because of you. Same thing, right? But there you have it. At my big age of thirty-three, I have a new favorite color.

You know what else I realized? Burgers aren't my favorite food. Contrary to what you think, I do have taste buds. Remember when we ate that dehydrated vanilla pudding you hated? Swear to God it tasted like heaven to me. Of course, it could've been because I could still taste it on your lips when I kissed you that night. Either way, 10/10 would eat dehydrated pudding from your mouth again.

Now this I already knew, but I feel it needs to be said: I can build anything. I'm not bragging. It's a fact. If you need me to prove it, I'll build you a bookshelf— no—a whole damn library. I'll fill it up with any kind of books you like. We'll start with the whole series for that werewolf book you let me borrow. But for the record, fingers are 10x better than tentacles.

In case you haven't realized it, all these changes are because of you. You make me want to be a better man. Because of you, I want to be a better man. Do you know how life-changing that is for a man like me? For that I want to say thank you. If I never get the chance or the courage to say it to your face, I also want you to know that you're amazing and I have fallen so in love with you.

And now I know it's not over for us. How can it be, when I help to bring out the best in him and he lets me just be *me*? He's my perfect match.

I turn off my engine and bolt out of my car.

I run inside, trying to decide which way Roman would have gone. I take a gamble and head toward the administration offices. I see him coming out of the office and into the hallway. He stops when he sees me.

I'm still clutching the journal. Breathless, I hold it up. "Did you mean everything you wrote in here?"

"Every single word," he confirms without reservation.

I close my eyes as relief washes over me. I take in a deep breath and open my eyes. I straighten my shoulders, sure and confident in what I'm going to say next. "How about we start over? After we met, it seems like things got off on the wrong foot. Let's do it right this time. All of it."

Roman's throat moves as he swallows and lets out a quiet "Okay." He walks up to me and shoots the friendliest and most open smile my way. "Hello, I'm Roman. It's nice to meet—"

Before he can finish, I do exactly what I wanted to the first time we met, a year ago. I stand on my tiptoes, wrap my arms around his neck to bring him to my level, and smash my lips into his.

When we pull apart, I'm breathless, but my heart is so full. "You had me at hello," I say against his lips before we kiss again.

"I'm so sorry about everything. But thankful you're willing to give me a second chance. I swear I won't let you down again," he says.

"The only way you could let me down is if you started hiding who you are. You may think I bring out the best in you, but I'm only helping you see the man who is already there. The man I love."

As we go in for another kiss, we hear clapping. Roman quickly swipes at his cheek and we look around to see that the people who were in the administration office are now peeking from the doorway and looking at us.

Angie is there. She clasps her hands together and tilts her head up to the ceiling. "Lord, I see what you've done for others. Please do it for me!"

Amen, girl.

I kiss Roman one more time before pulling away. "I think we've let them see enough of our lives. What do you say we take this somewhere away from prying eyes?" I say.

"You read my mind."

Roman interlocks our hands and we walk out of the school together.

EPILOGUE

Movie!"

"Four words!"

I wordlessly nod as the guesses begin rolling in for my turn at charades. I've got something I'm pretty sure is going to stump everyone.

"*Honey, I Shrunk the Kids*," Jordan guesses.

"That's five words, not four," Angie says.

"*Lady and the Tramp*," Simone tries, and I shake my head.

"*Deliver Us from Eva*! *Planet of the Apes*! *The Mask of Zorro*!" Jordan calls out in quick succession.

I smile, shake my head, and throw my arms out, palms up.

Angie did call me to set up the book club, and after hearing about it, not only did Simone join, but so did Roman and Jordan. Today's book features another one of Angie's favorite tropes: touch her and die.

As has become habit, we decided to do a few rounds of charades after. Jordan is determined to get the most right, but his guesses are always so off-the-wall.

Case in point: "*The Muppet Christmas Carol*," he calls out. Just loud and wrong.

"*Across the Spider-Verse*," Roman says, his tone indicating it should have been obvious to everyone else.

I point at him. "You got it!"

I love how he gets me.

"Aww, man, does that mean it's his turn again?" Jordan complains.

Roman rises from his spot on my couch. Angie and Simone prefer to meet at my house since I have the biggest home library.

"Not this time. We don't have time for any more rounds," Roman says as he approaches me. He smiles down at me as he takes my hand. "Ready?"

"I've been waiting for this my whole life," I say. I turn to our friends. "Y'all are coming too, right?"

"Of course," Angie says. "We wouldn't dream of missing it."

We all leave my house, with Roman and me riding in my car and everyone else following along in their respective cars. Not that they need to follow. They know exactly where Juanita Craft Middle School is.

I pull into the familiar parking lot, and we get out and meet at my trunk. Roman reaches for the biggest box of books while I get the smaller one. We head inside, going straight for the library.

"Do you think we need a visitor's pass?" I ask him as we come upon the front doors.

"Not for after-school events."

I didn't know it at the time, but before I put in my resignation, Roman beat me to it. In fact, he'd been planning to leave the school even before the simulation began. The catalyst had been his dad canceling the library in favor of the football field. He knew his dad wouldn't stop trying to get his way and have Roman fill the vice principal role unless he did something drastic. So he transferred to Angelou

School of Arts. The school teaches all subjects, but they put an emphasis on arts and culture. He loves it.

As we walk down the hallway, my arms begin to ache from carrying the books, but I don't let it slow me down. It's finally time to see the new library.

Many familiar faces of teachers I used to work with fill the hall leading to the library. They greet Roman and me, making room for us to get through. I'm surprised they aren't inside already, but as we approach the entrance I see why. Whoever planned the library's reopening ceremony really went all out. There is a large black curtain hanging from the floor to the ceiling, blocking the entrance.

"Look at all this," I say to Roman. "I wonder how they talked your dad into doing such a big celebration."

He sets his box of books against a wall, then takes mine from me and does the same with it. "He couldn't get away with anything less." He leans down and whispers in my ear. "I hear he may have even ordered pizza."

I smile up at him as Angie, Jordan, and Simone make their way through the crowd.

Angie's nose is scrunched up as she joins us. "I swear, some of these teachers are just as bad as the kids. I'm about to start giving deodorant away like it's Halloween candy."

"Are you sure it's not your upper lip?" Jordan asks, and I don't hold in my laugh.

Angie cuts him with her eyes, and Jordan backs away, though he's still smiling.

After a few minutes of waiting around, I'm ready to agree with Angie: it does smell a little rank. I press my nose into Roman's side so all I smell is him.

"There they are," Roman says, and I look up to find

Superintendent Watts, Principal Major, and the school's new vice principal coming through the crowd. They stand in front of the curtain as the superintendent gives a small speech about the library remodel and the impact it will have on the kids for years to come.

I'm so happy to finally see this come to fruition that my eyes begin to mist. I take in a deep breath and try to hold back the tears.

As the superintendent nears the end of her speech, she thanks the crew and me for making it possible by joining the simulation. She didn't have a lot to say when the simulation was over. I thought she'd be upset and feel like she'd invested pointless time in mentoring me, but she happily wished me well on the foundation.

"Mr. Wilkerson," she says to Jordan, holding out a cord. "We'd like you to do the honors."

Jordan steps up and grabs the cord from her. He pulls, and the curtains fall to the ground to unveil the newly updated library.

There are gasps, clapping, and delighted whoops. When the noise dies down, Superintendent Watts speaks again. "Ladies and gentlemen, behold the Brianna Rogers Library."

The what? Her words don't register at first, but when they do, all I can do is stand there. "They named a library after me?"

"Look up," Roman tells me.

I do, and my jaw falls open. They *did* name the library after me. In large gold letters above the library's entrance, there's my name.

I turn to Roman. "Did you know about this?"

He smiles down at me and nods his head. "I did."

"Know about it?" Simone says. "It was his idea!"

I look at him with wide eyes. "Roman, I . . . I don't even know what to say. Except that I love you. This is unbelievable."

He strokes my hair, then bends down to kiss me. "I love you too. And if you think this is unbelievable from the outside, you should take a look at what's going on in there." He grabs my hand and leads me inside.

"What about the books?" I point to the boxes we brought in. Boxes of books from my foundation that I'm donating to the school.

"They'll be fine there for now."

The new library looks phenomenal. There are new shelves full of books. There is a computer lab with desktops for the students to use while here and laptops and tablets they can check out. In place of the area that was used for detention, there are round tables the students can sit at to read or do homework and floor seats for those who don't want to sit in a regular chair. I bet Principal Major just loves those.

Mrs. Yates comes up to me, clasping her hands and at a loss for words. She holds her arms out wide as if to say, *look at all this!* and I nod.

"It looks great," I say.

She hugs me before walking away, letting her fingers glide along the shelves.

As she walks away, Principal Major walks up to us. He nods in acknowledgment to Roman. Their relationship has been evolving since Roman resigned. At first his dad was furious. But little by little, Principal Major has come to accept that Roman has his own plans for his life and career, and they'll never include being a vice principal. He wants to repair their relationship, and Roman has decided to meet him halfway.

Roman realized his dad was never *un*interested in his life growing up, he just didn't know how to express his happy emotions. He didn't know how to feel. When Roman went into teaching, Principal Major saw it as an easy way to finally bond with his son. However, he went about it the completely wrong way by driving away many good vice principals and wasting thousands of dollars on unnecessary football fields, and he has a lot to atone for.

"What do you think?" Principal Major asks Roman.

"I think it's wonderful," I answer.

I never knew how spot-on I was when I told Principal Major to get used to seeing me. Of course, then I meant for him to get used to seeing me at school, but it's a great form of poetic justice that he's forced to see the one vice principal he could never get rid of whenever he wants to see Roman. And I love making my presence known.

"The library looks great," Roman says.

"I'll see you on Sunday for lunch?" Principal Major asks Roman.

"Yeah," Roman says.

"See you then!" I say, waving him off.

He lets out a sigh, but I swear I see a little smile as he turns and walks away.

"I think your dad likes me," I say to Roman.

"Are you just now picking up on that? You won him over a long time ago. At this point it's about keeping up appearances."

I squeeze Roman's hand, and we keep walking around. "I want to make sure those boxes we brought don't get forgotten," I say. "You know I had some books in there about hygiene the kids need."

As we walk toward the entrance of the library, I see two familiar figures. "Is that—?"

My unspoken question is answered by Jordan's distant gasp.

"Did you know they were coming too?" I ask Roman, pointing to Vincent and Camille.

Roman nods. "I thought your family should be here for this special moment."

We walk up to where Vincent and Camille are huddled together, and I pounce, wrapping my arms around both of them. "Are y'all talking about me?"

"Of course," Vincent says, returning the hug. "We were talking about how proud of you we are."

"I don't know how the library looked before," Camille says, "but this is amazing."

They turn to greet Roman, having met him when we all got together to set up the small—but not tiny—office I'm currently running my foundation out of. Jordan steps up to us, but I'm not delusional, thinking he's here to talk to me.

I smile, encouraging Jordan to come closer. "Vincent, I want to introduce you to my friend Jordan."

Jordan sticks out his hand, shaking Vincent's vigorously. I think he may be my brother's biggest fan. Or maybe second, after Amerie.

"It's an honor to meet you, Astronaut Rogers," Jordan says. "Or should I say Chief of the Astronaut Office?"

I gasp. "Vincent! You got a promotion? Why didn't you tell me?"

Vincent shakes his head. "Tonight isn't about me. We're celebrating *your* accomplishments."

There was a time when I would have felt so much envy that he's moving up yet again. But tonight it's all gone. "I'm proud of you, Vince. You are an inspiration, and I'm always happy to hear of your accomplishments."

As Vincent turns to Jordan to answer any of his burning questions, Camille turns to me. She reaches up to fix a misplaced braid strand and smiles. "So how are you feeling? About everything. Your new life, walking away from teaching, this amazing library?"

I look around the library, make eye contact with Roman, and my heart swells. "I feel like I'm ready to face the future." Finally.

———

"ARE YOU HUMMING 'ANGEL OF MINE'?" ROMAN ASKS ME AS I LIE draped over his chest the next morning.

After leaving the school, we came back to my house and shut out the rest of the world. We're supposed to meet with my family for lunch, but I'm tempted to send them a message saying we can't make it. I just want to spend the day wrapped in Roman's arms.

"I didn't realize I was humming," I say. "Do you ever miss the simulation?"

He thinks about it while wrapping one of my braids around his finger. "Do I miss finding dust in bad places and navigating from one crisis to the next? No. But do I miss being with you every hour and being able to glance around a small space and easily spot you? Yes."

"You're so sweet." I stretch my neck to kiss him. "It's what I miss the most too. I just want to spend every day with you. At least we have every night." I rest my head back on Roman's chest and sigh. After living with each other for six weeks in the Hab, it was an easy transition to spend every night together, alternating between his place and mine. "Well, I guess we'd better start getting ready to meet with my family."

"If my woman misses spending every night with me, what kind of man would I be if I didn't do something about it?" Roman asks, ignoring my comment about us getting ready. And really, I'm not mad. We can meet up with my family later and instead use this time for a little bonding.

"I said, what kind of man would I be if I didn't do something about my woman missing me?" he asks, and he's using *that* tone again.

"Not a very good man," I answer.

"That's what I thought. Now, move back to your spot on the bed." This time his tone is gentle, but I still scramble off Roman's chest and lie on my pillow.

"Close your eyes," Roman says, and I do, giddy with anticipation of where he'll touch first.

The bed shifts with Roman's weight as he moves. It feels like he's moving to the foot of the bed. If he's going to kick this off by trailing kisses up my legs, count me in.

"Now," he says. "Open them."

I do, then immediately sit up. "Roman?" I breathe.

He is at the foot of the bed, and he's holding an open ring box. Inside is the most beautiful ring I've ever seen.

"Brianna," he begins, then clears his throat and starts again. "Brianna Rogers, I love everything about you. Your smile. Your kindness. Your humor. The way you love and forgive. I'm ten times better than I was before, all because of you. Will you marry me?"

"Yes," I say. "Of course!"

I launch myself at him, nearly making us fall off the bed. Once he regains his balance, I grab his face and pepper his mouth with kisses.

Roman laughs. "I didn't put the ring on you yet."

"Fine." I lean back and hold my left hand out impatiently, eager to get back to his lips. When he finally slides the ring on, I take a moment to stare. It's the perfect fit, and we're the perfect match.

"I'm so happy," I whisper. "I feel like this isn't even real."

Roman tilts my chin up, and I fall over and over again when I see a tear rolling down his cheek. "It was always real," he says, then claims my lips in a kiss.

ACKNOWLEDGMENTS

I would like to thank all the wonderful people who helped get *The Love Simulation* out into the world. It takes a village, and I am so thankful for the support and encouragement I've received.

Thank you to my agent, Jemiscoe Chambers-Black, for your belief in my stories and for always cheering me on. Thank you to my amazing editor, Esi Sogah, for your expertise and keen eye, which helped bring out Brianna and Roman's story.

Thank you to my team at Berkley, who helped bring this story to the world: Genni Eccles, Kaila Mundell-Hill, Jessica Plummer, Kristin Cipolla, Elise Tecco, and Lila Selle. You all are wonderful. Thank you to the UK team at Penguin Michael Joseph.

To all my friends who offered encouragement or a listening ear, thank you.

Thank you to my family for being my support and inspiration for each love story.

And finally, thank you to every reader who has given my stories a chance!

Don't miss Etta Easton's debut novel

THE KISS COUNTDOWN

Available from Berkley!

Homeboy has ten seconds to divert his eyes from my ass before I lose it.

Ten . . . nine . . .

I face the pastry case filled with freshly baked donuts and scones, frowning at the reflection of the man behind me. I say *homeboy*, but in reality, he looks old enough to be my granddad, with his full gray mustache and a pair of reading glasses perched atop his shiny head. Like most patrons flooding Moon Bean this early, he wears a business suit with wide tan slacks and a black blazer that lends no credibility to his character. Not when he's eyeing my backside like it's one of the butter croissants on display.

One.

"This is my first time here. What do you suggest I get, sugar?" he says, close enough for his Brut aftershave to wrap me in a choke hold.

Nope. We are not playing this game. Not today, when I'm already on edge, anticipating the meeting that will help launch my new beginning—or see it fail at groundbreaking speed.

I whip my head around and glare, reaching deep into that ancestral pool of fortitude handed down from generations of resilient women who perfected the *mess with me and die* look. In two seconds he slides back to a respectable distance and raises his phone to his nose.

That's more like it. Satisfied, I pivot to face the front of the line once more, but it isn't long before another glance toward the glass case tells me he's back to ogling.

As the person in front of me moves up, I'm distracted when my phone buzzes. It's my best friend, Gina, texting that she's leaving her apartment. I let her know I'm already in line so she can grab us a table when she gets here.

Gina rarely makes the three-minute walk it takes to get from our respective apartments to the coffee shop more than twice a week, and when she does, I can always count on her to be at least ten minutes late. The conversion from Central Standard Time to Gina time works in my favor today. No doubt, if she'd witnessed the exchange between Pops and me just now, she'd be harping on me for not entertaining his nonsense and applauding his willingness to risk it all for someone half his age, all the while laughing her ass off.

"I can help the next person in line," a barista with a hotpink face mask says, and I move forward, dismissing the man behind me from my mind.

After ordering our drinks, I don't dare approach the pickup counter yet. Against the *burr* of multiple grinders and blenders going at once, a blockade of thirsty patrons watch the baristas furiously topping off drinks with pumps of syrup or oat milk, silently praying their hit of caffeine comes next. The only other time you see a crowd this anxious to get their hands around something hot is when it involves turkey legs at the rodeo. You can never know what someone is liable to do when deprived of coffee or poultry, so I keep looking around the shop until I spot Gina.

She waves at me from a table by a large window decorated with hand-drawn candy canes and Christmas ornaments, and I head that way.

The heavy green chair scrapes against the floor as I pull it out and sit across from her. "Hey."

"Good morning," she sings, and it's hard to believe she likely hopped out of bed five minutes before texting me.

Gina is one of those unnatural people who wake up with a good stretch and wide smile, ready to face the day. Not a drop of coffee in her system and she's brighter than a ray of sunshine in her long-sleeve white shirt and knitted yellow scarf.

Technically, I'm a morning person too. After years spent waking up before the sun to prepare for large-scale events, my internal alarm rarely allows me to sleep past six in the morning. But it takes me a nice long walk, usually around the golf course behind my apartment complex, and a cup of coffee before I'm ready for human interaction. Add in a couple of slices of bacon, and it's on.

"So, what's on the agenda for today?" I ask, keeping an ear out for my name to be called.

"I'm going to Sugar Land for a bridal party," Gina says. "The bride is seriously the sweetest. She's getting an updo, and I'm doing blowouts for the bridesmaids."

As Gina effortlessly uses the green silk scrunchie around her wrist to pull her curls into a low ponytail, I inwardly pout. My hair never goes up that easily. Certainly not without me feeling like I've just finished a full upper-body workout at the gym. I guess it's one of the perks of her being a hairstylist.

I try not to visibly shudder at the thought of brides and weddings. If I never have to attend another wedding in my life, I'll be just fine.

Gina's eyes widen. "Oh, I almost forgot. Don't you have that quinceañera consultation this morning? Look at my girl. Ready to take on her first client. How exciting! I take it after we're done here, you'll rush home to get camera-ready." She gives my hairline a pointed glance.

Since all I did was throw on a headband to liven up my worn bun, I'm not offended by Gina's blatant dig at my hair or at the concern evident in her brown eyes. I can't blame her when it's been only two months since I managed to claw my way out of a downward spiral that began when I almost lost my mom and worsened when my employer of eight years tossed me out like hot garbage. But being broken up with by my boyfriend was the exact push I needed to snap out of my despair and right my upended life. So I called Gina and told her I was going to start my own business.

Ever the queen to my bee, she didn't question if I was having a midlife crisis at the age of twenty-eight. She was at my door within minutes to congratulate me, then said I couldn't even think of starting a business until I'd swapped my sweat-stained sheets for new ones.

This morning I awoke to the sweet scent of lavender fields, knowing today was the day when, once and for all, I took control of my life. So, despite my current appearance, I'm ready.

"Don't look at me like that," I tell Gina. "When we're done here, I'm marching to my apartment—and yes, fixing my hair—then sealing the deal with my first client."

"You've got this, Mimi. And here's some extra good luck coming your way." Gina mimes throwing balls of glitter at me, and I indulge her by closing my eyes and basking in it.

"Medium roast and caramel latte for Amerie!" is shouted from the pickup counter, and I get up.

I maneuver around tables and furniture easily enough, but have to fight my way through two particular people who have zeroed in on the workers like their unmovable focus will make the baristas move any faster than they already are. It's a miracle more elbows aren't thrown in every coffee shop across America in the time between when customers place their orders and have to fight the masses to actually get them.

Relief comes when I finally reach our drinks, grab two cup sleeves, and turn to head back, feeling sorry for (and a tiny bit better than) everyone still waiting.

"I went with the cappuccino," Pops says from beside me, and I almost drop the drinks.

I knew he wouldn't be discouraged for long. These old-school dudes are a different breed of tenacious, but I've got no patience to deal with his foolishness today. I grit my teeth as I turn away from him without making eye contact.

I'm halfway to Gina when I realize I forgot to add cinnamon to my coffee. That won't do. I abruptly turn around, only to have my right elbow connect with something warm and solid, accompanied by a man's surprised grunt.

After catching my footing, I'm grateful the lids have held and neither of the cups in my hands spilled. As good as the coffee is, some of the baristas are notoriously awful at putting the lids on, so I always make sure to snap mine tightly before grabbing them. Foresight and planning for the win.

I'm ready to lay into Pops for his stalkerish tendencies when I look up and realize not only did I *not* collide with Pops, but the man I did bump into didn't fare as well as I did.

Coffee blots what I'm sure was once a pristinely pressed white shirt like paintball splatters, while dark spots coating the zipper of fitted navy slacks make it look like he had a suspicious accident in the restroom. The coffee stops mid-torso, so I let my eyes travel up to a wide chest and broad shoulders, then momentarily lose my breath once I reach my victim's face.

He's tall, standing a good head above me, with skin that's a rich, warm brown. He's clean-shaven, with the barest hint of a five-o'clock shadow, and gorgeous full lips that stand out in perfect proportion to a cut jaw. His eyes are a beautiful golden brown, like topaz. You'd think he'd once been foolish enough to stare into the sun long enough to capture its beams. I don't know how else someone would get eyes that brilliant. As our gazes hold, the ground begins to feel unsteady, like the earth might collapse right out from under me, and for a second, I wish I'd worn something more stylish than leggings and an old U of H hoodie. I tear my focus away from his face and focus on his shirt.

I blink, back on solid ground, then grimace at the mess covering his lower half. "Sorry about that."

In the silence that follows, I wait for him to say something like, *It's okay* or *Oh no, it was actually my fault for walking right on your heels.* But he says nothing, and I look up to find his eyes still rooted to my face. Though his stare appears a little dazed, my neck begins to prickle. What *is* it with people today? All I want to do is enjoy my morning cup of coffee. Not get hit on by old men who should know better, and definitely not bump into handsome strangers.

Under his piercing gaze, my annoyance hedges toward guilt, and I try to swallow my irritation. I am the one who turned around without being aware of my surroundings and should probably offer more than an apology.

"I can pay for your shirt to get cleaned," I say grudgingly. I hate the thought of adding a stranger's dry-cleaning bill to my already tight budget, but it *is* my fault he'll likely go around smelling like stale coffee grounds all day. "There's a dry cleaner's just a few stores down."

"Dry cleaning?" he finally says, and wow. That voice. It's as rich and smooth as my favorite brew. And judging by his slow response, he probably needed every drip of the coffee that just spilled.

"Yes. For your shirt."

He looks down, and I think he's finally snapped out of whatever trance he was in. Thick eyebrows shoot up as his eyes land on the white cup with a black lid that now sits askew and then his shirt cuff that's soaking wet.

His eyebrows draw together as he looks back at me, seemingly stunned. "You bumped into me."

I might've clapped if my hands weren't full. I settle for a nod instead. "I know. That's what I'm apologizing for." I sigh and look around, noticing how Gina has switched to the opposite side of the table and now has a straight line of sight to this spectacle. Great, she'll be talking about this for weeks.

That's it, dry cleaning is officially off the table.

"How about you let me buy you another coffee?" I offer instead.

He frowns. "But I don't have time to get a cup with you."

Something isn't clicking here, and I am holding on to my last shreds of patience with everything in me. "What is your name?" I ask slowly.

"Vincent. And you are?"

"Don't worry about that. Look, *Vincent*, I was offering to replace the coffee I spilled, *not* whatever it is you're thinking."

My answer amuses him for some reason, as he tilts his head to the side with half a smile. "'Don't worry about that' is an interesting name."

So he's got jokes. Not funny, and definitely not appreciated. But jokes.

"Do you want coffee or not?" I demand.

His eyes light up even more as he chuckles, and I roll my shoulders to deflect the pleasant sensation the sound tries to elicit. I am not about to be seduced by a nice laugh.

Tearing his gaze from me, he quickly sobers when he checks his watch, which, luckily for him, is still dry. "I better hurry home and change before I'm late for the Monday meeting," he mutters, then sighs and looks at me. "Maybe you can make up for the coffee another time."

My eyes bug out at his words. I am too stunned to speak. And before I can think of a good comeback, he's out the door.

"You can buy *me* another coffee if you want." Pops steps close and eyes me as he raises his cup to his mouth. "I know how you independent women these days like to pay for everything, so you can take me to breakfast too."

Heaven help me.

I look at the ground, where two drops of coffee lie on the light wooden floor. "Watch your step. Don't want to have you fall and break a hip."

Walking away, I shake my head. My mom would tear me a new one for not respecting my elders, even if he did deserve it.

Back at the table, I set our cups down and regard Gina sternly. "Do. Not. Even."

"What?" Her eyes are all rounded innocence. She takes a small sip of her latte, but I can see she's ready to burst.

I may as well have her get it out of her system now instead of badgering me later. With a sigh, I fold my arms across my chest and wait for her to crack.

It doesn't take long. She leans forward on the table and

covers one side of her mouth like she's telling me a big secret. "Okay, but did you see how fine he was?"

"He's still here if you want me to get his number for you."

"What?" Her eyebrows knit before she scowls. "Don't play. You know I'm not talking about Grandpa. I'm referring to Hottie with the Body."

"Oh, you mean the aggravating man with the . . ." Damn, I can't think of anything catchy like Gina.

She shakes her head. "Tell me you gave him your number, or at least got his?"

I grab my drink but set it down again, leaning back in my chair and shaking my head at Gina's ridiculous question. "Of course I didn't get his number."

"I don't see why not. You could do with a little love in your life now that you're done wasting time with Derrick."

"Now that Derrick and I have broken up, my focus is on me, myself, and my business. No distractions, especially from men."

"But—"

"Especially from *that* man."

Him and his *You can make up for the coffee another time.* That is not how this works.

Gina pouts and I sigh. I know she wants me to find the happiness she has with her boyfriend, Mack. It's the same kind of happiness my parents have. I used to want that too. Derrick hadn't been the love of my life. I knew it even when we were together, making plans to someday move in with each other and get married. But what if he *had* meant more? What if, when everything had ended, I'd spiraled even further and lost all of myself? For one, I wouldn't be here drinking coffee with Gina.

Which is exactly why I won't pursue any relationships. I can't afford to fall apart ever again.

"I'm just not in the market to get involved with anyone," I say.

"Fine. Get your business up and flourishing. *Then* we'll find the love of your life. You won't be able to run from the man you're destined to be with forever."

I shake my head at her and take a sip of my coffee. It's only then that I realize: After my run-in with the stranger—Vincent—I still forgot to get my cinnamon.

AFTER COFFEE, GINA AND I BID FAREWELL AS SHE SETS OFF TO MEET her client, and I head to my apartment, leaving behind thoughts of men and untimely collisions. I live in a nice little fusion of residential and commercial real estate. For a stretch of three blocks, the street is lined with boutiques, restaurants, and essential businesses. Gina and I live in the same apartment complex, but she lives with Mack and Mack Jr. (aka Human Mack and Dog Mack), while I live in a one-bedroom by myself.

On my way to my apartment, I pass through the courtyard. It's a large rectangle of Astroturf framed by metal tables and chairs, with a black marble fountain stretching across the front. The farmers market and other small vendors attract shoppers twice a week, on Sunday and Wednesday. I've set up a booth for the past two weeks. It's how my potential client found me.

My stomach tightens at the thought of what awaits me. Closing my eyes, I inhale deeply. I've got this. Planning quinceañeras is my jam. Planning anything is my jam. It's what made me such a valuable asset at Jacob and Johnson for eight years. My vision and legendary parties helped launch them into being one of Houston's top event planning firms. Just because I no longer work there doesn't mean I've lost my touch.

So today I will charm this client with my great personality. Wow her with my ideas. And dazzle her with my follow-through. Then, once I've made her daughter's big moment the event of a lifetime, she will recommend me to her friends, and everyone will know Amerie Price is back. And everything will make sense again.

When I climb the stairs and land on the second floor, I see bright pink papers attached to all the doors. Someone's been busy this morning. It's probably a notice about upcoming maintenance visits or reminders to the pet owners to clean up around the building.

God, I hope they're not reassigning the parking spaces again.

I unlock my door and step into my one-bedroom apartment. Once I place my keys down and turn on the lights, I read the paper, and the words threaten to derail me from the measured footing I just gained. It's a notice for the structure of new rent prices. Starting in the new year, my unit is going up by 30 percent.

I resist balling up the paper and throwing it in the trash.

With the money I've been saving up for years and the severance package I received from my old job, I have enough to ride out this price increase for another lease term, but not enough to pay for rent *and* help my parents.

How did this catch me off guard? I should have expected it when new management took over. The apartments were renamed the Hidden Palms three months ago; I'd just been too focused on my misery to care. It's always the same story. First, rebranding: new name, new paint, balloons out front. Next, they start promoting social events to "get to know your fellow tenants," along with perks like free massages on Wednesdays. A few months later—when they know they've got you—the price hikes kick in. Shit like this should be illegal.

This, however, is a worry for another day. In fact, an increase in rent won't be a worry at all if I get my business up and running with a bang.

On that thought, I place the pink paper beside my keys and head to my bedroom. My hoodie is exchanged for a cream silk blouse. Powder and lip gloss give my complexion a little life. With Gina's voice in my head, I put my hair in a low curly ponytail and smooth my edges, and I'm camera-ready.

I get out my brand-new computer. It was one of the pricey but necessary purchases I had to make when I decided to venture out on my own, since the one I'd been using for years belonged to Jacob and Johnson. I forked out even more money to load it with planning software.

Pulling up Zoom, I click on the link and wait with bated breath for my potential client to show up.

After ten minutes I send her a text message.

> **Me: Hey, I just want to make sure you've got the link. Here it is again. I can't wait to chat about your daughter's quinceañera!**

Right away, I see the message has been read, but she doesn't respond. Maybe she's running behind or just now waking up. Nine is still early for some, especially parents trying to shuttle kids to school and fight Houston traffic, so as I watch the clock in the bottom corner of my screen change from 9:14 to 9:15, I try to cling to the hope that she'll join me any second. Unable to help myself, I glance toward the front door, where the too-bright pink paper shouts at me from beside my keys, and force down the rising fear that wants to swallow me whole at the thought of what I'll do if this venture doesn't pan out. Then, after twenty more torturous minutes, I leave the virtual meeting. No one is joining me.

My reputation has preceded me, and not the one I painstakingly created over years of being one of the best event planners Houston has to offer.

I turn off my ring light, wash my face, and curl up in bed.

PHOTO BY ERICA SPIEGEL, STILLS FOR THRILLS

ETTA EASTON is a certified hopeless romantic who now writes contemporary romance. Her stories are full of humor, relatable heroines, swoon-worthy heroes, and Black joy. She lives in Central Texas with her husband and two young kids.

Ready to find
your next great read?

Let us help.

Visit prh.com/nextread

Penguin
Random
House